"*Bone Necklace* is exquisite—meticulously researched, culturally and historically authentic, and flat-out heart-wrenching. Sullivan's debut novel is an important contribution to the body of literature about America's last 'Indian War.'"

—Gary Dorr, former chairman of
the general council of
the Nez Perce Tribe

BONE
NECKLACE

Julia Sullivan

Brandylane
Publishers, Inc.
Publishing books since 1985

ISBN: 978-1-953021-53-3
LCCN: 2021922156

Project managed by Christina Kann

Printed in the United States of America

Published by
Brandylane Publishers, Inc.
5 S. 1st Street
Richmond, Virginia 23219

Brandylane
Publishers, Inc.
Publishing books since 1985

brandylanepublishers.com

To the ones who never gave up.

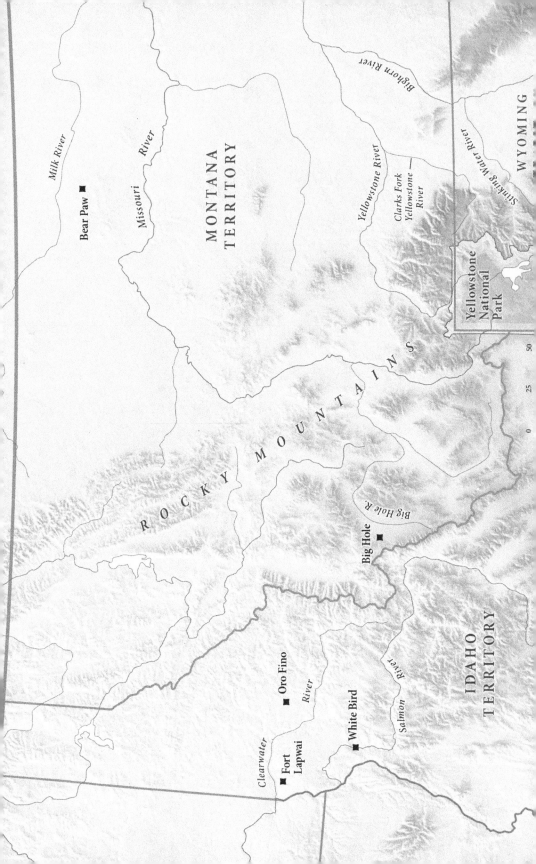

Milk River

Missouri River

Bear Paw ■

MONTANA TERRITORY

Bighorn River

WYOMING

Yellowstone River

Clarks Fork
Yellowstone
River

Stinking Water River

Yellowstone
National
Park

R O C K Y   M O U N T A I N S

50

25

0

Big Hole R.

Big Hole ■

Oro Fino ■

Clearwater River

Fort
Lapwai ■

White Bird ■

Salmon River

IDAHO TERRITORY

Part One

Chapter 1

At the sound of Chocolate Bar's deep-throated growl, Jack scrambled to his feet and grabbed the Hawken rifle leaning against a scrubby white bark pine. He found the dog crouched at the foot of a massive basaltic boulder, baring his teeth at a buff-colored mountain lion. The cat had been stalking Jack and his dog all day, all the way up a steep ridgeline overlooking Hells Canyon, but Jack was surprised at the predator's boldness now, venturing so close to his camp.

The cat let out a hair-raising howl, high-pitched and apocalyptic, the kind of sound Jack imagined he'd hear the day he finally arrived in actual Hell. The dog's growl was a low, dull rumble, like distant thunder gathering momentum. Jack's mule, Hammertoe, shuddered and bucked at the end of her picket line. Her instinct was to run, but the picket kept her moving in frantic circles.

Jack wedged the Hawken's worn maple stock between his shoulder and his cheek, aiming at the mountain lion's chest. He felt the rifle's cold trigger against his finger, but he didn't pull. The cat was such a beautiful thing, so sleek and daring and dangerous.

Jack had loved mountain lions ever since the day he saw one sitting on top of a giant saguaro cactus. For all their beauty, all the elegance in their movements, all the heat in their fiery eyes, cats sometimes made spectacularly bad decisions. Jack, whose life had been one bad decision after another, understood the astonishment, the bewilderment, the futile regret of that cat on top of the cactus, almost as if they were kin.

He hollered—"Hey! Hey! Hey!"—and fired the gun in the air. The muscular cat took the warning and bounded away. She flew to the top of a rocky outcropping, fifteen feet or more in a single leap, and disappeared in the fading light just as silently as she'd arrived.

Chocolate Bar, about the same size as the cat, chased after her, snarling and full of bloodlust, but the dog couldn't hope to match the mountain lion's retreating speed. He ran back and forth from Jack to the base of the high, bony shelf where the cat had escaped, moaning and sniffing every footmark she'd left. Hammertoe trembled, brayed, and reared against her picket line, which only tightened the knot.

Jack stood in a patch of wild buckwheat, holding the hot-barreled rifle, breathing in gun smoke. "You'd have died gloriously if you'd caught her," he told the dog, "but you'd have died all the same."

Chocolate Bar yowled and whined and refused to come when Jack called him.

"I'm not drunk," he told the insolent dog. "I missed her on purpose."

Chocolate Bar stared at Jack doubtfully, but it was the truth.

Jack sat down on a dusty boulder, surrounded by mountains with names like He Devil, She Devil, Ogre, Goblin, Devil's Throne, Mount Belial, and Twin Imps. Vertical walls of rock, covered with pictographs and petroglyphs, plunged thousands of feet from the high shelf where Jack had stopped for the night to the Snake River crashing through the narrow gorge below. He wondered how the ancient Indians had climbed those sheer canyon walls with their pots of ochre paint to record births and deaths and plagues on the face of the rock. He wondered how a spider could hang on there.

Jack took his supper from a pretty silver flask. Eventually, the truculent dog settled down beside him. Jack pulled pine needles, sticks, pebbles, and bits of grass from the dog's bushy tail and used oil to remove gobs of sticky sap from the thick black fur around his neck. Forgetting his grievance, Chocolate Bar rolled over so Jack could scratch his tummy.

"Sometimes I think God put cats and women on this earth for the specific purpose of humbling men like us," Jack told the dog, picking up their earlier conversation. "He knew full well how they'd taunt us."

The dog stretched and yawned.

"You mustn't ever let them see your desperation, though," he said. "No whining. No moaning. No panting if you can help it."

Chocolate Bar yawned and closed his eyes.

«———»

Three days earlier, Jack couldn't have imagined he'd soon find himself camped in the Seven Devils, chasing Indians. Then again, three days earlier, his father's house hadn't been burned to the ground by the Nez Perce. Rescuers had combed through the smoking wreckage with rakes and shovels, searching for Sally's corpse, but it had proven a futile task. If she was inside that house when the conflagration went up, her remains would never be identified. The fire had burned too blistering hot, reducing every shingle, every beam, every stick of furniture to cinders. Door hinges, jewelry, silverware, even pots and pans had been melted. Window glass had liquefied and cooled in iridescent pools beneath the ash. Two stone chimneys were all that remained, facing each other like forgotten sentinels.

Witnesses saw a Nez Perce flee the scene. Nobody mentioned a hostage, but that didn't mean the Indian hadn't taken Sally with him, in which case she might still be rescued. After sending a heart-breaking telegraph to his father, who was meeting with the governor in Boise at the time, Jack had gone out on his own, drunk as a boiled owl, vowing to bring Sally home. Now he was camped on the ridge overlooking Hells Canyon, which the local band of Nez Perce would have to traverse if they wanted to join the other hostiles.

Sally was the only mother Jack remembered, and though she could drop the temperature in a room ten degrees just by walking in, she and Jack had always shared a peculiar bond. When Jack's father beat him, Sally would bring cold compresses to his room, touching his brow with her elegant hands. When Jack's father spent the night with one of his whores, Jack would sit beside Sally on the porch, listening to her muffled sobs. They knew things about each other that neither one would ever share with another living soul. Wasn't that the essence of family?

Jack's father, Robert Peniel, had devastating flaws, but he wasn't a bad man entirely. When Jack was a boy, his father would rise early each morning to start the fires, which would be blazing by the time Jack stumbled out of his room with his clothes in his arms to dress before the kitchen hearth. Peniel would be scalding his throat with coffee by then, measuring flour and lard into a bowl for biscuits, which he insisted on making himself. Biscuits were too important to trust to Sally, who made them hard and dry. "Like turds," Peniel would say in an oft-repeated rant, which used to make young Jack laugh.

Breakfast would be a gluttonous affair, with eggs fried in butter, thick slabs of bacon slathered with maple syrup, and peaches fixed with cloves and soaked in brandy. Peniel's biscuits would come out of the oven hot and steamy so the honey and apple butter melted down Jack's chin.

Over breakfast, Peniel, who usually hadn't slept the night before, would read aloud from the *Lewiston Telegraph*, whose publisher was a friend, or from well-thumbed volumes by Tennyson, Keats, Wordsworth, Whitman, Shelley, and other sensualists, with his spectacles perched on his shark-fin nose. Jack loved the sound of his father's deep, baritone voice. The man could be charming when he wanted.

Jack's father had engaged in a number of vocations over the years—teacher, missionary, farmer, trader, lawman—but his real genius, the thing he truly excelled at, was lying. Peniel had a capacity for eloquence, camouflage, unverifiability, and inventiveness that was unequalled among even the most unrepentant charlatans. He'd once tried to tutor Jack in this industry, explaining that a good lie had to be delivered brazenly and unashamedly, with one's shoulders thrust back and chin tipped up. It needed a few small bits of truth woven into the tapestry so it resembled something that might have been true under other circumstances. A good lie had to be alluring. It had to seduce you, irresistibly. There had to be artistry in it—beauty, almost.

Jack only ever knew one person who didn't seem to understand, let alone appreciate, the occasional necessity of prevarication. Motsqueh and Jack had been six years old when they'd met at an orphanage where Jack's father had left him for a while. The two boys sat beneath a giant cedar tree for hours, companionably mute, until they were called for a cold supper. The next day they played "quiet" again, but this time Jack's new friend broke the silence, forfeiting the match.

"Take a breath," Motsqueh said. "Now let it out. . . . Now take another breath. . . . Now let it out. . . . Now take another breath but hold it."

Jack held his breath for one, two, three seconds.

"Now let it out. See? That didn't hurt, did it? My mother died just like that. She was breathing and then she wasn't. The next breath never came."

"I didn't see my mother die," Jack said.

"Maybe she's not dead."

Motsqueh was like that. Tell him the mountains were created by an invisible trickster named Coyote, or that Jesus was born to a virgin named Mary, and he believed it unhesitatingly, but tell him that the paint on the porch rail was wet, or that someone you knew had died, and he had to see it for himself, or at least interview three eyewitnesses.

If Motsqueh had been around after Jack went to live with his father, he never would have believed the ridiculous explanations for Jack's many injuries. The two boys would have played quiet, and Jack would have told his friend everything. Motsqueh would have told his older brother, Tiloukaikt, who would have done something about it. Maybe the two Cayuse would have helped Jack hide in the mountains. But Motsqueh died of measles when the boys were only eight, and his brother, Tiloukaikt, killed the doctor with an axe and was hanged before a cheering crowd. Years later, Jack whispered his secret into an empty tobacco tin, quickly tapped on the lid, and buried it next to Motsqueh and Tiloukaikt in the ground, hoping for supernatural intervention which never arrived.

After Motsqueh died, Jack found that he was one instead of two, and though he hadn't studied his numbers much at that point, he understood that one wasn't half of two. One wasn't even one billionth of two.

The more Jack thought about Motsqueh, the more other people disappointed him. At boarding schools, apprenticeships, church socials, Jack always found himself standing slightly apart. He was the fish in a jar. The white crow in a flock of black ones. The pine scion ludicrously grafted onto an apple tree. He was always carrying things—a block of clay, a plaster mold, an empty bucket sometimes—as a buffer between himself and the people he might bump into on the street. He stared down at his shoes a lot. When someone tried to be friendly, he stared down at their shoes.

As the years rolled by, Jack found that things were easier, and so much more lyrical, when the whiskey flowed. Sure, his art had suffered. Sure, he'd lost Jessica. Sure, his hands shook and his stomach hurt almost all the time. And yet the whiskey kept him company. It covered up an overwhelming sense of loneliness that sometimes felt catastrophic. It made him forget that his name was Jack and that he slept alone in a cavernous studio with only a kiln and a forge for warmth at night. Like a beautiful woman or a worthy lie, good whiskey demanded his appreciation. Then it kicked him in the teeth.

"Damn it all," he said out loud. He reached for the Hawken, poured powder down the barrel, added a patched iron ball, and pulled the hammer back to half-cock. He laid the gun in a rocky crevice, within easy reach, and pulled off his boots.

When the Nez Perce outbreak had begun, Jack had promised his father he'd drive Sally's carriage to Fort Lapwai and leave her there in the care of friends. Instead, he'd passed out on his straw mattress with an empty bottle in his hand. A messenger had woken him later that night with the news that his father's house had been torched.

The idea that Sally had been kidnapped rather than killed was a notion hatched by desperation more than rational thought. Jack sensed the cresting of a massive wave, and only this tiny, mad idea—that Sally was still alive—somehow kept it from breaking over and smashing him to bits.

He stripped to his cotton union suit and lay beneath the darkening sky. The canyon was noisy with tree frogs and boreal toads, screeching hawks and hooting owls, and the Snake River grinding through the deep gorge down below.

Lying in the unquiet dark, thinking about Sally, Jack fell into a hazy dream in which he'd somehow rescued her and delivered her safely back to Lewiston. In the dream, he could hear people murmuring that perhaps they'd misjudged him all those years, that perhaps he wasn't as frivolous as many of them had believed, that sometimes he acted as white as any man. He was wearing a hat that he'd constructed entirely from orange peels, and this, too, seemed to impress the people in the crowd. Even his father seemed pleased with him for once. But naturally, and in due course, he woke up alone in the wilderness, almost embarrassed by the absurdity—the transparent neediness—of the dream. Chocolate Bar looked at him with such sympathy, Jack suspected that even the dog found him pathetic.

"You probably dreamed you caught and killed that mountain lion," Jack said, "but you don't see me pitying you for it."

Chocolate Bar stood up and stretched.

"Half of life is hope, and that's the half that sustains the rest," Jack said. "She might still be alive."

The dog ambled to a tree, lifted his leg, and trotted off.

Chapter 2

Jack woke at the crack of dawn so stiff and sore from sleeping on the stony ground that he could barely move. With colossal effort, he sat up, dressed, and filled a hammered tin cup with cold coffee. Though it was mid-June, the high mountain air was brisk enough that he could see his breath. Still, he didn't dare make a fire, not with the Nez Perce headed this way.

The silver flask lay on his rumpled bedroll, nearly empty. It was a pretty little thing, nicely curved to fit the palm of his hand. It had been given to him by his father—a real irony considering how the old man used to beat him for drinking. Sheriff Robert Peniel drank at least as much as Jack did, which was to say, enough to float a steamer, but he went perpendicular if he caught young Jack passed out. "This hurts me more than it hurts you," the old man used to say as he bared Jack's buttocks and pulled the belt from his own trousers.

Every time Jack held the flask, he wondered why he kept the gift, and yet it was a lovely bauble. Besides, what was sobriety, anyway, but the most self-righteous form of insanity?

Jack uncorked the flask and breathed in the rich fragrance, like amber grain coated in chocolate and pecans. He poured the remnants into his cold coffee and took a swallow, feeling the liquor's warmth spread from his core to his fingers and toes. When the coffee ran out, his eyelids grew heavy. He was sleepy. So sleepy. The tiny new leaves of an aspen tree flipped like silver coins. The whiskey embraced him, lulling him, irresistibly, toward slumber.

Jack's head nodded, then snapped upright when he felt the drumbeat of hooves pushing up through the layers of granite and limestone and basalt. The sound of hoofbeats intensified, like an avalanche tumbling toward him. Chocolate Bar ran along the rocky ledge overlooking the river, whining and growling, a chipmunk wriggling between his teeth. Hammertoe trembled and brayed.

Jack pulled his field glass from a saddlebag and pressed it to one eye, waiting for the Nez Perce and their large herd of horses to come into view. Finally, he saw them, thousands of horses clattering pell-mell down a rocky defile, sliding through the gravel with whited eyes, tossing their long-maned necks while nearly naked warriors urged them forward.

Even in adversity, the Nez Perce looked resplendent, with shoulders, hips, and heels in perfect alignment and bodies beautifully formed by a lifetime of riding and racing in the mountains. The Nez Perce galloped their mounts across rocks and over stumps at breakneck speed to the edge of the thrashing river, and there, without a moment's hesitation, with no indication of apprehension or fear, they drove the screaming herd into the ice-cold, churning torrent, with riders clinging to the animals' backs.

To move invalids and children across the pummeling river, the Nez Perce used small round boats made from willow frames covered in hides, each one loaded with three or four passengers, and pulled through the water by strong horses. Jack watched one of the precarious boats swirling at the end of a rope like a leaf in a whirlpool. A small boy nearly toppled into the white water but was steadied by a fellow passenger. Somehow a bareback rider and his muscular horse got the little boat across, unloaded the children into their mothers' anxious arms, then turned back for another crossing, and another after that, and another, and another, for what seemed like hours.

Jack imagined himself in the bone-chilling river, riding a bare-back stallion, shell necklaces clicking against his bare chest, long hair flying loose around his shoulders. He imagined Motsqueh riding on one side of him and Jessica riding on the other, and a wide-eyed child smiling at him from a small round boat, reaching for him with tiny hands like daisies.

Sometimes the sound of hoofbeats would evoke a scene like that in his imagination, or a long-forgotten scent would thrill him for some inexplicable reason, and visions of some other, unlived life would seep like mist through a tightly locked door, evaporating when he looked too close. It was in these fleeting, almost ephemeral moments that Jack knew the rumors that had dogged him all his life must be true. Knew his dead mother was Nez Perce the same as he knew his hip was connected to his leg.

Jack's father readily admitted the absurdity of Jack's birth story, which involved a French beauty showing up in Idaho Territory at a time when the number of white women in the entire Pacific Northwest could have been counted on one hand, and yet the man swore, with a laugh and a toss of the head, that the outlandish tale was true. The fact that most people believed it most of the time was a real tribute to Robert Peniel's remarkable leadership skills. Jack, for one, disbelieved almost everything his father said in exact proportion to his father's vehemence, but this particular lie was no doubt intended as a kindness. Nobody ever called Jack a half-breed to his face, which counted for something.

Jack gripped the field glass with white knuckles, searching for Sally with a desperation that did his guilty conscience credit. As far as he knew, Sally had never traveled without a side saddle or a carriage and wouldn't have had anything like the skill needed to swim a horse across the Snake River this time of year, with the water so high and fast. If Sally was still alive and traveling with the Nez Perce, she'd be in one of those small, round boats, with the copper-faced children clutching their dolls and their feathered shields and their wriggling puppies.

Jack scrutinized every face in every little boat, hour after hour, but he never caught a glimpse of Sally. He followed the Indians for the rest of the day, watching from the ridgetop, slowly coming to terms with the fact that Sally wasn't down there. It became increasingly difficult to deny that Sally was dead, and he was responsible, which only proved, once again, how prescient Jessica had been in deciding to marry someone else. The vast, dark, infinite ache that had resided in him as long as he could remember, the insecurity and embarrassment and loneliness, became more intractable with each wasted hour of the search, and harder to bear.

When darkness fell again, Jack turned back toward Fort Lapwai to face his father and report to General Oliver O. Howard, the U.S. Army Commander of the Department of the Columbia, that the hostiles were gathering in increasing numbers in White Bird Canyon. If the government meant to confine the roaming Nez Perce to the reservation—and how could they not, now?—the job would have to be done by force.

Chapter 3

It took three days to get back to Fort Lapwai, which was bedlam by the time Jack arrived. Exhausted messengers passed each other at the wooden gate on lathered horses, shouting out the latest news about Scott Grooms, who'd been murdered, and Sam Benedict, who'd been murdered along with his hired man, and Harry Mason, who'd been murdered along with both of his hired men, and Henry Elfers, who'd been murdered along with his nephew and his hired man, and Richard Devine, who'd been murdered in his bed while his wife slept beside him, and Lynn Bowers, who'd spent two days hiding in the shrubbery, wearing only her bloomers. The telegraph line had been cut. The stages had been canceled. Businesses were closed.

Jack entered the fort and stepped off Hammertoe. He loosened the mule's cinch and scratched her ears while contractors unloaded pallets of milled wood, crates filled with guns and ammunition, and sacks of beans, coffee, and flour. Families that had been evacuated from nearby settlements were setting up makeshift shelters in whatever open space they could find. Soldiers had been posted to keep the parade ground clear, but with little success. The whole compound was strewn with dirty rags, cracked pottery, cheap wooden kazoos, crumpled copies of the *Lewiston Telegraph*, and every kind of string. Children chased kites, dogs, and one another through the already chaotic scene, bumping into everyone and everything.

Jack walked Hammertoe to a temporary stockade that had been hastily constructed to hold the civilians' stock, but it wasn't big enough. Over-crowded animals kicked at each other and bared their teeth, half-crazed. Jack feared that his mule would be kicked to death in there, so he kept Hammertoe with him on a long lead line. Chocolate Bar caught and killed a loose chicken whose red-faced owner demanded ten cents in recompense, an exorbitant price. Jack paid it just to end the shouting match after a pig walked up, grunted, and shat an eye-watering emanation. His head began to throb.

Upon entering the fort, Jack had been somewhat encouraged by the report that the Nez Perce had let Mrs. Devine sleep while they'd murdered her husband. It suggested that the Indians weren't inclined to harm innocent women, renewing Jack's hope that Sally might still be alive. But when he walked by the big canvas hospital tent, with its sides stretched out on a temporary wooden frame, he saw his former friend, Dr. Benson Graham, working on a woman who'd been shot in both legs. Next to her lay a woman with a bloody bandage around her neck, trying to quiet an infant whose tongue had been cut out. The sound of the infant's high-pitched wail and the pungent odor of dirty bandages boiling in a cast iron pot made Jack gag. He reached for the silver flask, then remembered it was empty.

A reporter from the *Lewiston Telegraph* spotted Jack near the hospital tent and walked a line to intercept him. The reporter pulled a pencil from his hatband and a scrap of paper from the pocket of his coat, which strained at the buttons like overstuffed upholstery.

"Jack Peniel? Fergus Dewsnap with the *Lewiston Telegraph*."

"I know who you are," Jack said, shaking the reporter's extended hand.

"Any word on Sally?"

"Still searching."

"Folks are saying she died in that fire."

"Some of us still hope she didn't."

"Why didn't she seek refuge inside the fort?"

"You can ask her yourself, once I find her," Jack said.

Dewsnap pushed his spectacles up the bridge of his nose, scribbled something into his notebook, tipped his hat, and wandered off. Jack wondered if the reporter already knew that Jack was the one who'd been asked to deliver Sally safely to the fort. The truth was bound to come out eventually, especially with a hound like Dewsnap around. There was no situation so terrible, Jack realized, that it couldn't be made even worse by the prospect of public censure and shame.

Jack uncorked the empty silver flask and inhaled deeply. He wondered if the quartermaster might sell him a bottle, just to settle his nerves before he faced his father. The quartermaster would want to save the whiskey for the officers, but Jack wasn't particular. He'd settle for a cheap bottle of wine or a pint of stale beer or a goddamned teaspoon of cough syrup if that was all he could get. After that, he'd square his shoulders, find his father, and tell him—what? That he'd gotten drunk? That he'd failed to appreciate the urgency of the situation? That he was sorry?

Whatever he said, he knew it wouldn't be enough.

Chapter 4

"Well, by the mercy of Sweet Saint Fuck, there you are," Peniel said. He had a voice that could punch a hole through a wall if it wanted.

"In the flesh," Jack said.

He'd found his father at the parade ground, handing out surplus Springfield rifles to a crowd of civilian volunteers. Jack had always felt wary around his father, but the tension between them now was palpable.

Well aware that he was in for an epic tongue-lashing, Jack stared at his shoes, hoping it would be over quickly. The volunteers waiting for their new Springfields shook their heads and looked at Peniel with expressions of sympathy and bewilderment, confirming that Sally's tragedy and Jack's unfortunate role in it were by then common knowledge. Hammertoe tried to imitate a donkey's bray, but it came out sounding like a band tuning up.

It was the first time Jack and his father had talked since the fire. They were both accustomed to ignoring hideous truths, but this one, it seemed to Jack, would have to be confronted before one of the other men brought it up.

"I'm sorry," was all Jack could think to say.

Peniel looked at Jack like a person might look at an animal that had something wrong with it—a broken-backed horse or a three-legged dog or a pig foaming at the mouth. "You were drunk, weren't you?"

"I'm going to quit drinking," Jack said.

Peniel laughed. "That might be the biggest lie since Jonah told his wife he was three days late on account of getting stuck in the belly of a whale. You were drunk when you should have been taking care of Sally, and you're drunk right now. Don't you even know how obvious it is?"

Jack doubted it was obvious at all. More like a lucky guess and not even all that lucky, the odds being so strongly in that direction.

"I looked for her in Joseph's camp."

"The Indians don't have her," Peniel said. "Why would they take her? What would they do with her? They'd have to carry her up and down mountains and through white water rivers like a sack of sand, and for what? They'd sooner fuck a jellyfish in the surf than Sally. Plenty of times in our marriage I'd have preferred the jellyfish myself, to be perfectly honest. I'm quite sure she died in that fire, a martyr like she always wanted, God rest her soul." He doffed his hat for that last bit.

Poor Sally, Jack thought. If only she'd been penniless, his father would have left her alone.

"Witnesses saw an Indian flee the scene," Jack said. "Any idea who it was?"

Peniel stared at Jack with eyes so pale in the bright sunlight he looked almost blind if not insane. "I asked you to do one thing, Jack. One. Thing. I could have had my hired man drive Sally's carriage to Fort Lapwai, but no. She said it wouldn't be 'proper' to travel with a man who wasn't family. She said she wanted you to do it, even after I reminded her you're about as reliable as a wet paper sack."

Jack couldn't deny his own shameful part in Sally's tragedy, but if he was going to rescue her, it seemed important to know who might have taken her.

"Any Nez Perce who might bear a grudge?"

Peniel narrowed his eyes to slits of glacial ice. His jaw muscles flexed like the gills on a cold fish. "You are warm milk toast, Jack," he said. "A bucket of sopping sponges. An unmatched sock, stiffening in the dirt. You and I have so little in common, I think God must have been joking when he made you my son. I'd question your mother's fidelity if you didn't have my mark upon your hip. That and the fact that we both have ears makes a total of two things we have in common."

"You know exactly who did this," Jack guessed.

Words flew out of Peniel's mouth like wasps. "I'm the goddamned sheriff, Jack! Every Indian in this country who ever stepped across my threshold nurses some kind of grievance against me. That's why my house was such an obvious target. That's why I told you to evacuate Sally to Fort Lapwai! Don't you dare try to shift the blame here onto me!"

Jack felt himself flinch from the latent violence coiled in his father's body and building behind his eyes, which changed colors when he was angry like the sky before a thunderstorm. Now they were almost violet.

The night of Sally's tragedy, Jack had only planned on having one small glass of whiskey. Just a drop for the road, really. But as he'd learned with brutal repetition, one sip tended to lead to another until the bottle was empty. While he slept it off, precious time had slipped away like a fistful of sand. It wasn't his first or probably his last ruinous decision, but this time someone else had paid the terrible price. It forced him to consider the possibility that he might have a problem with alcohol. He might have to quit, or at least cut back, for real.

"I'm sorry," he said again.

"As if those words ever solved anything," Peniel said. His sharp, angular face seemed to have been designed for the specific purpose of expressing contempt. "You always want the easy way out."

"I can fight when I have to," Jack said evenly. It was the closest they'd ever come to talking about Jack's fifteenth birthday, the day they'd nearly killed each other. Peniel had never laid a hand on Jack again after that.

"If you really want to go looking for her in the Indians' camp, you can come with us," Peniel said.

"Join the militia?"

"You won't find her, but at least you can help us chastise her killers. You owe Sally that much."

Jack would have preferred to hold the target for a blind man's archery, but he knew when he was cornered. What else could he do? People already thought he was a drunk. He didn't want them thinking he was a coward too. Besides, his father had a point. He owed it to Sally to join the attack.

"All right," Jack said.

"What?" Peniel always needed confirmation when Jack agreed with him about anything.

"All right," Jack repeated.

"You'll be under my command. I've just been elected captain."

Jack had studied his father's face enough to recognize the satisfaction spidering across it. "Congratulations," he said.

Peniel grinned, then eyed Jack's mule skeptically. "I've got a good stallion you can ride."

"I'll ride Hammertoe here," Jack said, stroking the animal's shaggy neck. "Mules are smarter than horses. Stronger. More sure-footed."

"If you want an animal to submit to you completely in battle conditions, the last thing you want is a mule. I guarantee that mongrel will balk."

"I'll take my chances with Hammertoe."

Peniel's eyes went cold again. "I'm trying to help you."

"I said I'd join your militia. I didn't say I'd give up my mule."

"I swear, Jack, every flea, leech, and hookworm in all creation couldn't aggravate me half as much as you do. It's because no self-respecting Indian would be caught dead riding a mule, isn't it? You think that big-eared, slow-footed, recalcitrant, ornery bag of hair proves you're white."

"Don't tell me what I think. You know I don't like it."

"That mule's going to get you killed. You're hoping to die a hero, aren't you? Even though I'm the only one who'd even notice you were dead, and I'd call it a suicide."

Peniel always knew just where to stick the knife and twist the blade.

"I won't argue with you now," Jack said.

"That's what you always say when you know I'm right."

"It's what I say when I'm tired of arguing. When do we move out?"

"Tonight."

Peniel took one of the Springfields from a wooden crate and held it out to Jack. It smelled like gun oil and the sawdust used for packing.

"No, thanks," Jack said.

Peniel sighed, seemingly exhausted. "A muzzleloader's useless for fighting Indians," he said. "They'll get three or four arrows off in the time it takes you to reload that old Hawken once."

"I'll use my own gun."

"It's because I'm the one who procured the surplus Springfields from the governor, isn't it? It galls you to accept any kind of assistance from me."

"You're doing it again."

"Then tell me your own obstinate self why you won't take a superior gun!"

"I've had this old Hawken a long time. I know its quirks. Besides, I spent a lot of time decorating the maple stock with these here little brass tacks, and I like the way it came out. I doubt there will be much fighting anyway. Once we make a sufficient show of force, the Indians will hand over the killers and go to the reservation as ordered. What else can they do?"

"You're an expert on Indians now?"

"I'll bet you a nickel we don't have to fire a shot."

They shook hands on the bet.

"There's grub at the mess," Peniel said. "Beef and potatoes. The officers' wives made pies. Better eat now. You won't get another chance for a while, other than hard tack, which isn't hardly worth the trouble unless you're starving, in which case you'll be too weak to chew the stuff anyway. May as well eat your own saddle at that point, if you don't mind ruining the pretty tooling, which in your case—"

"I spent a lot of time on this here tooling," Jack said, touching his saddle. "I like the way it came out."

Peniel spat on the ground. "Be ready to go at sunset," he said.

"All right," Jack said.

"All right?"

"All right."

Chapter 5

General Howard dispatched a hundred and twenty-five regulars plus Peniel's thirty civilian volunteers under the command of Colonel David Perry, with instructions to wait in Mount Idaho for reinforcements, but the ambitious colonel insisted on pressing forward, lest the hostiles escape. Jack had expected to refill his flask in Mount Idaho, but when the column kept moving, he didn't get the chance. He should have packed an extra bottle, but he never was the sort to plan ahead. Now, after thirty-six hours in the saddle, he was well into the throes of alcohol withdrawal—trembling hands, dry heaves, and a headache so astonishing he thought his hair would fall out. When a hapless bugler blasted his instrument not three feet from Jack's ear, Jack grabbed the musician by the back of the collar and said, "You do that in my neighborhood again, I'll wrap that horn around your neck." Jack was a large and unusually quiet man, so when he spoke, it tended to get people's attention. The bugler apologized and hastened away with his eyes bulging like a bat's and his shirt bunched up around his ears.

Peniel had insisted that the civilian volunteers wear surplus army uniforms, which made Jack feel like a marionette. It didn't help that Jack was fiercely allergic to the wool. It felt like his entire body was crawling with homicidal ants. He tore at his flesh with fingernails chewed to the quick, but the more he scratched, the more he itched. An angry red rash crept from his neck to his ankles, covering every scrap of skin.

"Just a precaution," Peniel had told the men when he'd

distributed the ill-fitting uniforms, which had clearly been designed by someone who'd never experienced Idaho's afternoon heat or else was just plain sadistic. "I don't want any of those cow-brained regulars mistaking one of us for a Nez Perce," Peniel had explained, making Jack conscious, again, of his own dark features. Jack wondered if his father would have insisted on the uniforms but for him. He guessed that some of the other men had the same question, though none would openly challenge their captain.

Jack recognized most of his fellow militiamen from Hooey's saloon in Lewiston, which seemed to confirm that war seduced the same broken, greedy, needy men that whiskey did. These were hard-bitten men who'd lost fingers and toes and fragments of their sanity in the secession war. Men who wanted nothing more than to prove the existence of others weaker and more miserable than themselves. Men who'd been in so many bar room scuffles and scrapes their ears looked like cauliflower. Men who'd lost most if not all their teeth to violence or decay or some combination of the two. Men with lice not just on their scalps but also in their beards and eyebrows and probably their pubic hair.

There were men with breath so bad it could knock down a tree. There was a midget with leather-framed spectacles strapped to his head, picking his teeth with a thorn. A boy with carrot-colored hair and ears that angled away from his head like leaves sprouting off a branch. A bald, beardless man with two square postage stamps of hair on either side of his face where other men wore their sideburns. A preacher with a hook nose and a guitar slung over his back in lieu of a rifle.

There were white men, Chinamen, Frenchmen, Russians, Africans, and even a few reservation Indians who were given only three bullets apiece. There seemed to be every kind of man represented in that small army, and yet Jack stood apart as if he were some other kind of being altogether, trembling and scratching and retching at the back of the column.

The soldiers rode four abreast, rifle straps taut across their shoulders, ammunition belts slung about their waists. They traveled through a hazy swath of dust kicked up by the horses and black smoke billowing from houses, barns, outbuildings, wagons, and fields the Indians had set ablaze to signal the position of the advancing army. From a distance, Jack imagined the little army looked like Noah's flood crashing down White Bird Canyon, intent on wiping the Indians out.

Those who still had whiskey drank it to make themselves brave. Those whose flasks were empty chewed on coffee beans to stay awake. Sleep deprivation made the men slouch and stutter, but as far as Jack could tell it produced not the slightest inclination to shut their ever-loving traps. Despite the humidity and heat, despite bloodshot eyes, despite tree branches whipping their faces and poorly constructed army boots driving screws into fleshy toes, not a one of the sagging men, other than Jack, seemed able to abide silence in any measure. Every utterance, no matter how inane, no matter how filled with drivel, became a matter of heated and pointless debate. Hammertoe was as ornery as the men, pinning her ears and swishing her tail and pulling against the bridle and bit.

Jack couldn't stop thinking about the things his father had said back at Fort Lapwai. The man could be as blunt as a spoon. Some of the insults were undoubtedly true, but was it fair to say that Jack was looking to die a hero? Maybe. He couldn't deny his own susceptibility to that kind of romanticism. If he died in the upcoming battle, would it cancel out his great mistake in abandoning poor

Sally? Was there some kind of scorecard God tallied up at the end of a flawed man's life, where the pain he'd inflicted upon others could be counterbalanced by the pain he'd inflicted upon himself? Words like "redemption" and "atonement" drifted through his head, but he didn't find much comfort in them, not without a drink to wash them down. Was it any surprise that Jesus the Savior chose as his very first miracle the transmutation of water into wine?

"I never met a bigger lunkhead than our colonel," Peniel said, riding up beside Jack on a steamy stallion. "Look at this place. I never saw anything so superbly designed for an ambush. We could be assassinated from any direction. You're shaking like a leaf, Jack. People are going to think you're yellow."

"I don't care what people think."

Peniel laughed.

"Must you provoke me even now?" Jack said.

Peniel produced a flask from his own coat pocket and offered it to Jack. "It's admirable if you've really decided to quit drinking, but now is not the time. You'll need a steady hand today."

Jack stiffened at his father's condescension, but he accepted the elixir, a fine Kentucky bourbon, and managed to keep some down.

Peniel rode up and down the line, leading the men in a popular show tune. He was irresistible sometimes. Even Jack found himself singing along.

> When a pair of red lips are upturned to your own,
> With no one to gossip about it,
> Do you pray for endurance to let them alone?
> Well! maybe you do, but I doubt it.
> When a sly little hand you're permitted to seize,
> With a velvety softness about it,

Do you think you could drop it with never a squeeze?
Well! maybe you can, but I doubt it.
When a tapering waist is in reach of your arm,
With a wonderful plumpness about it,
Do you argue the point 'twixt the good and the harm?
Well! maybe you do, but I doubt it.

When the column reached the narrowest stretch of the gorge, the men bunched up like cattle in a chute.

"We're lining up for a slaughter, here," Peniel fumed. "Forward! Forward! Keep moving forward!"

But Colonel Perry's bugler, maintaining a respectful distance from Jack, blew two bars of a little ditty: *Come to halt! Stand fast men!*

"Not here!" Peniel said, but the volunteers halted anyway, their path blocked by Colonel Perry's regulars.

"Indians in sight," the colonel called back.

Two mounted Indians slowly emerged from a tumble of boulders.

"Steady, now," Peniel said, pushing his way up and down the column. The air was close with roiling dust and sweaty horses and nervous men touching their rifles.

Jack focused his field glass on the two Nez Perce chiefs, whom his father identified as Joseph and White Bird. Both of them wore elegant military-style coats decorated with brass buttons and beaded epaulettes. Joseph's forelock was swept straight up in the shape of a wing, a showy pompadour style common among his band. White Bird held an eagle's wing before his face so that only his small black eyes were visible. Each one carried a ceremonial pole with a white flag fluttering from the tip. They didn't appear to be armed, but Jack couldn't tell for sure.

Colonel Perry stepped his big sorrel forward, flanked by his officers. The column fell mostly mute except for a few men who wanted to change their bets on the likely duration of the war. Jack maintained that it would all be over by noon, including the hangings. Others thought there would be mopping up to do into the following day. Treetops wavered as sporadic raindrops began to fall.

Peniel cautioned that it might be a trap—"There's fuckery afoot," he warned—but Jack thought the Indians' white flags were genuine. Before the outbreak, Chief Joseph had given General Howard a list of twelve white criminals he wanted punished, but the general had demurred. Now all twelve were dead. Innocents had been caught in the violence too—mostly relatives and employees of the wanted men—but Jack guessed that was largely a matter of wrong place, wrong time, and passions stoked too hot. The Nez Perce had made their point and would likely surrender enough men to buy peace now.

Jack left his Hawken rifle in its scabbard and wiped his brow. The bourbon had settled his stomach and steadied his hands. The pounding in his head had receded to an occasional throb. The negotiations between Perry and the chiefs might take some time, but in the end, they'd get Sally back, if she was still alive, and hang the Indians responsible for the recent butchery.

Jack was glad he'd come. He pictured the gallows they'd build right there in White Bird Canyon. Perhaps he'd be given the privilege of placing the hoods over the prisoners' heads or the nooses around their necks. Once the hoods and the nooses were placed, Peniel would pull a hatchet from his belt and chop at the rope that held the platform on which the condemned men stood. There would be a *thwang!* and then a *clunk!* as the rope flayed high and the platform dropped and the bodies fell straight down, then yanked up like the lash of a whip. If the knots weren't placed just right, the prisoners' necks wouldn't break, and they'd flail and kick for four or five minutes. Jack had seen it happen before and hoped it wouldn't be like that. Motsqueh's brother, Tiloukaikt, had died like that. If Colonel Perry put Jack's father in charge of the ropes, the hangings would be done right.

In the corner of his vision, Jack saw the boy with the carrot-colored hair raise his rifle to one shoulder. He'd heard the boy say he hoped the war would last all summer because he needed the fifty cents a day.

Jack realized what the kid was about to do and shouted "No!" at the same time the kid's rifle flashed. Some of the other militiamen didn't know who'd fired that first shot and discharged their own weapons, too.

Hammertoe began to buck. Jack pulled her nose around in a tight circle and got her under control, but barely. Peniel shouted obscenities at the "flea-bitten, maggoty mongrel," which improved the mule's attitude not at all. Even some of the cavalry horses skittered sideways with their metal shoes slipping across rain-slicked rock.

After the initial shots were fired, the chiefs, unhurt, rolled their horses back over their haunches and ran for cover. Colonel Perry accused the volunteers of insubordination and every other kind of idiocy which Peniel did not take kindly at all, answering with his own torrent of invective. Peniel seemed to be winning the war of words until he was interrupted by a high-pitched, blood-curdling war cry as seventy Nez Perce warriors emerged from cover.

Through some terrible anthropomorphism or alchemy or witchcraft, the boulders and tree trunks and waving grass surrounding the men seemed to come alive in the form of shrieking

Indians coughed up straight from Hell. Colonel Perry had marched the column right into an ambush with mounted warriors concealed almost within spitting distance. Whether the chiefs' white flags were a ruse or the Indians had merely anticipated the possibility that the soldiers would fire on the unarmed chiefs made no difference now. The battle Jack assumed would never take place had just begun.

Chapter 6

"Sweet Jesus," Jack said.

The first arrow hit one of Perry's buglers in the neck, cutting short whatever instruction he was about to blow. The second arrow hit Perry's other bugler in the chest, leaving the command rudderless. After that, the Indians targeted the officers with their brass insignia, proving the madness of such frippery on a battlefield.

Jack's heart pounded so hard he thought it might bruise his chest from the inside. He fumbled with his rifle, pulling the hammer to half-cock and shoving the ramrod down the barrel to seat a patched ball. Every few seconds, he heard another man shout, "I'm hit!" and drop to the ground in wounded agony. Riderless mounts ran through the canyon with empty stirrups slapping against their sides, tripping on their reins, screaming and bucking as the rain beat down.

The soldiers outnumbered the warriors and were better armed, but the disparity in fighting skill was so stark that Jack knew right away his side was in trouble. It felt like he'd been tied into a sack full of cats and tossed over a waterfall. It was hard to even take a shot with the fighting so close, for fear of hitting one of his own. When he finally thought he had a clean line, he missed the Indian he'd been aiming at and struggled to reload while the insolent mule tried to buck him off.

Colonel Perry ordered the men to form two lines and fall back to a steep hill, saying, "We'll hold up there until dark."

"Colonel," Peniel said, incredulous, "do you know it's seven in the morning, not seven in the evening, and we'll be out of ammunition by noon?"

"Oh my God," Perry said, inspiring no confidence at all. He ordered Peniel to take the hill he'd mentioned and admonished, "Do not give it up!"

The rain fell in a torrent now. Peniel charged up the hillside with his militiamen, including Jack, following close behind, slipping and sliding in the mud. Peniel was quite possibly the worst father in the history of fornication, but Jack couldn't help feeling a flash of pride as he watched his father now, with his trim waist and his sapphire eyes and his fine black stallion at least a hand taller than any other horse on the battlefield.

Jack struggled to keep up on Hammertoe, who had her own opinions about taking the hill. He saw an Indian sharpshooter in a wavering treetop and took the shot. The Hawken's maple stock kicked against Jack's shoulder, but the bullet flew past the warrior ineffectually.

"That was your fault," Jack told Hammertoe, who wouldn't stand still.

Before Jack could reload, he felt a hard blow to the back of his head that knocked him from his saddle. When he lifted his head from the wet plate of rock where he'd landed heavily, the goddamned mule kicked him square in the face and bucked away, trailing her reins. A bullet scratched Jack's neck as he scrambled for cover beneath a rain-soaked sage.

Jack took a moment to catch his breath and assess his injuries as the battle raged around him. He had three knots on the back of his head, each one already the size of a plum. He'd broken his collar bone and probably some ribs when he'd fallen off the mule. Hammertoe had broken his nose when she'd kicked him in the face. That hurt. That *really* hurt. The scratch on his neck didn't seem too serious; the bullet had missed the artery.

Jack had dropped his rifle when he'd fallen off the mule. Now he watched helplessly as a naked warrior hanging off the side of his horse scooped up the gun and tossed it to another Nez Perce who'd been fighting with nothing but a club. Jack had heard jokes about bringing a knife to a gunfight, but here was a man who'd brought nothing but a club with three bloody stones tied to the business end with rawhide cords. It seemed like a stupendously poor choice of weapon for a battle against the U.S. Army, but who was hiding in the sagebrush now?

Jack spotted a riderless horse and tried to catch it, but the terrified animal bucked away, half-crazed. Meanwhile, Peniel and his volunteers kept moving up the hill, leaving Jack further and further behind.

Injured and alone, with no horse and no weapon, here was Jack's chance to die a hero. The Indians would gladly finish him off. Instead, Jack took cover in the shrubbery again, disgusted with himself. He pressed his blue neckerchief against his face to staunch the bleeding from his nose, astonished that he could feel so much excruciation and not die from it.

From beneath the silver sage, Jack had a good view of the battlefield. Every muscle in his body tensed and cringed as he watched his father and the other volunteers try to hold the hill that Perry wanted, but it was hopeless. Mounted warriors snatched rifles and bayonets right from the hands of Peniel's stunned men and killed them with their own weapons. Colonel Perry sent six regulars to reinforce the civilians, but it wasn't enough. Peniel's men fell back, leaving Jack behind on a hillside now swarming with Indians.

Once the Nez Perce got control of the hill, Colonel Perry's whole line collapsed. The colonel tried to establish an orderly withdrawal, but with two dead buglers, coordinated movements proved impossible. The battle became a rout, with soldiers abandoning their posts in a panicked, chaotic, and undisciplined retreat. Perry's men were shooting wildly now, wasting ammunition, desperate to escape the pursuing Nez Perce.

Jack saw his father, still riding the fine black stallion, whipping the animal's flanks with the knotted ends of the reins. The men who could keep up with Peniel—most of them half the captain's age—followed him out of White Bird Canyon and back toward Mount Idaho.

While Peniel and the others escaped, Nez Perce warriors rounded up the stragglers on the slowest and most used-up mounts. They herded the prisoners into a narrow coulee, from which every avenue of escape was blocked by giant formations of rock. Jack watched the color drain from rain-soaked faces as the doomed men realized they would never leave that battlefield. A few of the soldiers crossed themselves. Some of them clutched rosaries and tintypes. One wept.

Jack watched in horror as the Indians executed the trapped men one by one. Some died with one or two arrows. Others required three or four. Toward the end, Jack covered his eyes with his hands, unable to watch the continued slaughter, but he couldn't block out the screams as each arrow hit its target. The sickly-sweet smell of blood and the stink of excrement mixed with rain from the gunmetal sky.

Jack had expected the battle to end with Indians hanging from a scaffold, not soldiers lying on the ground with arrows sticking out of them. He cursed Colonel Perry, who'd been in too much of a hurry to wait for reinforcements—not to mention a few hours of rest—at Mount Idaho. The colonel might not have expected the Nez Perce to fight, but wasn't it his job to be prepared in case they did?

Jack wriggled out of his boots when he realized they were sticking out from beneath the sagebrush where he'd taken cover. He'd just pulled his knees up to his chest, sending sharp stabbing pains through his cracked ribs, when two bullets sent the empty footwear flying. He heard a cacophony of voices as warriors swept the battlefield, collecting guns and ammunition from the dead.

Jack held his breath, terrified he'd be discovered. These were the men who'd cut out an infant's tongue. He trembled to think what they might do to a man like him.

Chapter 7

Jack lay in the shrubbery, shaking and retching, until the Indians rode off on their colorful horses, leaving the battlefield eerily quiet. With painful effort, he raised himself up on all fours, panting and hanging his head like a wounded dog. Blood drenched his face and shirt and dripped from his nose to the sodden ground. He knew there was no easy way to get up onto his feet, so he gritted his teeth and, with one great push and a string of expletives, stood himself upright.

He stumbled through the battlefield, half-dazed from a combination of dehydration, alcohol withdrawal, loss of blood, and a terrible swelling on the back of his head. He found his damaged boots and gasped at the grinding pain in his ribs and collar bone as he pulled them on. One big toe poked through a bullet hole in the leather, exposing a muddy sock.

The only sounds now were the rain and the howling wind, pushing dark clouds across the sky, and the hollow ringing in Jack's ears. From clamor and chaos, the battlefield had gone grimly, hauntingly silent.

Jack counted thirty-four dead on the field with vacant eyes and open mouths. All thirty-four were soldiers, which meant that the Indians had either suffered no casualties or had carried their wounded off the field. Horses lay dead with their lips curled back, their teeth bared, and their bodies coated with salt and blood and rain.

Having never seen such carnage, Jack found it difficult to avert his eyes. If he'd been lying there among the dead, he wouldn't have wanted people to see him that way, but he wouldn't have wanted them to pretend they didn't see him, either. There ought to be an undertaker in such situations. Someone to make the dead look peaceful and happy.

Jack's stomach gave a dry heave. God Almighty, he needed a drink.

Jack found the boy with the carrot-colored hair who'd fired on the chiefs' white flags. He was dead on the field with a bullet hole in his forehead. The day might have ended differently if the kid hadn't fired that first shot, but he'd paid the ultimate price for his mistake. Jack searched the boy's pockets for two coins to cover his eyes, but all he found was a single copper penny plus a pair of dice, a marble, and a dented tin whistle. He put the boy's penny onto one eye and a penny from his own pocket onto the other eye and covered the smooth-skinned face with his own wool coat. He didn't know if the kid would need the coins for Charon or not. What he did know was that, once the eyeballs dried out, the eyelids would snap open again. It had happened to Motsqueh, and Jack had been haunted by his dead friend's ghost ever since.

Jack found the bugler who'd blown his instrument in Jack's ear. Someone had taken the arrow from the dead man's throat—probably an Indian, who would refurbish it for the next battle. Jack searched the dead bugler's pockets and found an odd assortment of coins—gold doubloons minted in Mexico and gold Napoleons minted in France and gold dollars minted in Georgia and gold nuggets straight from the mines—but he couldn't find two matching coins. He reached into his own pocket again and found two nickels, which reminded him he owed his father a nickel, assuming the old man had gotten away safe. Jack unbuttoned his linen shirt and shrugged it off with a grimace, then used it to cover the bugler's face. He felt the cool rain against his skin and saw where his ribs had started to bruise dark purple.

Jack didn't have enough coins or clothing to cover all the faces. He collected a great assortment of rain-soaked hats and tried to match them to the bodies, but he couldn't remember which hat belonged to which man and had to keep switching them around. The wind blew the hats off the faces almost fast as Jack could place them, so he finally decided to wait until the storm had passed.

There should have been a preacher to say a few words, but there was only Jack, and he hadn't brought a Bible. Despite the years he'd spent at the orphanage, memorizing Bible verses, all he could summon at the moment was a passage from Whitman, which his father used to read at the breakfast table. "I am not contain'd between my hat and boots," he recited beside each body. It would have to do until someone more qualified arrived.

He wondered how long it would take him to dig thirty-four graves in solid rock with broken ribs and a broken collar bone and no shovel. Surely General Howard would send a burial party with pine boxes and grave markers. Certainly they would get here soon.

Except for Jack, there were no survivors on the field. While he'd hidden in the bushes, thirty-four men had died fighting. It made those dead men harder to face, and Jack more anxious to get them covered up.

He found his own hat trampled in the mud where Hammertoe had thrown him. He brushed it off, put the wrecked garment on his head, then staggered and lurched to the top of the summit his father had tried, and failed, to hold. He pressed a field glass to one eye and saw the plume of dust thrown up by retreating soldiers. They'd probably run all the way back to Mount Idaho, where

Colonel Perry's reinforcements would just be arriving.

From the summit, Jack could also see the Indians ferrying elders and children across the Salmon River, which the storm had whipped into a perfect torrent. Again, he looked for Sally in the small round boats. Again, he didn't find her.

He saw his mutinous mule in the water, swimming across with the Nez Perce horse herd. There wasn't a mule ever born that wouldn't hitch up with a horse if it got the chance, and Hammertoe was no exception. It meant that Jack would have to walk back to Mount Idaho with his throbbing head and his broken bones and one muddy toe sticking out of his boot.

Jack's heart jumped into his throat when he noticed Chocolate Bar out in the river with the Nez Perce horse herd. Jack had left the dog at Fort Lapwai, but he must have escaped somehow and followed Jack all the way to White Bird Canyon. Now the dog was trying to follow Jack's mule across the swirling rapids with floating branches smashing into his head, shoulders, and hips. All four of Chocolate Bar's legs paddled furiously against the current, but the dog, always a strong swimmer, got no closer to the opposite bank. The river churned and slammed the weakening animal repeatedly into the sharp rocks. Blood foamed and dissipated as Chocolate Bar continued to flail.

In the scheme of things, with the war now promising to be longer and harder than anyone had anticipated, some might consider a dog's life unimportant, even trivial, but Jack didn't see it that way. There were few people in the world he'd choose for company over the amber-eyed dog. In fact, there was only Jessica, and she'd married Dr. Benson Graham instead.

Chocolate Bar went down and came back up near one of the Indians' small round boats. A young girl pulled the limp animal into the crude ferry, somehow managing not to sink the whole precarious craft. Jack could see others in the boat gesticulating at her—probably telling her to let the animal drown—but she held the panting dog firmly in her lap with a stubbornness that won Jack's admiration. It was almost as if the Indians were gathering up the puzzle pieces of Jack's broken life—his Hawken rifle, his obstinate mule, his loyal dog—to see what might still be made with them. *Good luck with that*, he thought.

Wind hissed through the canyon with a poisonous viper sound. Jack felt suddenly overcome. The all-night ride from Fort Lapwai, the rush of the battle, the hard blow to his head, the broken ribs and collarbone, the kick in the face, the tremors and shakes that had resumed in full measure now—all of it crashed down on him at once. He leaned his back against a tree and felt the rough bark against his skin. He bent his legs, lowering himself carefully to the soggy ground. He was thirsty. So thirsty. He sniffed the empty darkness of his pretty silver flask, then fell asleep among the open-mouthed corpses, pelted and numbed by rain.

Chapter 8

From the depths of sadness and sleep, Jack experienced a great flash of calm. He heard a woman humming—*Hmmmmmm-Ah-Ah, Hmmmmmm-Ah-Ah*—or maybe he just imagined it. The rain was just a soft drizzle now. Tiny white flowers, bowed by the storm, lifted their faces toward the dissolving clouds.

Jack would have given ten years off his life to extend the unexpected feeling of serenity just ten more seconds, but instead he felt a jolt of excruciating pain, like he'd been struck by lightning. His heart fluttered like a bird trying to break through the cage of his cracked ribs. His eyes rolled back and his head bumped against something hard, a rock or a tree or maybe just the stony ground. His whole body seized and convulsed as if possessed by demons. The bird from his chest crawled into his throat, strangling him. He bit his tongue, hard, and choked on his own blood.

The air broke apart into multicolored grains of sand, scattering. Images flashed through his mind, too fast to comprehend. He saw people, but he couldn't make out their faces. He heard voices, but he couldn't make out the words. He was cold, so cold, like the blood in his veins had turned into ice. Somebody asked his name. He found that he couldn't speak, which didn't matter, because he also couldn't remember his name.

Two shadows speaking words he could not comprehend lifted him onto a travois and strapped him down with a stick wedged between his teeth. They jounced and jarred him over rocks and stumps and then transferred him to a springless wagon, which jolted many hours more over muddy hills and trails. He raved like a lunatic with broken thoughts and broken bones. All he could think about was his name. He couldn't remember his own name, which seemed like a particular tragedy. The wagon stopped outside a hotel in Mount Idaho that was being used as a temporary hospital for war casualties. The driver left Jack there, gibbering.

He had six or seven more seizures, each one preceded by the same fleeting aura of ecstasy. During one hallucination, Jessica came to lie beside him. She was wearing a loose shift made entirely from braided daisies and violets, humming a tune he could not place as she stroked his tangled hair. He knew that the sweetness of the moment, forged by years of loneliness and despair, wouldn't last. It was a flash in the pan, to be followed by the now-familiar bolt of excruciating pain, and yet the suffering that came before, and would surely come after, seemed only to make the moment itself more poignant. He developed a new respect for pain.

He traced the perfect line from her ear to her chin with his shattered mind and his nail-bitten fingers. She smiled back at him the way she used to do. He recited a stanza from Tennyson, which he'd once engraved on a lovely gold medallion with a blue star sapphire in the center:

> *My heart would hear her and beat,*
> *Were it earth in an earthly bed;*
> *My dust would hear her and beat,*
> *Had I lain for a century dead,*
> *Would start and tremble under her feet,*
> *And blossom in purple and red.*

"Did you really marry Benson Graham? Tell me it was only a dreadful dream," he said.

"Did you really join the militia? What in the name of all that's good and holy were you thinking?" she said.

Jack didn't want to tell her about Sally and the shameful part he'd played in her demise. Instead, he said, "Run away with me."

"You have to let go of what might have been," she said.

"I can't," he said.

Jack was afraid that if he blinked, she'd disappear, and the lightning would seize him again, and sure enough, that was exactly what happened. It was almost funny because he'd always been afraid of lightning, always afraid it would strike him down, and now, in a way, it had.

The next time he opened his eyes, Motsqueh was there, sitting on the window sash with his pock-marked face and his arms folded across his chest, which did not rise or fall like a living boy's but stayed perfectly still.

"They were holding white flags," Motsqueh said in a tone more hostile than Jack had ever heard from him. "They tried to hand over the guilty men, which is more than your side ever did."

"It was a trap," Jack said.

"You're fighting on the wrong side, trying to prove you're white."

Jack awoke from these and other eccentric dreams feeling fatigued beyond all prior experience. He had a headache so wearisome it made everything seem off-scale, like the oil lamp that looked twice the size of his hospital bed, and the ceiling that looked half the size of the room. He felt like a chicken whose neck had just been wrung by the cook.

On his fourth day at the hospital in Mount Idaho, Jack felt somewhat stronger and asked for some whiskey. The nurse, whose face looked exactly like a boiled dumpling, gave him weak broth and a Bible instead. Disgusted, he found his blue wool trousers and his bullet-torn boots, put them on beneath his hospital gown, and walked out.

Mount Idaho hadn't changed much in the six years since Jack had left. The settlement straddled a forty-five-mile toll road into the mining district, with rows of wooden storefronts surrounded by forested peaks. Jack and Jessica had been happy there, at least for a while. After she'd married Benson Graham, he'd gone on a bender for which even a three-month spree in 1864 offered no precedent. When he'd finally sobered up enough to pack, he'd moved to Lewiston, about eighty miles north, never intending to return.

Jack walked to the barbershop and paid for a bath and a shave. Sitting in the chair with his feet on a stool and a hot towel around his neck, he could almost have been convinced that the man staring back in the mirror was a blue-lipped corpse. Jack's eyes were dull and vacant and grotesquely blacked. His nose sat crookedly on his face, like a misshapen potato. Every movement, every breath sent stabbing pains through his ribs, contorting his face into a permanent grimace.

After the barber, Jack bought a new set of civilian clothes, then strode a familiar path to the Doubloon Saloon. He pushed through the flap of leather that served as the door and waited for his eyes to adjust to the semi-dark. The place hadn't changed much in Jack's long absence. He recognized the barman with his gaitered sleeves, and the African playing *Nelly Bly* on a piano wheeled over from the church. The floor was made of hickory, a scent that always reminded Jack of breakfast meat.

Jack placed a shiny coin on the paneled bar, which had been polished to a high gloss.

The barman pocketed the coin and produced a clean glass and a bottle of Jack's favorite Kentucky bourbon. "You look even worse than last time I saw you, Jack," he said.

"I can assure you I feel even worse than I look," Jack said.

Jack filled the glass to the rim and quaffed it down, then poured himself another. He pulled up a stool and rested his new boots on the shiny brass foot rail, settling in while the bourbon worked its magic. The trick was to stop drinking when he reached the euphoric state. If he kept going after that, he'd find himself in the painful state, nursing old grievances, starting useless fights. Despite extensive practice, he rarely stopped in time.

About halfway through the bottle, Jack found himself thinking about Jessica. He remembered lying on a blanket beneath the stars, spinning fanciful tales about Orion the hunter and Pegasus the flying horse. He still didn't understand how things had gone so horribly wrong.

"Damn it all," he said to no one in particular.

←———→

Staggering from the saloon, Jack crossed Main Street and turned down a twisty side road which took him to a one-room schoolhouse, red with white trim. The schoolhouse door was tightly closed, but Jack could hear children shuffling their desks and chairs inside and Jessica warning a boy named Nicky that if he disrupted her class one more time, he'd clean the floors and the chalkboard for a month.

Jack waited in the yard until the school bell rang and the children spilled out, talking all at once, running and skipping toward home. He stashed his nearly empty bottle in a barberry bush and stood in the open doorway, holding his stiff new hat, trying not to make a sound lest the teacher send him away.

Jessica dropped the eraser when she saw him, scattering a layer of white chalk over small muddy boot prints on the rough-hewn floor. "Jack? Is that you? How long have you been standing there?"

"Not long."

Her curly black hair was pulled back into a ponytail and tied with a pale green ribbon that matched her calico dress and her eyes. The air was sweet with the scents of roses and lilacs gathered in a ceramic jug on the teacher's well-worn desk. The walls were covered with colorful maps, drawn in her familiar hand.

Jessica picked up the eraser, frowning at the mess on the floor, then lifted her chin and studied Jack more closely. "You look awful," she said.

"So I'm told," Jack said. "Goddamned mule kicked me in the face, on top of which, I am grossly under-intoxicated."

"Hammertoe? Again? I assume you had it coming."

"Apparently she thought so. I should thank the Indians for taking her."

A small boy with Jessica's dark curls burst through the door, squeezing past Jack.

"Can I go to Nicky's house?" the boy asked. "Please?"

"Be home in time for supper."

"I will."

"And stay away from the creek. Promise me."

"I promise."

After the boy scurried off, Jack took a deep breath and stepped into the room. "I—I just need to know," he stammered. "Did you ever love me, Jessica?"

She placed her flat palms on her desk and leaned toward him with an expression that could have frozen hot soup. "That's a strange question, Jack," she said. "You're the one who walked out, remember? I haven't seen or heard from you in six years. I wasn't sure you were still alive until Benson told me he'd seen you at the hospital."

"Because I still can't figure out why you married that pompous ass barely six weeks after we—"

The flower jug flew past his head and smashed against the wall, scattering shards of pottery and cut flowers across the floor.

Jessica walked over to him and stood so close he could smell the peppermint on her breath. "You just walked out of here with your mule and your rifle without even saying goodbye!"

"Why would I say goodbye? I was coming straight back! And when I did, I found out you'd already married that puffed-up—"

"I was pregnant!"

Jack felt like he'd just been punched. He stared at her, struggling to catch his air. "Sweet Jesus," he whispered.

Jessica turned away from him. "Benson was my doctor," she said. "I guess he saw his chance when you went missing. We named the boy Charlie. I guarantee that, right now, he's standing in the creek with his friend Nicky, ruining his shoes."

Jack's head was swimming. His peripheral vision went black. He dropped his hat and flattened his palms against the schoolhouse wall. Waves of longing and regret swelled and broke, bringing him almost to his knees. He'd come so close to the life he wanted. So close. He fished for words, but his mind was too battered, leaving him incapable of anything resembling complete sentences.

"Sweet Jesus," he whispered again.

"Where were you, Jack? Where did you go?"

"It took two weeks to get from here to the Sapphire Mountains, two weeks to get back, and a month in between to find the stone I wanted," he managed to say.

Jessica stared at him. "You disappeared without a trace for two months to look for a sapphire?"

He lifted a thin gold chain over his head and placed the medallion in her hand. It was a masterpiece, ornately carved with a blue star sapphire in the center and smaller sapphires all around it in shades of saffron and violet and green, and colorless ones all around the edges shining like diamonds. He'd carved Tennyson's poem on the back in small, evenly spaced letters. "I wanted to propose properly," he said.

Jessica turned the medallion over in her hand with the chain dangling between her fingers. "You never had one ounce of sense," she said raggedly.

Jack wanted to kiss her more than he'd ever wanted anything in his life. Instead, he backed away. "I shouldn't have come," he said.

"It's time you knew about Charlie," Jessica said. "And I haven't felt enough passion to throw anything in years. So, thank you for that." Her eyes crinkled at the corners when she smiled.

She handed back the medallion, but Jack wouldn't take it. He shoved his hands into his pockets. "I made it for you," he said. "It won't ever be for anyone else."

Jack heard heavy bootsteps on the walkway outside and looked through the open doorway. A quiet groan escaped his throat as Dr. Benson Graham strode into the room sporting small round spectacles, mutton chop sideburns, and the disposition of an undertaker.

"I heard shouting," Graham said. "Is everything all right?"

Jessica stiffened, almost imperceptibly, when her husband touched the small of her back. She'd tucked the medallion into a pocket. "Darling, you remember Jack Peniel?"

"Of course." Graham said, shaking Jack's extended hand. "I saw you at the hospital, Jack, but you were still unconscious. That's a nasty bump on the back of your head."

"I don't remember much since the battle," Jack said.

"I heard it was an ambush," Graham said.

"They rode their horses off the edge of the earth and left me there, not knowing my own name," Jack said.

Graham cocked his head. "You're not out of the woods yet, Jack," he said. "You shouldn't even be out of the hospital yet. Take it easy, all right?"

The last thing Jack wanted was Graham's pity. It was excruciating. He made his excuses, put on his hat, and shambled toward the door.

As he crossed the threshold, he felt like he'd just left so many pieces of his heart behind in that one-room schoolhouse that there might not be enough of it left to keep him alive. He headed toward the creek, desperate for a better look at Charlie, then stopped himself, knowing it wouldn't be fair. Not to Jessica, not to Graham, not even to the boy.

It's time to let go of what might have been, Jessica had said in his dream.

"I can't," Jack said out loud. "I just—I can't."

Chapter 9

Fergus Dewsnap, "FEDERAL TROOPS CUT AND RUN AT WHITE BIRD CANYON," *Lewiston Telegraph* (June 17, 1877)

Colonel Perry's command was slaughtered after federal troops broke rank and ran at White Bird Canyon. The officers could not rally the men or make them face the fire. Had it not been for Captain Peniel and his civilian volunteers, many more would have been massacred. "The savages regard the regular soldier with open contempt," Peniel said, "but they are justly terrified by our western frontiersmen, who have personal interests at stake and know how to use a gun."

General Howard falsely implied that the Nez Perce outbreak was sparked by the conduct of lawless white men. In fact, it was General Howard himself who gave offense with his haughty delivery of the order to stay inside the reservation. The real cause lies, however, in the mutinous and conniving character of the Indian.

Recent events demonstrate to a fineness the impossibility of improving, to any great degree, the moral status of the Indian. More than forty years ago, missionaries settled with the Nez Perce, giving them all the advantages Christianity and education could bestow. But there is something about the Indian, his singularly narrow, perverse, and stiff-necked nature, that places him beyond all efforts at improvement.

When we contemplate the repeated horrors that have been perpetrated upon pioneer settlements from the Atlantic to the Pacific, we are almost ready to advocate extermination as the only safe and permanent treaty that can be concluded with Indian treachery. Colonel Chivington, an experienced Indian fighter, said it simply is not possible for them to obey or even understand the law. "To kill them all is the only way we will ever have peace and quiet."

←——→

Fergus Dewsnap, "Evidence of Ineptitude Accumulates," *Lewiston Telegraph* (June 18, 1877)

Each succeeding day brings new evidence of the wholly unprepared condition of the military to protect the settlers in this country against hostile Indians. The coolest, most experienced, and most reliable frontiersmen say the present situation promises a long and bushwhacking war.

The whole region is sparsely populated, with miners, herders, woodsmen, and farmers scattered in small groups all over the territory. This manner of settlement has been brought about by a long season of peace, which engendered feelings of security exceeding common precaution, and by the supposition that the government would secure us against any outbreak.

In fact, General Howard is powerless, owing to the fact that there is no military force in the neighborhood adequate to the task of chastising the murderous Nez Perce. He is gathering troops from various posts and will probably be in a position for effective operations about the time the savages have wiped us all out entirely. Meanwhile, the local populace can only anticipate with painful suspense news of the next disaster.

←———→

Fergus Dewsnap, "GENERAL HOWARD KICKS A HORNET'S NEST," *Lewiston Telegraph* (July 3, 1877)

General Howard's most recent blunder was spectacular even by military standards. Two days ago, he ordered Captain Whipple, with two companies of Cavalry and two Gatling guns, to arrest Chief Looking Glass and all his people. The famous buffalo hunter was camped well within the boundaries of the Nez Perce reservation, but Howard didn't trust the chief to remain neutral in the fight.

Through superior generalship on the Indian's part or total incompetence on ours, Looking Glass evaded Whipple and joined the hostiles in the Salmon River country—the very thing Howard had been aiming to avoid. Looking Glass has just twenty warriors, but they are among the best in the tribe, and their savage will has been provoked by the loss of a woman and her child when Whipple opened fire on the Indians' peaceful camp.

General Sherman, Commanding General of the Army, was boiling mad when he learned of this latest fiasco. "Perhaps I was not clear," he telegraphed Howard. "The idea is to put the Indians on the reservation, not chase them off of it. These Indians require to be soundly whipped, the ringleaders of the present trouble hanged, their ponies killed, and such of their property destroyed as will make them very poor. You had promised, at the outset of this campaign, to make 'short work' of it."

‹———›

Fergus Dewsnap, "NEZ PERCE SHOW CONTEMPT FOR GENERAL HOWARD," *Lewiston Telegraph* (July 15, 1877)

Three weeks after taking to the field with 400 men, assembled at enormous taxpayer expense from outposts as far away as Alaska and Atlanta, General Howard is exactly where all this started, in White Bird Canyon, and no closer to catching the villains.

Ever since the battle, the Indians have been running General Howard in circles. They cross and recross the Salmon and Clearwater Rivers at will, knowing that a crossing they can accomplish in half a day will take our infantry and artillery two or three. So far, our panting epaulettes have barely gotten within spyglass distance.

Following the Indians' most recent crossing, Howard found himself without a cable long enough to construct a ferry to the opposite shore. His chief engineer, a pear-shaped lieutenant, scratched some figures in the sand with a stick and proclaimed that the cavalry's lariats, strung together, would work just as well. "No way that's going to hold," Captain Peniel told Howard, but the engineer pushed his spectacles up his nose and said he'd "worked it all out mathematically," pointing at the scratch marks in the sand.

Sure enough, the lariats snapped like a piece of thread. The men aboard the untethered ferry paddled furiously, but it was useless. Overloaded with passengers and equipment, they pounded into submerged boulders, launched over huge breakers, and swirled through eddies before finally disappearing around a bend in the river and smashing to bits, sinking Howard's Gatling gun. It's a miracle nobody was killed. The Indians watched the entire spectacle from perfect safety on the other side of the river, showing Howard their bare buttocks and taunting him with contumacious gestures.

So far, the Indians have killed 68 of ours without losing a single buck. It should be obvious to everyone that Howard doesn't know how to fight Indians, and he cannot learn. When Howard was sent to us, it was on the supposition that there would be nothing for him to do.

General Sherman's loss of confidence dripped from his most recent telegraph to Howard. "Perhaps I will catch these Indians for you," he wrote. "I depart tomorrow for two weeks in Yellowstone Park before proceeding with an inspection tour of the proposed route of the Northern Pacific Railway. With my trav-

eling party of five men (including the cook), I sus-
pect I could inflict greater losses on the Nez Perce
than your assembled forces have done to date."

«————»

Fergus Dewsnap, "President Considering Howard's Removal,"
Lewiston Telegraph (July 17, 1877)

The greater part of the cabinet session yesterday
was devoted to the Nez Perce outbreak. There are indications that the president intends to replace General Oliver O. Howard, who has long been known in
administration and army circles as "Uh-Oh Howard,"
due to his disastrous performance in the Secession
War.

«————»

July 18, 1877
From General William T. Sherman, Commanding General of
the Army
To General Oliver O. Howard, Commander, Department of the
Columbia

It is a great source of stupefaction for me and others that you cannot keep up with Nez Perce women,
children, and invalids. If they can make twenty-five
miles a day, why can't you? You must deliver results,
and soon, or I cannot defend you.

«————»

July 19, 1877

From Major Henry Clay Wood, Adjutant General, Department of the Columbia

To General Oliver O. Howard, Commander, Department of the Columbia

> A Nez Perce chief named Red Heart came onto the reservation today with 39 men, women, and children, and 400 horses. They have been hunting in Montana Territory since last year, having no part whatsoever in the hostilities.

←———→

July 20, 1877

From Major Henry Clay Wood, Adjutant General, Department of the Columbia

To General Oliver O. Howard, Commander, Department of the Columbia

> Pursuant to your instructions, we have chartered a steamship to carry Red Heart and his peaceful band, numbering 39, from their reservation in Idaho to the prison in Fort Vancouver, and confiscated all 400 of their horses. Perhaps you could recommend a supplier of irons suitable for the three and four-year-olds? Or do you think 19 guards can manage a few Nez Perce toddlers for the length of a boat trip?

←———→

July 21, 1877

From General Oliver O. Howard, Commander, Department of the Columbia

To General William T. Sherman, Commanding General of the Army

We struck the enemy hard in a deep canyon on the South Fork of the Clearwater River. They fought us mounted and dismounted, from ravines and behind rock barricades, for seven hours. We shelled them rapidly from the high bluffs until they escaped by crossing the river again. They fought as well as any troops I ever saw.

We captured 39 prisoners, who have been sent to Fort Vancouver in chains, along with 400 Indian horses. Our losses were 13 men. I have denominated this as the "Battle of the Fork of the Clearwater River." I now believe we are in fine condition to subdue these hostile Indians.

←———→

July 24, 1877

From General William T. Sherman, Commanding General of the Army

To General Oliver O. Howard, Commander, Department of the Columbia

Your enemies in Washington, D.C. have been quieted (for now), but I think that they, like the Nez Perce, will rise again.

←———→

July 27, 1877

From General Oliver O. Howard, Commander, Department of the Columbia

To General William T. Sherman, Commanding General of the Army

> The Nez Perce are on the Lolo Trail, a narrow track that traverses the Rocky Mountains from Idaho to Montana. With my force pushing them from Idaho and troops from Fort Missoula ready to intercept them when they reach Montana, their destruction is now inevitable.

Part Two

Chapter 10

Running Bird first met General Howard shortly before the war began, at what was supposed to be a peace council. Arriving at Fort Lapwai ahead of the rest of the Nez Perce delegation, Running Bird and his brother, Black Hoof, saw the general's gray shape standing on a slight rise in the prairie with his empty right sleeve flapping in the wind, whacking an aide who was missing a foot. While the secession war veteran wrestled the phantom limb back into its pinned position, the two Nez Perce galloped their horses straight toward him and skidded to a stop, scattering dust on the general's polished brass buttons and thick gold shoulder braids.

Running Bird stared into Howard's flinty gray eyes in a way that was intended to be neither friendly nor haughty, but rather was meant to convey that if Howard wanted the Indian's respect, he would have to earn it.

The general appeared unimpressed. "You're three days late," he said.

"I didn't want to come," Running Bird said.

"It's the middle of the salmon spawn," Black Hoof explained.

The rest of the Nez Perce delegation arrived over the course of the hot afternoon, circling Fort Lapwai's high wooden palisade before entering the toothy gate. The Indians' arrival added splashes of bright color to the otherwise drab interior of the fort. The Nez Perce wore scarlet red, cobalt blue, lime green—colors that complemented their dark skin and mocked the dusty gray uniforms of their hosts.

At the compound's center was a quadrangular parade ground, surrounded by squat buildings made of logs chinked with plaster or mud. Open areas were thronged with people talking all at once, raising their voices to be heard above the din of blacksmiths hammering, horses whinnying, and young calves, separated from their mothers, lowing in dry paddocks. The hot, stagnant air smelled of coal dust and fetid sewage, boiled cabbage and unwashed men, and the reek of pigs in unmucked sties.

Running Bird and some of the other warriors had displayed their horsemanship coming in—standing up in their saddles, hanging off the sides of their horses, flipping from side to side at a full gallop—and General Howard reciprocated with a demonstration by his infantry. The chiefs joined Howard on an elevated viewing stand while Running Bird and the rest of the Nez Perce—nearly eight hundred souls in all—pressed together on freshly-sawn benches of yellow pine.

The infantry assembled in formation at one end of the parade ground, wearing wide-brimmed hats and expressions so blank Running Bird wanted to paint a picture on them. Sweat rolled down the soldiers' faces, but they didn't dare move an arm to dab the salt from their eyes.

"I've known lizards who appeared more interesting and intelligent," Running Bird said.

"It's called discipline," Black Hoof said.

An army drummer tapped out a monotonous two-beat refrain while a bugler played short musical strains to communicate the sergeant's commands: *forward, double quick, halt.* The regimented movements of the soldiers and the rhythmic sound of combat boots pounding the dry earth gave the impression of machinery more than men, reminding Running Bird of the wooden cogs in the grist mill back at the old mission house. He could feel the soldiers' locked-step marching reverberate through the ground and into the soles of his moccasined feet as a dull throb.

"Watch this," Running Bird said.

After viewing a similar military exercise at an earlier council, Running Bird had purchased a bugle from a secession war veteran and learned how to play a few commands. Now, when the army bugler blew *forward*, Running Bird played *lie down*. When the army man blew *double quick*, Running Bird played *retreat*. Every time the army man blew a new command, Running Bird countermanded him, so that the soldiers walked in stutter steps, like dogs that wanted to jump into the water but were too afraid. They tripped and fell and swore like drunks.

General Howard's face was a red splotch of heat and indignation, but Running Bird's friends were delighted, laughing and slapping him on the back.

"He'll have you arrested," Black Hoof warned.

"He should thank me for pointing out the folly of marching into battle with men who can't think for themselves," Running Bird said. "I'm doing him a favor."

From the viewing stand, one of the chiefs gave Running Bird a subtle hand signal, urging him to end the game, but Running Bird had been looking forward to this for too long, and had put too much effort into learning the bugle calls. When the army man blew *forward*, Running Bird played *lie down* again, three short notes that ground the general's parade to a chaotic finish.

In deference to the chiefs, Running Bird offered no resistance when the sentries arrived. The one-armed general ordered him jailed for "insolence," but only for one night. The Indian had humiliated the general, and now the general would humiliate him in turn. Still, Running Bird felt he'd gotten the better of the exchange.

He watched the general's artillery display through the rusty iron bars of his triple-padlocked cell. Two mules pulled a brass-plated Gatling gun into position and pointed the barrel at a red blanket strung between two poles. When a soldier turned the hand crank, rotating barrels spewed out bullets in a horrific, deafening on-slaught. Nez Perce women huddled together between the yellow pine benches, hiding frightened children beneath colorful shawls. The Indians' horses bucked and snorted, outraged as much by the fences penning them in as by the gun's terrible noise.

When the shooting finally stopped, a soldier walked out and picked up what remained of the target, which was nothing but red threads. Wide-eyed warriors gathered around the smoking gun bar-rel, which was now too hot to touch. Gunpowder, smoke, sand, and sweat suffused the air.

"From the people who brought us cholera, a gun with diarrhea," Running Bird said later, when his brother came to visit him at the jail. "To cart out such a weapon at a peace council—"

"You forced his hand," Black Hoof said.

"He has no sense of humor."

The two brothers faced each other through the iron bars, Running Bird inside the darkened cell, peering out, and Black Hoof in the fading sunlight, peering in. It used to be just the two of them, racing horses from sunrise to sunset, placing exorbitant bets, throwing their blankets down, but ever since Black Hoof married, a crack had opened up between them. The older brother had two wives and two babies on the way, and they were all he cared about now.

"We've been ordered onto the reservation," Black Hoof said.

The same order had been issued countless times—ever since

gold was discovered on Nez Perce land—but the chiefs always managed to talk their way out of it. What alarmed Running Bird most was the way Black Hoof was avoiding his eyes.

"We swore we'd never go," Running Bird said. "We cut our palms and swore an oath."

"We were children," Black Hoof said, rubbing his face. "I have a family to think about now. You will, too, someday."

"Maybe your wives could just cut off your balls and dangle them from your ears, like earrings."

"Grow up!"

Running Bird sat down on the cell floor of square-cut logs, pounded close and rubbed smooth by the press of previous inmates. He worried that Black Hoof might walk away, leaving him alone in the lock-up, but instead his brother sat down too, so that they were positioned back-to-back with the iron bars between them. Running Bird could feel his brother's steady breathing and smell the cedar oil he'd rubbed onto his skin to keep the biting insects off. The prisoner synchronized his own breaths with his brother's, like he used to do at night when he was afraid. It still soothed him.

Black Hoof slipped a smoked salmon through the iron bars and a handful of camas bulbs cooked the way Running Bird liked, buried beneath a steady fire for tens of hours until the sugars caramelized and the husks turned black. Running Bird popped one of the bulbs into his mouth, then two more. The taste was smoky and sweet.

"We've been given thirty days to enroll with the Indian agent," Black Hoof said. "Any fighting age man caught outside the reservation after that will be shot."

Running Bird stopped chewing. "Shot?"

"That's what General Howard said."

Running Bird put his elbows on his knees and balled up his fists, cutting deep half-moons into his palms. Years earlier, the government had appointed a head chief over all the Nez Perce, then bribed him to sign a treaty purporting to relinquish millions of acres that Running Bird's band had always claimed as its own. Following a lengthy investigation, President Grant had corrected the error by issuing an executive order setting aside the Wallowa Valley for Running Bird's people, but the governor had objected, insisting that Oregon was "too cold for keeping Indians." Never mind that Running Bird's people had lived there more than ten thousand years.

The Nez Perce didn't resist when the president revoked his executive order and Congress opened up the Wallowa Valley to settlement under the Homestead Act, but they didn't move to the reservation, either, resulting in an uneasy truce. For all his life, Running Bird's people had lived side by side with the Big Hats—selling them horses, shopping in their markets, even refraining from vigilante justice when crimes were committed against them. General Howard's threat marked the end to this long period of integration and peace.

"It's dog shit wrapped in horse shit and served up on a skewer," Running Bird said. "There aren't enough soldiers in the world to make me eat it."

"Listen to me," Black Hoof said.

"Not until you look at me," Running Bird said.

They faced each other squarely, eyes shining through the prison bars like chips of black obsidian.

"We're the last tribe in America still living in peace on our own land," Black Hoof said evenly. "We've avoided disaster for longer than anyone else. Longer than we had any reason to expect. We're the endlings. Now it's over."

"I won't go," Running Bird said, folding his arms across his chest.

"You might be able to evade the white man's law for a little while," Black Hoof conceded. "You've always been clever and quick. But they'll catch up with you eventually, Running Bird, and when they do, they'll shoot you down or hang you from a tree. Until then, you'll be always on the run. Always trying to beat the odds. Always consumed by fear and suspicion and secrecy. It's no way to live and no way to die. I'm telling you three times!"

Running Bird couldn't help picturing himself swinging from a rope, kicking his feet and soiling his pants, trying to release his spirit with his last strangled breath. The image horrified him.

But what kind of life would he have on the crowded reservation? The day Running Bird enrolled, if he enrolled, the Indian agent would give him a new name—something preposterous, like Orville or Ruprecht—marking the end of his life as a free man and the beginning of his new life as the property of the government. He wouldn't be allowed to leave the reservation without a written travel pass, which, as a fighting-age man, he wouldn't be able to get under any circumstance. As a further precaution, his horses and his weapons would be confiscated as tools of war, which meant that he wouldn't be able to supply his family with meat.

He would be given a plow but no mules or oxen with which to pull it. He would be given seed for planting, but the best of it would go to men who agreed to become Christians. He would work from dawn to dusk, scratching out a bare subsistence from a dry patch of ground, growing increasingly dependent upon government handouts that would arrive unreliably or not at all. He would live in a condition of permanent want.

Running Bird was barely seventeen. Perhaps it was pure vanity, but he couldn't accept that his life was meant to be so squalid and unremarkable. He had always believed that he was being shaped to some purpose, and while he could not say toward what pinnacle he was moving, he felt sure he could never achieve it with an Indian agent's boot sole on his neck.

Running Bird wanted to travel, explore, climb, think for himself, work out on his own what he believed and how he wanted to live. He wanted to choose his own religion, his own teachers, and his own vocation. He wanted to follow his own path, not the one that others tried to force upon him. He wanted to make his own decisions, even if others disagreed.

If he went to the reservation, he would live a life of regret, feeling that he had wasted his chances and given up his power too easily and too soon. Instead of writing his own story, he would become the victim in someone else's. Tragedy would hang about him like a motheaten coat.

"They won't catch me," he said.

"I heard the Indian agent pissed his pants when a snake fell out of a tree and landed on his head," Black Hoof said. "We could have some fun with that. We're both good with snakes."

Running Bird felt an overwhelming affection for his brother in that moment. It was the kind of prank they might have planned together in the days before Black Hoof married.

"You could just piss on the Indian agent yourself," Running Bird said with a smile. "It would be easier."

"Just give the reservation a chance," Black Hoof pleaded. "If it's as bad as you say, we'll escape together, after the babies are born."

"I don't need to try it on for size," Running Bird said. "I can't live there. I won't."

"What about Prairie Dove?"

Running Bird closed his eyes and thumped his head against the rusted iron bars, rattling his cage.

Was it only a few days ago that he'd stood at the edge of Split Rocks Lake, watching her walk toward him through the meadow, swinging her arms so her fingers barely touched the purple tips of the grass? He remembered how she'd tilted her head so that a slight breeze swept across her face, which was flushed and damp from the afternoon heat. He'd pressed his hips against her, felt the tension building inside, lifting him to a steep precipice, then pulled back, relaxing his abdomen and thighs, diffusing the sensation with a few deep breaths. He remembered how ragged he'd felt, his body twitching from long, fierce control. They'd agreed to wait until she turned fifteen.

"She'll be better off marrying someone else," Running Bird said. "And I'll be better off without a woman slowing me down."

"You don't mean that."

"She can pass for white, which means she can still have her freedom, so long as she doesn't do something stupid like marrying an Indian. Like I said, she'll be better off without me."

"You can't make that kind of decision for her."

"I just did."

←———→

When the cell door creaked open the following day, Running Bird caught his favorite horse and mounted up with just the bare essentials: a long-range hunting rifle in a scabbard, a quiver and bow slung across his body, a knife holstered at his hip, a powder horn, a bullet pouch, and enough food and water to get him through a day or two.

He pressed his heel into Confetti Cloud's side and felt the stallion's muscular response. He asked for more speed and the Appaloosa willingly gave it, tearing up the ground with sharp, powerful hooves. He charged forward at daredevil speed, jumping sagebrush and broken logs, yellow grass whipping against his legs. It felt like he was flying, soaring like a hawk.

Running Bird didn't know if this day would mark a beginning or an ending for him. Maybe the one-armed general would catch him and hang him from a tree, like Black Hoof said. So be it. Until then, at least he would be free. At least the fire within him would burn bright. And at least when he died, he would go with a bang and not a whimper.

Chapter 11

Running Bird followed the creek from Fort Lapwai to the Clearwater River, then followed the river into the Clearwater Mountains, looking for a sheltered place to spend the night, which had turned stormy and wet. The rugged country was still beautiful, but seventeen years of mining had left its ugly marks. Majestic ridgelines had been reduced to rubble by pulsing jets of water, diverted from muddy streambeds. Quicksilver pooled beneath trees that were no longer green and gave no shelter. Abandoned equipment lay in rusting heaps.

Running Bird smelled the stench of death and found the source, a corpse hanging from a skeletal tree with a faded sign around his neck that read "theef." The dead man had been swinging there for a while but still had flesh enough to stink up the neighborhood following a hard rain. The Indian watched the body twist and turn as a gray mouse worked its way down the rope and into the raw hole of the cadaverous mouth.

Two years ago, when Running Bird's father was gunned down, he'd threatened to administer vigilante justice in much the same way that the miners so often did, but the chiefs had talked him down. They'd insisted that the Nez Perce must never kill a white man—no matter the provocation. They'd argued that forbearance was the only way to ensure that the Big Hats never sent soldiers against Running Bird's people.

At the time, Running Bird and Black Hoof had been persuaded to follow the white man's law. They'd delivered their father's killer to Sheriff Robert Peniel in Lewiston rather than administering justice themselves, only to be told that the law prohibited Indians from testifying against whites. According to the sheriff, without white witnesses, there wasn't any evidence of a crime. Running Bird had pointed out there was a dead body, then beat up two deputies. He'd woken up in jail, where he'd spent the next seventy-three days in chains. Meanwhile, Scott Grooms had walked free.

It had been a thorn in Running Bird's side ever since. Now the government was sending soldiers against his people anyway. Running Bird could think of no reason why he ought to care what the white man's law said now. What was the law anyway but a set of rules purporting to bind the Indian while offering him no protection? Rules that came, not from Running Bird's people or from his own conscience, but from the self-interest of his oppressors? Rules that were designed to break the Indian's spirit and grind him down to nothing?

Fuck the white man's law. Running Bird made his own law now.

←———→

Running Bird slept a few hours, then traveled from dawn to dusk and into the following day, arriving at Scott Grooms's claim on Orofino Creek shortly after sunrise. He painted two red stripes on his cheeks, oiled his bare skin, and tied his hair in a knot, leaving nothing for the killer to grab. He staked Confetti Cloud in a tumble of granite boulders surrounded by aspens and spruce, then crept as close as he could to the miner's dilapidated shack, moving silently from tree to tree.

Running Bird spotted Grooms's hunched back shoveling gritty tailings into a wooden rocker, washing the sand into an apron below in hopes that a few gold flakes might catch on the riffles. The thing

Running Bird remembered most about his father's killer was his pinched and deeply folded face, which looked exactly like a bulldog who'd just bitten into a toad. Seeing that dog face again sent a jolt through Running Bird's chest, radiating out into his limbs.

The miner still looked strong enough to overpower a woman or shoot a man from a safe distance, but hand-to-hand, Running Bird didn't expect much of a contest, and he found this vaguely disappointing. Grooms's arms and legs were twig-thin, and his clothes looked more like cobwebs than garments. There was nothing even mildly imposing about the man's physical presence. He was a weakling who'd taken down a giant. It still didn't make any sense.

Running Bird crouched in the trees, drawn down and coiled like a rattler ready to strike. He'd hoped for clouds, but the sky remained insolently clear, which meant that he'd have to wait for the sun to drop so his shadow would fall behind and not in front of him as he approached his prey. He was tempted to shoot Grooms from the trees and be done with it, but he forced himself to wait. He wanted Grooms to know who was killing him and why. He wanted it to feel like a proper execution, not murder.

His chance finally came when Grooms put his back to the trees to relieve himself in the creek. Running Bird sprinted forward on the balls of his feet. When he got close enough to smell the miner's dark urine and unwashed body, he grabbed Grooms from behind and put a knife to the wrinkled neck.

"You're under arrest," he said.

As soon as Grooms heard Running Bird's voice, his body went limp, as if he'd known this day would come and had resigned himself to the outcome.

Running Bird hadn't expected Grooms to shoot his father that tragic day, and Long Walker hadn't acted like a man who expected to be shot. The jowly American had asked permission to plant an orchard in the family's summer pasture, and unholstered his pistol when Long Walker politely but firmly declined. It hadn't seemed possible, at the time, that such a petty disagreement could really end in violence. Weren't there countless other hillsides where Grooms could plant his trees? Running Bird had raised his rifle reflexively, but Long Walker whispered, "*Elew*, easy," so Running Bird had stood down. It was the kind of mistake he still couldn't figure out how to live with.

Running Bird had never seen an actual trial, but he knew the accused was supposed to be given a chance to defend himself, no matter how strong the evidence against him.

"Why did you do it?" Running Bird said.

"Why does it matter?" Grooms asked.

"Defend yourself!" Running Bird demanded. "It's how it's done!"

The miner sighed, as if his own trial required too much effort. "You ever lived in a mining camp?" he said, jutting out his chin. "No. Of course not. I'll tell you, then. In the wintertime it's bitter cold and the snow's so deep your mules all die and your toes turn black and there's never enough to eat, you're just teetering on the edge of starvation, so sick of squirrel jerky you start to think death might be the better option, and you don't even dare play a game of cards with the other fellows because if you're unlucky enough to win, somebody calls you a cheater and shoots you down, so instead you just sit in your flimsy shelter and shiver and gnaw your fingernails and you don't even have any books, which doesn't really matter because you never learned how to read because you've been on your own since your father got hanged for beating your mother to death when you were seven. In the summer it's a hundred degrees in the shade, and you're puking your guts out with dysentery, and the whole country is swarming with claim jumpers and Orientals, and your claim isn't producing worth Jessy but you just keep working it anyway, long after it makes any sense to continue, because you don't have anything else to do, or anywhere else to go, and you're so tired of smoking willow bark you'd gladly sell your soul for a pinch of real tobacco except not even Lucifer's buying. Finally, you scrounge up enough odd coins to buy a few saplings and you get your mouth all ready for some hard apple cider, not so much of it that people might notice you have something they might like to steal but just enough to get you through the hard days and nights. You decide to plant your trees in some remote corner where the other fellows won't ever find them. Then a goddamned Indian gets in your way."

Running Bird stared at him. He'd expected an apology. Instead, he'd allowed the miner to wound him again. He tightened his grip around the handle of the Bowie knife and pulled the miner's head back by the hair.

"You killed my father for some apples?"

"I killed him because for once in my life I wanted to be the hammer instead of the goddamned nail!"

Running Bird slit the miner's throat. When Grooms started making hideous gurgling sounds, Running Bird pushed his face down into the creek to hurry his dying. Grooms's skin took on a bluish tinge, like the moon shining through a veil of clouds.

Running Bird knew that once he'd killed a man—once Grooms finished dying—there would be no turning back. No thinking about himself in the same way ever again. He looked into the terrified hazel eyes staring up at him through the moving water and sensed that he and the killer were crossing a terrible threshold together, leaving the only world they knew and entering their own separate corners of Hell.

In three or four minutes, it was over. Running Bird stood in the thigh-deep water while Grooms's corpse floated downstream, caught on some woody debris, then pushed through. The Indian watched the body slowly disappear around a bend in the creek. He listened to the water and the locusts whirring in the grass, one taut note striking against his skin like a million tiny pins. The sun beat down, still hot.

Running Bird had expected to feel, if not glad that Grooms was dead, then at least satisfied that justice had been done at last. Instead, he found himself wondering if the dead man had anyone who ought to be notified—an estranged sister, a fellow desperado, maybe the orchardist who sold the miner those saplings. Running Bird wished he'd thought to ask.

Perhaps it would have been different if he'd killed Grooms on the battlefield, but to kill him here, with piss dribbling out of the old man's cock—it didn't feel like warrior's work. It felt like an ugly job that the sheriff should have done himself. He looked down at his chest and arms, slick with the dead man's blood.

He took a deep breath and sank to the cold, stony bottom of the creek. He felt the heat steaming off his body, and the crimson rage he'd carried for so long bleaching out into something more ambiguous. He came up for air and went back down, muscling his way against the current with powerful whip kicks, but it was no good. The miner's blood would never come off. In throwing off the role of the victim, he had become the killer.

Chapter 12

After General Howard attacked Looking Glass's peaceful camp, Black Hoof packed up his family and left the reservation for good. Three weeks later, he and Running Bird were reunited on the narrow ridgetop trail from Idaho to Montana. They were joined by the victorious Nez Perce from White Bird Canyon, who, after running General Howard in circles, had finally decided, after many tears, to abandon their land, their ancestors' graves, and their cached supplies, and go to the buffalo country until some kind of truce could be reached.

While Black Hoof mostly blamed the war on General Howard, he reserved a specific slice of his anger for Running Bird and the other young men who, in uncoordinated fashion, had gone out looking to avenge past wrongs.

"It's the last thing our father would have wanted," Black Hoof said. "He told you to stand down."

"He was shot down like a dog!" Running Bird said.

"How many Big Hats do you want to kill, then? All the criminals? All the lawmen who protect the criminals? All the people who elect the lawmen and serve on the juries? All the women and children who happen to get in the way? We have eight hundred people. They are as numerous as the stars. We are like deer. They are like grizzly bears. How do you think this will end?"

They rode in silence but for the *clip-clop* of horse hooves and the sound of loose stones sliding down the steep hillside. The space that had opened up between the two brothers felt more like a chasm now. It made Running Bird wonder if he would ever be able to share his heart with Black Hoof again in a great gush of words, or at all.

Killing Scott Grooms had changed Running Bird. It made him aware of a ruthlessness inside him that he hadn't fully recognized before. It made him realize that he and Black Hoof were different, and that Black Hoof was the far better man.

After the trial and execution of the miner at Orofino Creek, Running Bird had burned down a fine clapboard house belonging to Sheriff Robert Peniel, against whom his grievances were too numerous to list. A feeling that was almost satisfaction had spread across Running Bird's chest as he'd watched the sheriff's estate burn. But satisfaction had quickly turned to horror when he'd heard a high-pitched wail and looked up to see the sheriff's wife standing in the dormer window on the second floor. He hadn't looked under the bed when he'd searched the house; she must have been hiding there. He remembered the scent of lavender and the sound he'd taken for a mouse scratching across the floor.

After he'd seen Sally Peniel in the dormer window, he'd run back toward the house, but by then it had been too late. He remembered the violent *whoosh!* as the house had reached its tipping point and buckled in a giant fireball. Something exploded inside the house, probably ammunition or booze. Stone and glass and burning chunks of wood had rained down, striking Running Bird on the head and back. At his feet, the torch he'd used to ignite the fire glowed orange against a bed of coarse black gravel.

"It was such an obvious hiding place," Black Hoof said now, drawing his eyebrows together in an angry V.

"Don't you think I know that?"

Running Bird didn't need Black Hoof to explain, again, the enormity of his mistake. He'd already condemned himself—first by volunteering to surrender at White Bird Canyon in exchange for peace, then by wearing a blood red shirt into battle, making himself an easy target—but he didn't think it was fair that he should also be condemned by his own brother, who had no power to offer absolution.

He wished it could all be erased with a stale cracker dipped in blood red wine, but he didn't believe in any of that rubbish, and he doubted anyone else did either, except when their conscience demanded it. The only person who could forgive him—Sally Peniel—was dead. The sound of her scream was a stone in his belly. The scent of lavender, the sound of a mouse, would forever set it churning.

Yahahiya, he thought.

The two brothers rode in silence, staring straight ahead. Running Bird uncorked his canteen, but it yielded only a few precious drops of water. His mouth was so dry it felt like he'd swished it with ash, but the Nez Perce were miles away from the nearest creek. The horses, too, were half crazed with thirst, their tongues lolling out the sides of their mouths.

When Running Bird had first imagined life on the run, he'd assumed he would be traveling alone. Instead, the Nez Perce were spread out for miles along the Lolo Trail with young people, old people, sick people, dogs pulling heavy travois, and thousands of horses, including hundreds of foals who were too weak for the brutal pace of the march. There was no way to hide the movements of such a large convoy. The Indians simply had to move faster than the pursuing force, which meant that food and rest came at a heavy price. It was the exact thing Black Hoof had hoped to spare his two pregnant wives, who were so exhausted they had to be tied to the high pommels and cantles of their saddles so they wouldn't come off if they fell asleep.

"I'm sorry," Running Bird said. "I know how much you were willing to give up to avoid this war."

"It was the dumbest of all the considerable dumb things you've ever done," Black Hoof said.

"Do you still love me?" Running Bird was embarrassed by the question. It was the kind of thing he used to ask when he was a little boy. But he felt desperate for some kind of bridge across the bleak abyss that gaped between them.

"If I didn't love you, I doubt I'd even talk to you, useless as it generally is."

Running Bird smiled.

←———→

Running Bird and Black Hoof painted their bodies and faces with streaks of green and white to blend into the summer leaves and light, then tied deer hides to their backs with tails, legs, and antlers intact. They crept through the trees on the balls of their feet, careful not to bend or break any branches, pausing now and then to take turns with a field glass they'd camouflaged with mud and leaves.

The Big Hats had constructed a crude breastwork, three or four logs high, blocking the narrow footpath into Montana's Bitterroot Valley. Running Bird counted thirty uniformed regulars and fifty militiamen huddled behind the barricade. Some of the soldiers lay on their bellies, sticking their gun barrels through chinks in the logs, waiting for the chance to shoot an Indian. Others huddled in small groups, checking their guns and gnawing on their fingernails.

The breastwork effectively blocked the footpath on which the Nez Perce had been traveling, but the soldiers had failed to consider the thickly forested hillside overlooking their entrenchment.

From the cover of the trees, Running Bird and Black Hoof could fire right into the soldiers' ranks, killing them like ducks in a barrel. Thirty of their warmates were also positioned in the trees, with rifles aimed at the soldiers.

"I'm beginning to think Howard's whole army is nothing but a gigantic bluff," Running Bird said.

"I doubt those farmers ever killed anything except their own pet pigs," Black Hoof said.

This time, the chiefs didn't carry white flags, which would only be perceived as weakness. Joseph, Looking Glass, and White Bird rode right up to the breastwork and told the Big Hats that the Nez Perce would go peacefully to the buffalo country if they could, but that they would go anyway.

The soldiers whispered among themselves. A few tense moments passed. Finally, the captain extended his hand to the three Nez Perce chiefs, promising safe passage.

Running Bird and Black Hoof watched from the hillside as eight hundred Nez Perce and two thousand Nez Perce horses stepped over and around the soldiers' breastwork, exchanging friendly greetings with the men who had been sent to stop them.

"It's over," Running Bird said when the last of the Nez Perce had gotten through.

"We're still homeless," Black Hoof said. "Winter is coming, and we have no cached supplies—"

"But the war," Running Bird said, squeezing his brother's shoulder. "It's over. We're free."

Chapter 13

Running Bird sat on the parched bank of the Big Hole River, carving an arrow shaft with long, languorous knife strokes. So full of ruthless energy at White Bird Canyon, he felt fatigued beyond all comprehension now, bleary-eyed and scraped out. Although the war was over, Running Bird could not rest yet, not with Black Hoof pacing circles around the red maternity lodge, wearing down the grass to a thin dirt track.

In the first few hours of Corn Tassel's confinement, Black Hoof was full of bluster, talking excessively about things like fatherhood and legacies. As the screams from the red lodge became more frequent and more desperate, cutting the hot, heavy air like shards of broken glass, Black Hoof talked about how strong Corn Tassel was, how stubborn and strong-willed, how she'd spent her whole life preparing for this ordeal. After a day and a night and another half a day, Black Hoof had just enough words left to state the obvious.

"Something's wrong."

Running Bird wanted to offer his brother encouragement, but he wasn't a liar and Black Hoof wasn't a fool. Running Bird was afraid to say too much, or feel too deeply, and so he simply clasped his brother's hand, helplessly. He imagined the infant's small pink face puckering in a silent wail, the little fists opening and closing in quiet desperation, unable to turn back to the safety of the womb or pass through the darkness to be born.

Running Bird was the kind of man who would do almost anything to exert some semblance of control when things started sliding toward disaster. If he was afraid of losing the woman he loved, he would push her away. If he was going to be hanged, he would place the noose around his own neck. If the sky was going to fall, he would give it permission to fall directly on him. He would stand like a beaten anvil and ring out his final song. Embracing his fears gave Running Bird at least an illusion of power. But there were times—and perhaps this was one of them—when all a man could do was to put his faith in the constant presence and mercy of the divine and resign himself to its will. If only he had that kind of faith.

Corn Tassel let out a feral, raw-throated cry. It was the sound of desperation bordering on panic. It reminded Running Bird of Sally Peniel, standing in the dormer window. Black Hoof buckled to his knees.

Amidst the mounting desperation, the Nez Perce medicine man ascended a hummock overlooking the red lodge with his pigeon-tailed coat buttoned backwards. When he reached the summit, he cupped his hands to his mouth and shaped a sound such as Running Bird had never heard a human voice produce. It started out as a whisper, then grew and grew until it sounded as if the creative power itself had taken up residence in Cedar Smoke's androgynous body. The song throbbed and pulsed, rippling across the grass like an invisible spirit.

Men who were pulling fish from the Big Hole River dropped their nets. Women who were collecting sunflower seeds put down their colorful baskets. Children throughout the camp stood still and hushed their dogs.

Each person added their voice to the medicine man's song, becoming part of it and part of each other and part of creation too. The undercurrent was a steady chorus of ancient, wordless tunes.

On top of the chorus, grace notes, contributed improvisationally, mimicking the sounds of wolves, birds, bears, and other animals. Layered over it all, a storyteller, shouting to be heard, telling how Coyote created the world, how he killed all the bullies and the giants, how he would come back again someday to pass judgment on the Big Hats. Occasionally there were snatches of Christian hymns:

> *timneisze imki Jesus*
> *titmineze he imene*
> *etke im he ues*
> *tota num lyeuneuat*

Running Bird felt the voices enfolding him, voices that were there and voices that were not there except in his memory. Each individual note was a strand in the web that held them all together. The song was molten rock pushing through the earth to make mountains. It was rivers pushing through rocky defiles on their journey to the sea. It was a song that could summon a storm or an earthquake or a shower of volcanic ash. But could it summon life?

When Cedar Smoke raised his arms, the people quieted. In silence, they expressed the inexpressible. They were a still pool of water, cradling the unborn child, beseeching him to rise, at last, and fill his lungs. Hot air moved across Running Bird's skin, broken by a faint breeze coming off the river.

Corn Tassel let out another anguished cry, one that rooted everyone who heard it in their places and held them there in collective agony. A magpie stood on a bare branch with her wings unfolded, showing off her white wing patches. Black Hoof looked as if he might blow away.

Still, the baby did not come.

"It's no good," Black Hoof said, breaking the spell. His voice was ragged. His face crumpled up like paper. He held his head in his shaking hands as if he might tear it from his own shoulders, eyes glistening like jaspers.

Running Bird picked up a handful of gravel and threw it at the sky, at the spirits who supposedly lived there, but the stones just rained back down on his own head. His throat was a tightening fist.

The two brothers exchanged broken words that were nowhere near equal to the task.

"I can't—"

"Wait—"

"It's not—"

"No, no, no—"

Black Hoof let out a sob that sounded like wood cracking, like an oak tree battered and broken by a storm, its leaves torn away by howling wind.

Running Bird hadn't ever seen his brother cry. It hadn't ever occurred to him that it was possible. He held Black Hoof in his arms and let the waves of sorrow crash over them both. He tasted salt from the mingled tears carving hot trails down his cheeks and the blood from his own lip where he'd bitten it. He cried for his brother and for Corn Tassel and for their baby. He cried for Black Hoof's younger wife, Red Abalone Shell, whose own battle would come soon, who must be terrified watching her sister wife die. He cried for Prairie Dove and for himself and for the life they might have had if they'd been born in another time or place. He cried for his parents whose graves would be robbed, whose bones would grind for all eternity, never finding any rest. He cried for the land and the life he'd left behind, like smoke drifting away from the burned-out embers that created it, dissipating in the murk. He cried for the forest scarred by miners' picks and for the trees poisoned by quicksilver with their roots clutching at dried-out streambeds. He cried because he was forced to live at the mercy of a power he couldn't see or trust or understand. He cried because Coyote was either heartless or a lie, and it didn't really matter which one. He cried because killing Scott Grooms and Sally Peniel had only made things worse. He cried because his brother was slowly dying inside.

A small white feather, just a tiny fluff of down, wafted across the grass, and with it came another stifled cry. Black Hoof looked to be in shock as the sound became more insistent, more unmistakable.

A child.

The midwife stepped out of the red lodge with blood smeared up to her elbows. She wiped the sweat from her brow with a soiled cloth. "Black Hoof! Corn Tassel is asking for you! Come and meet your son!"

The two brothers jumped and hollered and whooped like madmen. Running Bird kept crying, but his tears were mixed with laughter now. Black Hoof flew to his family, feet barely touching the ground.

Then Running Bird was alone. He felt chastened. Toyed with. Grateful. Relieved. He still didn't entirely trust the spirits, but he didn't feel abandoned altogether.

We are pressed on every side, but we are not crushed. We are perplexed, but not driven to despair. Persecuted, but not forsaken. Struck down, but not destroyed.

His mother had recited the passage from Second Corinthians so many times, Running Bird could almost hear her now. He remembered her soothing song, *Hmmmmmm-Ah-Ah, Hmmmmmm-Ah-Ah,* and the smell of the sunflower oil on her hair and skin.

For one cautious moment, he surrendered to the feeling. *We are not crushed.*

Chapter 14

Running Bird awoke the next day to the sound of trumpets calling *charge!* and men screaming in ecstasy or agony, he couldn't tell which. He threw off his blanket and ran out of the lodge, barefoot and half-naked, to see two hundred soldiers splashing across a gravel bar in the Big Hole River with bayonets drawn. With mouths agape and eyes deadened by whiskey, opium, and cocaine, the soldiers looked like the roving undead from one of Cedar Smoke's legends, disinterred from some corner of Perdition and thirsting for human blood to preserve them against the Hellhounds chasing them down.

Before Running Bird could catch his horse, grab a weapon, or even decide which weapon to grab, the soldiers were already running through the Indians' camp, bayonetting people who were still half asleep, setting fire to grass lodges with whole families trapped inside.

People fell like heavy sacks, their bodies piling up in the trampled grass which soon became slick with battle gore. Soldiers pulled the dead and dying up by the hair, harvesting gruesome souvenirs, leaving the bodies raw-skulled. Dogs ran through the camp snarling and baring their teeth with eyes glowing red in the semi-dark.

Running Bird grabbed his bow and quiver of arrows and ran out into the mayhem. He saw a Big Hat shoot a two-year-old child in the chest with cold deliberation. The mother snatched up her dying boy and was bayonetted through the back. Running Bird's first

89

arrow sank to the fletching in that murderer's head.

A young girl fell to the ground with a bullet in her leg. The Big Hat who'd shot her hit her in the face with the stock of his gun, knocking out her teeth, then put a bullet in her sister's skull. Running Bird killed that Big Hat next.

A former slave whose owner had chained him out in the cold too long, costing him both feet, crawled on his hands and knees toward cover. A Big Hat killed the cripple with an axe. Running Bird loosed two quick arrows, killing No Feet's killer.

A naked little girl ran from the doorway of a burning lodge, holding out her arms in blistering agony. Running Bird loosed an arrow at the soldier chasing her down but missed. The soldier put a bayonet in the child's back, killing her instantly.

Over and over, Running Bird's arrows came too late or missed the mark while the bodies just kept piling up.

I am failing them.

What he saw next filled him with such horror that he dropped his bow on the ground, too stunned to move or even make a sound.

Four children had been trapped inside a burning lodge and now their nightclothes were in flames, and their hair, but their feet still had flesh and bone enough to run and flail in the narrow spaces between the lodges. Women wrapped blankets around the burning children to smother the flames, after which the small bodies collapsed in smoking heaps, moaning at first, then still as sticks.

Running Bird's world went completely silent but for the rush of black smoke billowing from the burning camp. He'd ferried those four little children across countless rivers in a little round boat. They'd rewarded him with sweet smiles, which were now just teeth with the lips burned off. He'd taught the oldest one how to tickle a fish from the creek.

"Running Bird! Behind you!"

Black Hoof's voice broke through like a clear, perfect note, but there was a heaviness in Running Bird's limbs that made it impossible for him to turn or look or pick up his bow. His vision darkened at the periphery until he could see but a pinprick of light, shining on the bodies of the four burnt children. He couldn't avert his eyes or move his hands, which felt clumsy as wooden mallets. At the edges of his vision, he saw shadowy men fighting and hot rifles flashing, but his body wouldn't respond to it.

He heard the *twang!* of a bowstring followed by the high-pitched *xit!* of an arrow flying past his ear. The arrow killed a soldier who'd been charging up behind Running Bird with a drawn bayonet. If Black Hoof hadn't been there, Running Bird would have been sliced in two.

"Don't weaken!" Black Hoof shouted. "Not now! Fight!"

Running Bird knew he had to pull himself together. He'd watched Scott Grooms gun his father down. He couldn't stand by while disaster unfolded again.

The Nez Perce had been caught completely by surprise. Half the warriors still didn't have their weapons. Many of the men had tied their rifles and bows to their lodgepoles and couldn't get at them now with the walls caving in around bullet holes. There was no plan, no strategy, only people fighting in ones and twos, surrounded by total chaos.

Black Hoof tossed his bow and quiver to a warrior who needed them, then ran straight toward a soldier, leaping from left to right. He snatched the rifle right out of that enemy's hand, killed him with his own weapon, then took the dead man's ammunition belt.

Seeing Black Hoof's bravery, Running Bird began to rally. He picked up his bow, nocked an arrow in the bowstring, and killed a soldier who was setting fire to more lodges.

Black Hoof delivered an endless stream of instruction—"Look right!" and "Cover me!" and "On my word!" and "Now!" Running Bird focused on his brother's voice and an imaginary red mark on each enemy's chest. Arrows fell aslant from the blue-black sky, quivering when they struck their targets.

The sound of men fighting hand to hand was like logs thrown into a whirlpool, smashing each other to bits. Some women had also joined the fight. A warrior's pregnant wife picked up her dead husband's rifle and shot the soldier who'd made her a widow. A young mother strangled her child's killer with her bare hands, her grief more powerful than anything that drunken soldier could muster. Running Bird's eyes were still in the habit of seeking out Prairie Dove, and he found her in the thick of it, carrying children into hiding among the dense willows along the riverbank.

An artillery shell flew over top of the camp and exploded harmlessly. Running Bird looked up and saw that the Big Hats had set up a Howitzer atop a forested bluff overlooking the battlefield. Flash and fire funneled from the gun's wide mouth as another shell flew overhead.

"They can't even aim that thing," Running Bird said.

"They don't care what they hit," Black Hoof said.

"Somebody stop that gun!" Chief Joseph shouted.

The two brothers climbed to the top of the bench and crept up behind the cannon-ballers. The soft, wet earth accepted their bare feet soundlessly, not that it mattered. The big gun was so loud, Running Bird guessed the men who operated it were mostly deaf and wouldn't have heard even if the two warriors had come crashing through the trees on horses.

Running Bird dropped one of the cannon-ballers with an arrow in the head. Black Hoof killed two more before the remaining three abandoned the colossal gun and ran.

From the top of the bench, Running Bird could see that the Nez Perce had killed or wounded about half the soldiers and now had the enemy on the run. An army bugler called *retreat!* in short, loud bursts. The tune evoked an image of sunset though the sun had barely risen.

The two brothers were taking the Howitzer apart, burying the pieces so it couldn't be used again, when Running Bird saw Black Hoof's face fill with horror.

"Oh, no," Black Hoof said. "No, no, no—"

Running Bird followed his brother's gaze. Robert Peniel had just emerged from the red maternity lodge, spattered with gore.

The two warriors raced to the bottom of the bench, tripping and sliding. Black Hoof went left, toward the red lodge, while Running Bird tackled Peniel. The lawman's face was a defiant mask, but Running Bird could smell his enemy's fear, like burned peppercorns mixed with sweat.

"What did you do?" Running Bird demanded.

"You killed my wife!" Peniel bellowed.

"The baby too? Answer me! Did you kill the baby too?"

"As Chivington would say, nits make lice."

Running Bird let out a scream that might have stopped the sun in its tracks. He knew Peniel was baiting him, hoping for a quick and painless death. The urge to put an arrow through the sheriff's heart was almost overpowering. Instead, Running Bird put arrows through each of the prone man's hands and feet, pinning him to the ground. Then he pressed his face an inch from Peniel's.

"Here's how this is going to work," he said. "All those lies you like to tell about Indian savagery? I'm going to make them true. And the more you talk, the longer it's going to take."

«———»

Running Bird found his brother standing numbly in the red lodge, his face a shattered plate. Corn Tassel and Red Abalone Shell had each been shot in the heart at close range. Their hands were burned from grabbing the hot barrel of the gun that had killed them. The newborn's chest had been crushed with a boot or the stock of a gun. A cradleboard made of cottonwood and willow, covered with elaborately embroidered hides, lay on the ground, broken and spattered with gore. Running Bird bent over and retched.

Black Hoof ducked out of the red lodge and walked toward the retreating Big Hats in a slow, straight, predictable line. He didn't use available cover or position himself in a way that permitted Running Bird to provide effective suppressive fire. Too late, Running Bird understood his brother's intention. Each man could endure a certain amount of pain and no more. Black Hoof had hit a wall.

"No! Black Hoof, no!"

The first bullet struck Black Hoof in the chest. He fell to one knee, aimed his gun, killed the soldier who'd just shot him, and reloaded.

"Black Hoof! Get out of there!" Running Bird yelled.

The second bullet smashed into Black Hoof's hip, dropping him to the ground. He propped himself up on one elbow, killed the soldier who'd just shot him, and loaded another cartridge with powder-blackened fingers.

"Brother, I am begging you!"

The third bullet hit Black Hoof in the arm. He switched the gun to his other arm, braced the rifle tight against his cheek and shoulder, aimed the smoking black barrel, and killed another soldier.

"Don't leave me here!"

The last bullet struck Black Hoof in the forehead. He reloaded and fired once more, but the shot missed. He slumped forward, blood pooling beneath his body, soaking into the ground.

Running Bird watched Black Hoof's breathing slow, become sporadic, then stop, like a whirring wheel coming to rest. He'd synchronized his own breathing with his dying brother's and now, unwilling to break that final bond, found himself holding his breath. His lungs began to burn, screaming for air. His stomach felt like he'd just been punched. His torso began to convulse.

He had the sense that his body was being riven in two, with one part of him silently watching his own body writhe, and the other part of him still clinging, desperately, to life. In the distance, he could hear the women keening in the burning camp, the children crying, the dogs whining. The soldiers were gone, now, chased back across the river by warriors who'd just seen their families murdered.

Running Bird lost consciousness, but only very briefly. He woke up gasping, gulping for air in a ragged pant. He retched and coughed, trembling on his hands and knees.

It was only with the greatest difficulty that he willed his hands to perform the necessary tasks—dig the hole, wrap the bodies, bury Black Hoof and his family beneath an old cottonwood, which would cover the grave each spring with a thin white shroud of pollen.

He placed no marker on that mound of broken soil. No wooden

cross or copper bell or cairn of pretty stones, which would only invite robbers. But if he ever returned to that graveyard, the footprints and the voices would still be there.

And the grass, Running Bird thought.

We are the grass.

Chapter 15

Running Bird staggered through the burning camp, calling Prairie Dove's name. He felt like a grizzly bear had torn apart his body and put it back together with important pieces missing. He turned over corpses to see if he would find her among the dead. His voice was hoarse and shaking by the time he finally heard her.

"Running Bird! Over here!"

He found her by the water, weeping over her grandfather's lifeless body. Blood dripped from her right shoulder onto the old man's bullet-torn shirt. Running Bird squatted down in front of her and lifted her chin so he could get a better look at her injury.

They'd barely spoken since he'd left the council at Fort Lapwai without a word. She'd called him a coward—the worst thing a woman could call a man—but she wasn't wrong. In a world where everything could be taken away, love terrified him.

There were so many things that Running Bird wanted to say to her now. *I'm sorry. I'm an idiot. I'm afraid.* But there was no time for any of that.

He cut the blood-soaked calico away from the bullet hole in her shoulder, which was small and symmetrical with a black ring of burned flesh around it. There was no exit wound, which meant that the medicine man would have to dig the bullet out with a knife. The threat of infection was like a green serpent, tightening around his chest.

"The soldier who shot me called me a cockroach," she said. "He said, 'I've killed seven cockroaches today, and you'll be number—'"

She stopped when she saw that Running Bird was wearing Black Hoof's bone necklace. "No," she said. "Please, no. Not him."

A sound escaped Running Bird's throat like a hard shovel cleaving stone. "We need to stop the bleeding," he managed to say, pressing against her wound with the flat palm of his hand.

She closed her eyes and moaned with pain, but there was nothing for it; he had to press down hard.

When the bleeding finally stopped, he carried her to the river and laid her in the water to wash the wound. She shivered with cold, but again, there was nothing for it. They had to clean the hole.

While the icy current ran over Prairie Dove's body, Running Bird covered her grandfather's corpse with willow branches. Then he walked to the river and splashed cold water on his own face, arms, and chest to wash away the battle gore. A bullet had grazed Running Bird's hip, only a flesh wound that he couldn't yet feel. He had various cuts, scratches, and bruises. Otherwise, he was uninjured, which was almost farcical. He'd been running through the camp, cursing at the Big Hats, calling them dung heaps and devils, doing everything he could to draw attention to himself and away from the non-combatants, and yet it was the women and children who'd suffered the most, making up two thirds of the dead.

"I'm freezing," Prairie Dove said. Her lips, hands, and feet were blue. Her whole body shivered and shook so hard she could barely speak.

Running Bird picked her up, trying not to jostle the injured shoulder, and carried her to Cedar Smoke, who'd already set up a makeshift hospital at one end of the smoldering camp. Running Bird wrapped two blankets around her while the medicine man examined more critical patients, trying to work out who he could save, who he could only comfort. There was a three-year-old boy with a bullet in his abdomen. A six-year-old boy with a knife in his back. A young girl with a bullet in her leg and most of her teeth knocked out. A warrior with blood gushing from his leg, begging Cedar Smoke to get him back into the fight.

Every time Running Bird blinked, another tragedy unrolled before him—people who'd lost parents and siblings and children. Ninety dead Indians lay where they'd fallen, covered with branches and blankets until their families could get them buried. Thirty dead soldiers were being tossed into a grisly pile outside the camp. Running Bird covered his mouth with his hand to muffle the awful sounds coming out of him. He listened to Prairie Dove cry.

Many of the wounded lay in shock, their skin unnaturally pale. Cedar Smoke used anything he could find to splint broken and battered limbs: pot-handles and tree branches, hairbrushes and corn cobs. Blankets and clothing were torn into strips for bandages. Willow branches were peeled for their painkilling bark. Gentle horses were tacked to carry the wounded in sturdy saddles with high pommels and cantles. Everybody worked frantically except for Running Bird, who felt like his limbs had been turned into wood.

The smoky haze from the burning lodges colored the sunrise an angry cerise. The day would be scorching hot when the sun finally reached its summit, but it was still semi-dark and chilly in the orange scratch of dawn.

An old woman gave Prairie Dove a mug of willow bark tea, but she couldn't drink it. She was shivering too hard. She tried to warm herself by holding the cup between her trembling hands. Running Bird watched the liquid spill.

There was no time to remove the bullet from her shoulder. Cedar Smoke bandaged the wound as best he could and fashioned a crude sling from calico and strips of leather. Running Bird buttoned his warmest flannel shirt over the sling and helped her mount the sure-footed mule that had followed them out of White Bird Canyon. He tied her into the saddle and handed the mule's lead rope to a healthy woman who promised to take good care of the patient. Before they'd gone ten feet, the loose flannel shirt already had a bright red bloom of blood on it. Prairie Dove's face was ashen and pinched, wincing with pain every time the mule took a step, and yet she would have to travel all day and all night to have any hope of survival.

Grooms had been right about one thing, Running Bird realized. It was every man for himself, each kind protecting their own, and when you'd finally suffered enough for someone to put you into a hole, someone else came along and invoked your name just for the pure malice of it, just to laugh while your poor bones writhed. Give them a horse and they wanted your pasture. Give them your pasture and they wanted your grave. Give them the graveyard and they wanted your soul, and then they wanted you to thank them for it. There was no God anymore. No Great Spirit. No Coyote. People had killed them off.

"Don't weaken," Black Hoof had said, right before he'd lost his mind. He was always better at giving advice than taking it.

Running Bird wished he could dive into the dark heart of the earth and float out to the saltwater sea. He wished he were made of water because water knew how to change its form without ever losing the essence of itself. Water knew how to rise and fall and rise again. How to quench fire and clear debris and get where it wanted to go, even if it meant drilling a hole through the middle of the earth. Water never relented, never gave up, never got scared, never lost a fight.

Running Bird painted two red stripes on each cheek. He took an ammunition belt from a dead soldier and put it on. He slung a quiver of arrows across one shoulder and the long-range hunting rifle across the other. He picked up his curved bow, strapped on his Bowie knife, and mounted Confetti Cloud.

"I am not crushed yet," he said.

Chapter 16

Two months after the disaster at White Bird Canyon, Jack lay prone on his back in a shallow rifle pit overlooking the Big Hole River, itching and retching and staring up through thick pine boughs at the black smoke rising from the wreckage of the Indian camp. The knee-buckling stench of burned flesh and scorched buffalo hides was so dreadful, even the trees scrunched up their deeply creviced faces. The sun was an enflamed ball of blistering red. It was barely eight in the morning, but already the temperature was starting to climb. By afternoon, it would be hotter than Hades.

After the fiasco at the breastwork on the Lolo Trail, dubbed "Fort Fizzle" by the press, Colonel John Gibbon had been ordered to capture the Nez Perce. Before the battle, Gibbon had insisted that the Indians would surrender quickly, but since when did men throw down their guns when they saw their women and children being slaughtered? Gibbon had achieved complete surprise, catching the warriors not just unprepared but sound asleep, and yet within minutes the Nez Perce had turned the tide and driven the soldiers to the top of the forested hill where they now lay entombed in their rifle pits.

Jack suspected that gaining the hill had really been a forfeit. If there was a place as perfectly designed for an ambush as White Bird Canyon, this was it. The soldiers were surrounded by thick pines that served as perfect cover for Nez Perce sharpshooters. Warriors moved quietly through the trees, never shooting from the same place twice, never wasting a bullet. Shots came from every direction until finally Jack and the rest of the men just lay in their trenches like corpses, afraid to raise their heads, let alone take aim and shoot. The sound of Nez Perce women wailing over their dead added to the gloom.

The ravings of Tennyson's madman ran through Jack's addled mind:

> *For I thought the dead had peace, but it is not so;*
> *To have no peace in the grave, is that not sad?*
> *But up and down and to and fro,*
> *Ever about me the dead men go;*
> *And then to hear a dead man chatter*
> *Is enough to drive one mad.*
>
> *Wretchedest age, since Time began*
> *They cannot even bury a man;*
>
> *O me, why have they not buried me deep enough?*
> *Is it kind to have made me a grave so rough,*
> *Me, that was never a quiet sleeper?*
> *Maybe still I am but half-dead;*
> *Then I cannot be wholly dumb:*
> *I will cry to the steps above my head,*
> *And somebody, surely, some kind heart will come*
> *To bury me, bury me*
> *Deeper, ever so little deeper.*

Jack had murdered a little girl. "Shoot low into the teepees," Gibbon had said before the charge began, and Jack had done it in spite of all damnation, knowing full well there would be women and children in there. Three days ago, he wouldn't have believed himself capable of such butchery. Now he'd become Thoreau's wooden man, marching into a loathsome business against common sense and scruples, with no independent exercise of the moral judgment God gave him. Blood still flowed in Jack's veins, but the weight of remorse pressed so heavily against his chest it was a wonder his lungs continued to draw the acrid air.

If Jack had been forced to face his victim sleeping in her mother's arms, he couldn't have done it. Instead, he'd fired blindly into their teepee. He'd been willing to kill, but he'd wanted to do it in the most anonymous way possible, to make it less painful for himself. What if Sally had been inside that teepee? What if, instead of rescuing her, he'd accidentally killed her?

He lay in his earthen pit with the stillness and rigidity of the recently dead, thinking about all the things the little girl with the pink nightgown would never do, now, because of him. She wouldn't learn to swim, or chase blue-winged butterflies, or tie feathers into her pony's tail and mane. She wouldn't hug her parents or plant a garden or weave a basket or fall in love or have a child of her own.

After Jack shot the girl, he'd seen her mother carrying the corpse through the camp, wailing, until a man with a shining face and his shirt buttoned backwards took it away. Jack felt like he'd just witnessed something sacred—something he had no right to see—and yet he couldn't pull his eyes away. He wanted the mother's forgiveness and the shining man's blessing, but he might as well ask for stardust in a porcelain teacup.

Jack tried to imagine what that mother would endure in the weeks and months to come. She'd ride from dawn to dusk as if in a dream, glassy-eyed. When she stopped for the night, she'd pound roots into biscuits she didn't want to eat. She'd swallow a few crumbs with water when friends insisted, then lay in the dark, exhausted beyond all endurance, unable to sleep. She'd still look young, but she'd feel ancient and crumbly inside, her joints grinding like a broken wheel over gravel. Jack wanted to comfort her, and yet he was the instrument of her suffering.

He knew about other massacres where women and children had been slaughtered: the Apache at Camp Grant, the Piegan Blackfeet at Marias River, the Cheyenne at Washita and again at Sand Creek. Nobody ever got punished or even prosecuted for those atrocities, but that didn't make it right, or explain why Jack went along with it, or help him understand how exactly he'd become such a monster. He remembered his own horror when he'd seen the baby at Fort Lapwai with its tongue cut out. Now he'd murdered a Nez Perce child.

He was the only man bivouacked alone on that forested bench. He had diarrhea from the too-rich pork he'd eaten the night before the attack and had to use part of his shallow rifle pit for a latrine, which effectively kept the others away. He was still the white crow, listening to the disembodied voices of the black ones all around him, chattering and nattering like the dead men haunting Tennyson's madman.

Several of Gibbon's men claimed to have seen Jack's father die, but Jack still couldn't believe it. Peniel would cheat Beelzebub just like he cheated everyone else or charm him if trickery didn't work. Yet Jack couldn't deny that thirty men didn't make it to the top of the forested hillside, and Peniel was among the missing. If the Indians had him, he was better off dead.

All Jack's life, he and his father had crossed each other like a pair of sharp scissors. Peniel was the kind of man who pretended knowledge he didn't have, denied facts that were obvious, and never was so implacably insistent as when he was patently wrong.

He was more a force of nature than a man, possessing a relentlessness that could drive the sun itself to final darkness. Like Jacob's angel, he seemed to have an almost supernatural power to drive Jack mercilessly to exhaustion. It seemed impossible that the man had been killed, and by a mere mortal at that. If the river started running backward and the fish walked out wearing combat boots, Jack would have found it no less surprising.

His mouth was the kind of dry it usually took a hangover to achieve. Black dirt gritted between his teeth. His tongue felt like a used dustpan. He was desperate for a drink, even if it was only water.

He could hear the river not fifty yards away, but there wasn't any way to get there without being shot. A grievously wounded man moaned for water so piteously that Jack couldn't help wishing God would hurry and take the poor wretch home. When had he become so unfeeling?

Dozens of men had bullets and knives and arrows in their bodies with no water to ease their misery, no bandages to stop the bleeding, no splints for broken bones. General Howard was supposed to pick up supplies and bring them forward, but Howard was notoriously slow. It could be days before he arrived. Who could have guessed, when the battle plans were being drawn, that it would be the soldiers and not the Indians who got pinned down?

Jack stripped off his blue wool blouse and let the sharp gravel cut into his reddened flesh. Every so often, he raised an empty uniform sleeve with a stick, which would invariably be snapped in half as a bullet tore through the fabric. His ribs and collarbone were mostly healed but they still ached. Everything ached.

A tiny red-faced squirrel emerged from a dome-shaped burrow and stared at him, as if to ask what he was doing there. "I don't know," he told the squirrel. An instant after he spoke, a bullet flew past his trench and embedded itself in a tree. The squirrel went back into its hole.

Jack had joined this war in hopes of rescuing Sally, but he'd been chasing these Indians for more than two months without the slightest evidence that she was still alive. The notion that Sally had been kidnapped rather than murdered, in the face of so much evidence to the contrary, wasn't just delusional: it was disrespectful. Sally's tragedy was bad enough, but then to drag it out by indulging his own weakness, when he should have been planning her funeral, was shameful. There would be no heroics, no parade when he got back to Lewiston, no pat on the back from his father.

Jack drifted in and out of sleep, with his dead friend Motsqueh haunting his murky dreams.

"Forgive me," Jack said.

"You expect too much of me, and too little of yourself," Motsqueh said, arms folded across his pock-marked chest, which was disconcertingly still.

Chapter 17

On the third day of the siege, the Nez Perce set fire to the hillside where the soldiers lay entombed. Gibbon urged calm, but to little effect. The soldiers had no water to fight the fire, no tools or time to build a fire line, no rockslide to ride it out, no room to retreat. The conflagration moved toward them from every direction, gathering speed and strength until the sound was almost deafening, like a speeding train. Jack felt the heat close in and started to panic. Malachi's prophesy came to mind: *Every evildoer will be chaff and set ablaze.* He didn't want to burn.

Jack realized he was about to die in a grave he'd dug for himself, already soiled with his own stinking excrement. It was hardly the romantic ending he'd hoped for when he'd set out to rescue Sally at the start of the war.

He had the sense, again, that he'd lived the wrong life, or lived his real life wrongly. He didn't know if the Lord had any purpose for him, but if so, it seemed clear that Jack hadn't fulfilled it. He'd leave behind a pile of ash on the forest floor. A woman he loved and then abandoned. A child he didn't know. A few pretty sculptures which, in time, would be broken and lost and then forgotten. It turned out he was an even worse father than his own, something he wouldn't have thought possible if he hadn't already achieved it. He hadn't even gotten a good look at Charlie that day in Jessica's school room.

"Damn it all," he said.

Jack watched the tops of the pine trees sway one way and then the other as if the wind couldn't make up its mind. The blaze was closing in inexorably, smoke searing his lungs. He covered his mouth and nose with the stinking wool blouse, its sleeves torn away by bullets.

The heat raised blisters on his bare chest, arms, and face. He thought about Sally, trapped inside that burning house, and the Nez Perce families trapped inside their burning teepees. He understood, now, the terror they'd faced. He couldn't think of a worse way to die.

Jack dropped the blue wool blouse from his face and took deep breaths of the thick, black air, coughing and retching, hoping to pass out before the flames could reach him. If unconsciousness didn't come in time, he'd shoot himself with the Springfield rifle he'd carried since he lost the Hawken. He put the hot barrel beneath his chin and placed an unbooted toe on the trigger.

The smoke seemed to be doing the trick; he felt nauseous, dizzy, and out of breath. He was teetering on the edge of consciousness when the fickle wind shifted again, blowing the fire back upon itself, opening a narrow passage of escape. He stood up too fast and lost his balance, then stumbled through the burned-out section of the forest with one bare foot. He half expected to be ambushed on the other side, but by then the Indians were gone. The fire, it turned out, was their parting shot.

Jack fell to his knees and buried his head in his hands. Some of the other men said it was a miracle. They wanted to believe that God was on their side, but the Devil was just as powerful.

Jack stood at the edge of the river and watched the sweet, cold water lapping at a bank of blood-stained gravel. He stripped off his remaining clothes and stepped into the moving water. He drank too much, too fast, and started to cough. He slowed himself. He cupped his hands and sipped for a long time. He couldn't remember when water had sated him so thoroughly.

He lay back and let the river wash over him, carrying the grit, grime, smoke, sweat, and blood downstream. He thought about the woman whose child he'd killed. What would he say to her if they ever met? What would he say to Sally?

I'm sorry. I'm so sorry.

He could almost hear his father's retort: *As if those two words ever solved anything.*

Chapter 18

Entering the abandoned Indian camp, Jack saw that the Nez Perce had buried their own dead and tossed the fallen soldiers into a crevice. He tied a scarf around his nose and mouth and walked among the dead, beating hissing vultures out of his path with a stick, looking for his father. He heard Peniel before he saw him, growling at one of the scavengers.

"Sweet Jesus," Jack said, swatting at a black-caped bird.

"Water," Peniel croaked.

The man looked more in need of a taxidermist than a doctor, and yet he was, undeniably, alive. He had an arrow sticking out of his chest and another in his neck that had damaged his vocal cords, so his milky tenor voice sounded a whole octave lower with a gravelly rasp in it. Both of Peniel's hands and both feet were broken, along with God only knew what else. Jack could almost see the blood boiling in black pools beneath his father's skin. His whole body, including his face, was covered with fat green blowflies.

The Indians hadn't just wanted him dead. They'd wanted him to suffer. *Why?*

Jack held his father up and pressed a canteen to his cracked and bleeding lips.

Peniel drank greedily.

"What did you do to them?" Jack asked.

"What did *you* do?" Peniel croaked.

"What?"

"You murdered a little girl. I saw."

It was a line weakly tossed across the bow, but the barbed hook found its mark, sinking deep into Jack's raw flesh. He stared at his father's swollen and sunburned face, blackened with blood and smoke, his pale eyes mirroring the scorched and burning hillside. It wouldn't have surprised him one bit in that moment if his father's body split in half and bats flew out.

"The difference between my sins and yours," Peniel rasped, "is that I can look in the mirror and face mine, while you try to hide yours behind a pasteboard mask."

"Don't tell me what I think."

"Show me a drunk," Peniel wheezed, "I'll show you a man with a mask, pretending to be something he's not."

"I won't argue with you now."

Peniel's victorious grin revealed broken and blood-stained teeth. He closed his eyes, exhausted by the effort of speaking.

Jack covered his nose with a handkerchief, moved the nearest corpses away from his father, and constructed a shade with sticks and rags while they waited for General Howard, whose command finally arrived a few hours later. Dr. Benson Graham showed up with the general's medical detail, but thankfully he didn't mention the embarrassing scene at the school.

"Help me get him onto the stretcher," the doctor said. "Gently, now."

They carried the canvas stretcher into a hospital tent that had just been staked. Jack watched Graham administer chloroform and cut away his father's blood- and mud- and shit-stained clothes. When the physician picked up his scalpel, Jack went outside to wait.

Howard had arrived with nearly six hundred men, including several companies of cavalry, infantry, and militia; Indian scouts from various reservations; two Howitzer cannons; a medical team; a burial detail; and dozens of wagons loaded with food, medicine, ammunition, tents, and other supplies. Local citizens tagged along as Howard lumbered through the Bitterroot Valley, pulling carriages filled with fresh chicken and mutton, jars of jam and pickles, and cases of whiskey and brandy. The quartermaster distributed rations of salt beef, hard tack, and soap, while the cooks got to work making coffee and a hot meal.

Details were formed to set up Howard's headquarters, dig latrines and fire pits, gather wood and meat, and await the general's next move. Where the Indians' hide and grass lodges had stood at the start of the battle, Howard's infantry now laid out four neat rows of canvas shelters, each one about the size of a chicken coop. Where the Indians had gathered around small cooking fires, telling stories and playing games, Howard's men now reclined in the blood-stained grass, cleaning and oiling their weapons. Where the Indians' large herd of colorful, athletic horses had grazed, Howard's sturdy pack mules now stood, big-eared. Instead of chirping birds and playful raccoons, the river was lined with carrion eaters now, and graves.

When the chow bell rang, Jack stood in line with a tin bowl and received his ration of stew and fresh baked bread. Most of the men ate together in groups of three or four, but Jack ate alone. He was struck by the fact that they all looked so ordinary, with their tangled hair and bloodshot eyes and unremarkable clothes. If Jack hadn't seen it for himself, he would never have believed they were all murderers, much like himself.

Jack's hands shook so hard he nearly spilled the stew. For a moment he thought he was having another seizure. The food helped. When he finished eating, he rinsed his tin bowl in the river, then sat on a log outside the hospital tent, waiting for news of his father, who was still in surgery.

Hours passed. Graham was a good doctor, but Jack became increasingly doubtful that he'd be able to save Peniel, and he felt himself succumbing to despair. For all his father's insults and hypocrisy, all his grandiosity and outrageous vanity, the fact remained that Jack needed him. Peniel was the one person Jack could measure himself against and almost always come out on top. All he'd ever been was a repudiation of Peniel, and it wouldn't do to rage against some impotent ghost. He needed Peniel himself, in the flesh.

Finally, Graham emerged, eyes red with exhaustion, surgical gown smeared with blood. Jack stood up, searching the doctor's face.

"It's a miracle he survived," Graham said.

"If Noah threw him off the ark, I swear the waters would sneeze him back up," Jack said.

Graham tossed his bloody surgical gown into a giant iron pot of boiling water and washed his hands in a bucket. "He'll have aches and pains the rest of his life," he said. "Limited use of his hands. Difficulty walking. I imagine his days as sheriff are over."

"He'll probably run for governor."

"He'll probably win."

"Is he awake?"

"Let him rest," Graham said, removing his small round spectacles and rubbing his face. "I need coffee."

They walked to the mess tent, where Graham filled two tin cups, handing one to Jack. "There's more sand than coffee in it," he said after taking a noisy sip.

Jack couldn't stop thinking about the scene at the school. He wanted to ask about Charlie, but he didn't know how. "I shouldn't have shown up unannounced like that," he said.

Graham looked at him skeptically. "What were you doing there?"

"I don't have a good answer," Jack said. "I haven't gotten over her, I guess."

Graham didn't seem surprised. "I wish she hadn't told you about Charlie, though I suppose you had a right to know. I'm the only father the boy's ever known. It would be extremely upsetting to him—"

Jack waved this off. It was too excruciating. "He won't find out from me."

Graham stared at him, as if trying to decide something. For all his pomposity, he'd always been a decent man.

"I don't want to cause any more unhappiness than I already have," Jack assured.

Graham looked satisfied. "It must have been a shock," he said.

"My father once said I was too dumb to tie a shoelace. Told me to buy a pair of those boots the cowboys wear so I wouldn't have to lace them up."

Graham finished his coffee and refilled the cup. "She doesn't love me. I won't pretend she does. But I'm hopeful that she will, eventually. We both love Charlie. He's a sweet boy and smarter than all three of us."

Jack tried to picture Jessica's life with this man. "Does she ever throw things at you?"

Graham seemed to consider it a strange question. "No."

"She used to throw things at me all the time."

"Still does, evidently."

Jack shrugged that off. "I had six years to get used to losing Jessica. But Charlie—I just—you know—I didn't—I don't suppose . . ."

"You want to see him," Graham guessed.

Jack wondered if it was better to deny his need than to hear the inevitable rebuff, but somehow he found the courage to say, "More than anything."

Graham gripped his coffee cup. "I knew this would happen. It's why I didn't want her to tell you."

"It's—if not—you know, of course," Jack said.

"Jessica and I already discussed it," Graham said. "You'd have to stop drinking."

Jack's heart skipped a beat. He thought he must have misunderstood. "Wait. You're saying yes?"

"On that condition."

One minute earlier, if someone had asked Jack what scared him more than anything in the world, he would have said, without hesitation, sobriety. But that was before he dared to hope he'd have a chance with Charlie. "I'll never drink again," he said.

"If you cheat, I'll know," Graham said.

"I won't."

"You stay sober six months. Then you can meet him. We'll tell him you're a family friend."

"I'll do anything you say," Jack said.

"I'm only agreeing so Jessica will think I'm a better man than I really am," Graham said.

"You were there for them when I wasn't. I ought to thank you, but I can't."

Both men smiled. Graham extended his hand. Jack took it.

The doctor tipped Jack's chin up and looked inside his nose. "You left the hospital before we set your nose. Can you breathe all right?"

"Not really. I thought it would improve when the swelling went down, but it hasn't."

"I can fix it. I'll have to break it again."

Jack sighed. He supposed Graham had every right to break his nose.

They walked back to the hospital tent. Jack lay down on the surgical table, which still had smears of his father's blood on it. Graham rested a metal bar against Jack's nose and picked up a wooden mallet.

"This is going to hurt," the doctor said.

"Go ahead, then."

"I can give you chloroform."

"Save it for the men who need it."

Graham gripped the mallet.

"Graham?" Jack said.

"What?"

"Thanks."

"You're welcome."

Then the hammer came down. *Wham!*

«———»

"Motsqueh, do you believe in redemption?"

"I believe it's possible to find beauty in the things that make us weep."

"I want more than that."

The dead boy raised one eyebrow. "Forgiveness?"

"A clean slate," Jack said.

"I was only eight years old when I died," Motsqueh said. "The worst thing I'd ever done was take more than my fair share of the meat. I don't see how you can expect me to know so much."

"I wish I didn't know half of what I know," Jack said.

"Find the beauty in it," Motsqueh said.

Chapter 19

If Jack had realized how painful breaking and setting his nose was going to be, he would have taken the chloroform. Getting kicked by Hammertoe hurt, but getting hit by the mallet, when he knew exactly what was coming, proved incalculably worse. His nose felt ten times its normal size. His head throbbed.

He walked off the surgery table and headed toward the canvas tent that served as Howard's headquarters, intending to muster out. He was done with the army, which had bungled this war at every turn. First Perry had led them into an ambush, then Gibbon had given that damnable order to shoot low into the teepees, and now "Uh-Oh Howard" had arrived in the flesh, which meant it was only a matter of time before disaster struck again.

Besides all that, Jack's father was badly wounded, not to mention homeless. Jack didn't relish the thought of becoming his father's nursemaid. Robert Peniel was sure to be the worst patient in the history of blood. He was not the sort to suffer quietly or alone. Nevertheless, Jack couldn't abandon him.

Rounding a corner toward Howard's tent, Jack almost tripped over three pickle jars with human heads inside: a man and two women with long black hair swimming in the brine. The man's face was so hauntingly familiar, Jack could almost have been staring into a mirror, but for the corpse's greenish pallor. A fourth jar held a dead newborn whose chest had been crushed with the stock of a gun or a boot.

"Fucking Hell!" Jack said, jumping back. He lost his balance, nearly falling flat.

"They're for the phrenologists at the Army War College," a pimply-faced orderly said. "You draw two lines, see? A horizontal line from the nostril to the top of the ear, and a vertical line from the upper jawbone prominence to the forehead prominence. In the ideal man, the angle of the two lines is ninety degrees. Whites are eighty to ninety degrees. Negroes are seventy degrees. Orangutans are fifty-eight degrees. They're still doing the math on Indians."

Jack wanted to shake the orderly and smash the jars and return the pickled heads to the ground, where they surely belonged, but instead he raised his arms in disgust.

"Must we rob them even when they're dead?" Jack said.

"The general said to harvest as many heads as—" the orderly began.

"Is there anything you wouldn't do if General Howard gave the command?"

The orderly scratched his head. "If he told me to piss in my own bathtub, I'd be mighty reluctant."

"I catch you scratching around my grave after I'm dead, I'll tear you limb from limb," Jack said.

"It's just Indians the army wants," the orderly assured.

Jack walked on. He found General Howard hunched behind an ivory-inlaid field desk the size of a large suitcase, seated on a packing box fitted with a quilt. A candle stood next to nib and paper, flickering against the general's blue velvet cuff. He'd traded his infantry boots for sheepskin slippers.

Jack removed his hat and cleared his throat at the entrance to the tent.

Howard looked up from his correspondence with bloodshot eyes. "Come in," he said sharply. "Where's your uniform?"

Jack had traded his scratchy wool uniform to a Flathead scout for canvas pants and a comfortable buckskin shirt. "I'm mustering out," he said.

Howard dipped his nib into a pot of ink, still intent on his unfinished correspondence. "The war's not over."

"It is for me."

"This is still the U.S. Army, last I checked. That means you muster out when I say so and not until."

Jack didn't appreciate the general's haughtiness. He was a volunteer, after all. After two battles and more than two months on the march, he could go home having done his part, and that was exactly what he intended to do. Howard could keep his fifty cents a day and his stupid war.

"I didn't sign up to murder women and children," Jack said.

Howard put his steel nib down and straightened his back. He nodded to a canvas chair in the corner of the tent. "Have a seat."

Jack looked at the low-slung chair. It seemed like too much effort to fold himself into it and then raise himself all the way back out. He intended to keep this conversation short. "If you don't mind, sir, I'll stand."

"Murder is a serious charge."

"It's a serious crime."

"Gibbon said the women were carrying rifles."

That was interesting. It meant that Howard had already questioned the colonel.

"Gibbon ordered us to 'shoot low into the teepees,'" Jack said. "He gave the order long before the charge began, signaling that women and children were fair game. I saw five children shot in the head at point blank range. The oldest couldn't have been more than eight years old, and he did not—I repeat, did *not*—have a gun. I saw a soldier bash a young girl's head in with the stock of his rifle while she cowered in a bush. I saw a soldier shoot a toddler in the chest with cold deliberation. I saw a whole family, including four little children, burned alive. Do you want me to go on?"

Howard didn't answer.

"When those mass murderers get back to the settlements, I'll bump into them on the street corners. They'll be in the saloon and at the market. They'll be on the ferry and at the bank. And every time I see those killers, I'll see the people they killed. I'll hear their horses and their songs. The idea of it makes me want to heave. I wish I'd never come here and never seen half of what I saw."

"You like to leave it to other people to deal with all the ugliness," Howard said. "Like a woman who buys meat in a white paper package and then calls the butcher a brute."

"And you're a soldier who gets down on his knees and recites Mark Twain's 'War Prayer,' not realizing it was a joke. 'O Lord our God, help us to drown the thunder of the guns with the shrieks of their wounded, writhing in pain; help us to lay waste their humble homes with a hurricane of fire; help us to wring the hearts of their unoffending widows with unavailing grief; help us to turn them out roofless with their little children to wander unfriended the wastes of their desolated land in rags and hunger and thirst, broken in spirit, worn with travail, imploring thee for the refuge of the grave and denied it. For our sakes who adore Thee, Lord, blast their hopes, blight their lives, protract their bitter pilgrimage, make heavy their steps, water their way with their tears, stain the white snow with the blood of their wounded feet! We ask it, in the spirit of love, of Him Who is the Source of Love, and Who is the ever-faithful refuge and friend of all that are sore beset and seek His aid with humble and contrite hearts. Amen.'"

"Tell me," Howard said, squaring his shoulders with a

disapproving look. "What did you do when you saw those Nez Perce women and children being killed?"

There was no good response. Jack was no better than the rest of those murderers. He'd killed a little girl and done nothing to stop the carnage. He was astonished to realize he'd become as hypocritical as his father. The heat rose in his cheeks as the general stared at him, waiting for an answer.

"You should be cross examining Gibbon, not me," Jack said.

Howard came up over his desk and roared at Jack with fiery eyes. "Don't tell me how to run my command, you insolent fool!"

Jack was a big man, but Howard was too, and his empty right sleeve made him all the more terrifying. It was as if the arm had been removed without losing one trace of its compacted wrath.

Jack wondered if he'd made a mistake, speaking so plainly to a powerful man he barely knew. Why didn't he just say he had to take care of his father and leave it at that?

Jack retreated to the low-slung canvas chair. Howard sat back down behind his desk. Both men were flushed with anger, breathing hard. The candle wick threw a weak circle of light against the tent wall.

"I'm just asking to muster out," Jack said.

"You're an idealist," Howard said coolly. "So I'll forgive your impertinence. This time."

"Thank you, sir."

"I don't know what rock you've been living beneath," Howard continued, "but let me bring you up to date. This isn't the first time Indian women and children have been massacred. The commanding general of the army isn't going to do anything about it. If you think you're going to take General Sherman down with your stories, or change his course, or change one single opinion he's ever voiced—and there are some corkers, believe me—you're delusional. We just ended reconstruction in the south, knowing full well what's going to happen to the Negroes. We're not going to foment rebellion in the west for the sake of a few hundred Indians."

Jack noticed that Howard didn't deny or defend what had happened. He sensed that the general might even agree with him, at least in principle, though perhaps he couldn't say it out loud.

"Wrong's wrong, even if everybody's doing it," Jack said. "Even if the commanding general of the army approved it. On Judgment Day, each of us stands alone."

Howard pointed an accusing finger. "You can pack your bags and walk out of here and pretend you're somehow better than the rest of us who dirty our hands. But if you really care what happens to these Indians, you'll help me do the hard work of putting them on their reservation. Right now, they're fair game for any number of ambitious young officers looking to impress General Sherman. The best thing that can happen is they get caught by me rather than somebody else and go to the reservation before every last one of them is slaughtered. That's the cold truth of it. There is no other way to ameliorate their condition or preserve their existence."

Jack sat silent. He'd spent the last six years walking out, nursing his wounds. Howard was the first man who'd ever called him on it.

"War isn't about good versus evil," Howard said. "It's about evil versus greater evil. You want to wear a white hat? There are no white hats! Not in this war or any other."

The two men sat in silence, staring past each other.

"He's crazy, you know," Howard said.

"Who?"

"Sherman," Howard said. "'The only good Indian's a dead

Indian.' He said that. 'The more Indians we kill this year, the fewer we'll have to kill next year.' He said that too." Howard rubbed his face. "Look, I don't condone what happened here. I'll issue an order to all the men confirming that noncombatants mustn't be molested. But I'm not going to pretend it'll do any good, especially with the civilians."

"How does someone like that get to be commanding general of the army?"

"Sherman? He won the war. The big war. People love him. The president loves him. Both parties want him as their nominee in 1880. If he wants the job, we can skip the election and hold a coronation instead."

"I don't envy you, working for him."

Howard leaned back in his chair. "Gibbon thinks you have friends among the Indians."

It hadn't occurred to Jack until Howard mentioned it that he might have called unwanted attention to himself. He'd flown into a rage when one of Gibbon's men dug up the body of the little girl Jack had killed, looking for souvenirs. He'd snatched her back, whispered an apology, and reinterred the child where the grave robbers wouldn't find her again. Now Jack knew where to find the girl's grave but her grieving mother didn't, which felt like one more obscenity heaped on top of all the others. Only now did Jack stop to think of the impression he'd left with the other men.

"I don't have any friends," Jack said honestly. "Indian or otherwise."

Howard stared at him for a long moment, then seemed to make a decision. He leaned forward with his elbow on his field desk. "Gibbon and his men are needed at Fort Shaw," he said. "My command will continue the pursuit. Do you still want to muster out?"

Howard seemed sincere in his desire to avoid another massacre. And if staying on could really help the Indians, well . . . It wouldn't atone for abandoning poor Sally or killing the little girl, but at least it would sit on the right side of the ledger.

"My father was injured in the battle," Jack said. "He's going to need a lot of care."

"There's a hospital at Fort Missoula. He can convalesce there. He'll get excellent care. You can pick him up on your way back to Idaho, *after* the war."

Jack thought about it. He liked the idea of letting someone else take care of his father. He remembered that General Howard didn't allow alcohol in his command, which might turn out to be good for Jack as he adjusted to this new idea of sobriety.

"I'll stay on as a scout," Jack said. "I won't do any more killing. Call it mawkishness if you like. I haven't the stomach for it."

"You know the country?"

Jack nodded.

Howard picked up his nib again. "Where do you think the Indians are headed?"

Jack stared at his shoes, trying to imagine what he'd do in their position. "Yellowstone," he said.

Howard let out an exasperated sigh. "It's full of tourists!"

"The tourists will be gone in a month. In the winter, the park is sparsely populated. The Nez Perce are friendly with the Crow who hunt there when the Indian agent lets them. Yellowstone makes sense."

"General Sherman is in Yellowstone," Howard said. "He's on vacation."

Jack thought about that. What if the Nez Perce caught the commanding general of the army? Would they even know who they had?

"Sweet Jesus," Jack said.

Chapter 20

Fergus Dewsnap, "Who Are The Savages?" *Lewiston Telegraph* (August 11, 1877)

We have just learned that two-thirds of the Indians killed in Colonel Gibbon's battle at the Big Hole River were women and children, surprised and slaughtered while they slept. Joseph reckoned his chances of capture so contemptuously that Colonel Gibbon was able to achieve complete surprise, but within twenty minutes, our federal troops were in full retreat. Gibbon finished the battle pinned down ignominiously and precariously, cut off from his supplies, with half his men wounded or killed. The Indians moved off with perfect deliberation after they had buried their dead and packed what was left of their camp. The reports previous to this were that Joseph wished to pass peaceably through Montana, and it would appear that he was honest in his assertion, as he had already passed through the Bitterroot Valley without a collision, even stopping to pay old debts.

A remarkable feature of this war is the strategic skill with which the Indians have fought. According to Colonel Gibbon, "the Nez Perce are a match for an equal number of the best troops in the world." Whether the demand is for selection of the battleground, for skirmishing, for flanking, for threatening communications and supplies, for attacking in mass, for entrenching with rifle pits, for dispatching sharpshooters, or commanding key strategic positions, the Indians exhibit instincts and methods as strictly military as if they had been acquired at West Point.

Joseph and his band have been much underrated by many reports. He is no vagabond. He is neither bloodthirsty nor greedy. His braves are not a gang of besotted brutes. The Indians have a cause which, we regret to say, is too much founded in justice. With ordinary good sense and a sincere purpose to treat them fairly, the costly war now being waged could have been prevented. The mismanagement, fraud, and downright robbery perpetrated by our government and its rascally representatives drove the Indians to take up arms, and converted them into a fierce, dangerous, and relentless foe.

The Nez Perce are lighter in complexion than other Indians, with a general expression of features that is stern, often melancholy, but not as a rule harsh or repulsive. If not for their long hair, smooth skin, and imperviousness to pain, they could be mistaken for Europeans. Their average stature is equal to ours, with many of them standing six feet six inches in their moccasins. Their voices are strong and manly. They dress like all other wild Indians, but through superior industry, they ornament their costumes much more elaborately. They are persnickety about personal cleanliness. Joseph is in the full vigor of his manhood, about forty years old, a model warrior chief—tall, well-formed, of bold bearing, dignified demeanor, intelligent countenance, and every inch the leader.

«———»

August 14, 1877

From General Oliver O. Howard, Commander, Department of the Columbia

To General William T. Sherman, Commanding General of the Army

> We have made extraordinary marches, and with prompt and energetic cooperation from the eastern departments we may yet stop and destroy this most enterprising band of Indians. Without such cooperation, the result will be, as it has been, dubious.

«———»

August 17, 1877

From General William T. Sherman, Commanding General of the Army

To General Oliver O. Howard, Commander, Department of the Columbia

> The U.S. has no body of troops so near these hostile Indians as those immediately with you. You had, up to now, reported your force sufficient to contend with these Nez Perce. You will certainly be expected— by me, the president, and the country—to carry on the most active and persistent operations to the very end.

«———»

August 17, 1877

From General Oliver O. Howard, Commander, Department of the Columbia

To General William T. Sherman, Commanding General of the Army

I am sorry to be misunderstood. I did not wish to complain of want of cooperation, but to secure in advance that which would make our efforts most successful. My command, with jaded animals and men footsore and many of them virtually shoeless, shows signs of great discontent. The officers have complained to me officially of inability to maintain the current pace. I have been unable thus far to get any force ahead of the hostiles sufficient to hold them while my artillery and infantry catch up.

«———»

August 17, 1877

From General William T. Sherman, Commanding General of the Army

To General Oliver O. Howard, Commander, Department of the Columbia

I have no further instructions to give you.

«———»

August 20, 1877

From Major H. Henry Clay Wood, Assistant Adjutant General

To General Oliver O. Howard, Commander, Department of the Columbia

Do you recall the Nez Perce chief named Red Heart, who came upon the reservation a month ago with thirty-three men, women, and children, and four hundred horses, having had no part in the hostilities? He and his contingent are still being held in the stockade at Fort Vancouver, where they are being guarded by members of the military band, the regular soldiers being all out on field duty. Their trial has been canceled for lack of a single witness who can testify that any of them committed any crime. One of the detainees is a blind old woman, and four of them are little children, so it tests our most inventive prosecutors to conceive of a crime they could possibly have committed, even if we had witnesses willing to swear that they had done it. May we please send these peaceful Indians back to their reservation in Idaho?

«———»

August 22, 1877

From General Oliver O. Howard, Commander, Department of the Columbia

To General William T. Sherman, Commanding General of the Army

The hostiles have entered Yellowstone Park and begun robbing tourists. Suggest you cut your vacation short.

Part Three

Chapter 21

Nicole and her husband, Witt Lowsley, had been touring Yellowstone Park for the past three weeks. With two chocolate-colored mules, a Conestoga wagon, and a cantankerous guide, they'd followed the Firehole River through a forest of lodgepole pines and a succession of gigantic falls before finally reaching the highlight of their long expedition: a geyser basin filled with black sand, fluorescent pools, and geysers spewing hot water and steam through deeply fissured rock. The travel books called Yellowstone Park "Wonderland," after the fantastic world Lewis Carroll's Alice had found just a few steps away from the ordinary. Witt had heard about the park from another geologist and was almost giddy with excitement.

While Witt explored the curious landscape, Nicole stayed with the wagon and the guide, trying to paint a lone pine tree rooted atop a travertine boulder in a particularly turbulent stretch of the Firehole River. It seemed like a spectacularly bad decision for the tree to have laid its roots down there, where it had but a few inches of stubborn soil, and must spend its life battling through layers of rock to reach the steamy water below. The tree was barren on the windward side and bent over like an old woman coughing, and yet Nicole could see that it had persevered through many decades. Looking at the weather-beaten branches, she could well imagine the years of suffering, the storms endured, the lean years that made for the strongest wood, giving the tree a grandeur she'd hoped to capture on a scrap of linen. In hindsight, she was almost embarrassed by her own hubris.

Somebody else apparently admired the eccentric tree as much as Nicole did, and had festooned the sparse wood with colorful feathers and satin ribbons, so it sparkled in the sun like a *Christbaum*. In real life, the scene was sublime, exactly the kind of thing Nicole and Witt had traveled across the Atlantic Ocean and half the North American continent to see, and yet the painting looked ordinary. It didn't take one's breath away, like the real scene did. It didn't measure up.

She'd painted the tree on woven, hot-pressed linen paper sized with egg, but it couldn't hold the sparkle of the steam coming off the river, or the wet American travertine, or the rich colors of the tree's thick plates of bark, which looked like a collage made with broken bits of pottery in various shades of ochre with deep black crevices in between. She rubbed a finger across the linen and wondered if she should have washed it with a zinc oxide gouache instead.

Nicole dropped the uncooperative paintbrush into a porcelain cup and stretched her back, which was stiff from sitting too long on a three-legged stool in front of the easel. Her blonde curls were pinned in a loose French pleat, topped with a wide-brimmed hat to protect her face and neck from the sun, but her plump hands had been exposed all morning and were turning an angry shade of red; they might have belonged to an Irish washwoman rather than a professor's wife. She considered asking the guide, David Ford, to set up her parasol, but the fringe would block her view of the tree. She shoved her sunburned hands into her pockets. Such was her sacrifice to art.

Beneath the wagon's awning, Mr. Ford set up a folding table with a cheerful yellow oilcloth and turned out a pan of fresh bread, filling the air with a heavenly scent. Tea steeped in a hammered tin pot. Nicole wondered what was keeping her husband, who'd taken one of their mules and gone out on his own earlier that day. It wasn't like Witt to be late for tea.

She wished, again, that they had even the smallest drop of cream to cut the bitterness of the tea. She'd wanted to bring a milk cow on the trip, but the guide had flatly refused, and Witt hadn't pressed the point. For all his many good qualities, Witt vastly misunderstood the importance of cream. The guide, having won that opening volley, had been dismissive of her instructions ever since.

Nicole was enjoying Yellowstone's sublime landscape as much as her husband was, but she'd be glad to get back to London after such a long expedition. She missed the little shops in Piccadilly Circus, and her upholstered rocking chair, and the tri-colored tabby who'd appeared at the kitchen door one day and decided to stay.

Through a blur of steam coming off the river where a geyser fed into it, she saw figures crossing the windy basin and realized they were Indians, about a dozen of them mounted on horses much smaller and more colorful than the ones she and Witt rode back home. She grabbed a sketchpad and a charcoal pencil, and with quick, figurative strokes tried to capture the Indians' exotic appearance, with their painted faces and oiled bodies and long hair knotted at the backs of their heads.

"General Sherman gave us every assurance, when we saw him leaving the park, that the Indians wouldn't annoy us, so long as we stayed near the geysers," Nicole said to the guide. "He said they were very superstitious, and terrified of the geysers, and wouldn't go near—"

"I've got two ears," Mr. Ford said. "I heard him myself."

"They don't look terrified to me," Nicole said. "Terrifying, more like."

The warriors had smooth, finely-boned faces, almost womanishly pretty, but as they neared, Nicole saw that their expressions were ill-tempered, if not downright menacing. Rage seemed to pulse and seethe just beneath the surface of their skin, barely contained.

"Where's Witt?" Nicole asked, increasingly uneasy.

"I'm sure he's fine," Mr. Ford said, but Nicole could tell from the way the guide tightened his jaw that he wasn't sure at all.

Pinpricks of fear spread across her skin.

The Indians were well-armed with ammunition belts slung across their chests and rifles, bows, arrows, lances, and knives in various states of readiness. They didn't aim their weapons at Nicole or Mr. Ford, but they eyed the travelers closely. Nicole noticed dark spatters on their skin, the color of dried blood.

"Get your rifle, Mr. Ford."

"Don't be a fool," he said. "We'd be dead before I got the first shot off."

She was annoyed, not for the first time, by the guide's impertinence, though he might be right about their chances in a shoot-out with twelve mounted warriors.

The Indians trotted their horses right into the Lowsleys' camp, scattering dust on the tablecloth and the matching yellow napkins. They spoke brusquely among themselves in a language that sounded like cats or crows and would have been impossible to write with the English alphabet.

Nicole was almost paralyzed with fear, clutching her sketchpad with whitened knuckles, but she forced herself to meet the Indians' eyes. She'd read somewhere that one mustn't show an Indian the slightest weakness. Even the smallest prevarication could provoke their most savage instincts.

"Offer them something to eat," Nicole said.

The guide held out little scraps of the bread he'd made for the Lowsleys' tea, but it wasn't enough for twelve large men.

"Thank you," one of them said, accepting his share of the crumbs. He wore an unusual bone necklace and not much else.

"They speak English," Nicole said.

"I've got two ears," the guide reminded her.

She must ask Witt to talk to the guide about his impudence, but there wasn't time to think about that now. The Indian she'd decided to call Bone Necklace dismounted and turned out to be completely naked except for moccasins and a breechcloth which covered nothing in the back. Nicole was mortified by the view when he bent over to remove the hobbles on the chocolate-colored mule Witt had left behind.

"They're stealing our mule," she said.

Mr. Ford shouted at the Indian—"Hey! Hey!"—and tried to throw a halter line over the animal's neck.

Bone Necklace's smoldering anger flashed. He beat Mr. Ford brutally with his fists, dropping the guide to the ground.

Nicole tried to intervene—"Stop! Please stop! You can have the bloody mule!"—but Bone Necklace ignored her. The other warriors watched with little interest as the beating continued. Nicole covered her eyes, but she couldn't block out the sound of the heavy blows, like a fencepost smashing into a watermelon.

When Nicole looked again, Mr. Ford lay on the ground in pile of sharp angles. He raised his head unsteadily and tried to wobble to his feet.

Bone Necklace delivered another vicious blow.

"For God's sake, Mr. Ford, stay down! They can have the bloody mule!"

The Indians found an oak cask in the Lowsleys' wagon and treated themselves to a lovely, almost poetically fragrant French Armagnac, an extravagance that, unlike Nicole's milk cow, Witt had considered non-negotiable. She felt her cheeks blaze as the besotted men pawed through her whalebone corsets, lacy chemises, and thin silk stockings. Bone Necklace tied a strip of her fine swan's down around his head and raced his spotted horse around the camp, whooping like a madman. Another Indian tied her pretty pink mosquito netting into his horse's tail and mane. They seemed to be enjoying themselves at her expense, as if she were a person of no consequence. She tried to keep her face impassive. She commanded her lips not to quiver.

Where in the name of Christ on a biscuit is Witt?

When Bone Necklace picked up Nicole's unfinished painting of the tree, anger got the best of her. "Don't touch that!" she said, reaching for it.

The Indian took his time with the painting. His eyes gentled. Finally, he handed it back to her. "It's good," he said. "Very good."

They were the most mercurial people she'd ever encountered, which was saying a lot considering how much time she'd spent in France. They'd been brutal and playful, contemptuous and polite, all inside a few short minutes. They were beautiful to look at but also impulsive, unpredictable, alarming. Even General Sherman didn't seem to know much about them; the one thing he'd said—that they wouldn't go near the geysers—had turned out to be entirely wrong.

Bone Necklace's compliment appeased her. Like any artist, she liked nothing so much as admiration, regardless of the source.

"The colors are too flat," she heard herself say as he handed back the painting. "Too one-dimensional."

Nicole watched with dismay, worrying about Witt, while the Indians finished rummaging through the wagon and loading the tourists' supplies onto scruffy-looking horses. When the Indians had finished loading all the food and clothing, all the pots and pans, all the blankets and linens, even the spokes from the wagon wheels and the mahogany box that carried Nicole's art supplies, they set everything else on fire.

It wasn't until then that Nicole understood the seriousness of the situation. She and Witt would be stranded there, hundreds of miles from the nearest outpost, with no wagon, no supplies, and their guide beaten senseless. These weren't the traveling conditions she'd anticipated when she'd buttoned on her satin and kid-skin boots that morning. The boots wouldn't hold up for half a day walking in such rugged country. She felt exhausted by the very idea of what lay ahead.

Why had Witt insisted upon studying geology, of all things? Why couldn't he have chosen something more sensible—literature, for example—which wouldn't have beckoned them to this wilderness? She longed for the comfort and security of home.

Nicole felt something *zing!* by her head and heard shotgun pellets slam into the side of the burning wagon, spraying tiny splinters in every direction. She looked up and saw her husband galloping his big-eared mule toward the warriors, firing his bird gun with little aim or effect.

Nicole looked at him, incredulous. "Witt! Stay back!"

She realized he couldn't hear her and wouldn't have listened anyway. What would any man do if he saw his wife surrounded by a dozen naked men, his hired man crumpled on the ground, possibly dead, and his wagon burning? But how on earth did a geology professor with a mule and a bird gun expect to overcome twelve Indian warriors?

"Witt! Stay back!"

Bone Necklace took careful aim and with one bullet dropped her husband from his saddle. The professor's neck twisted at a horrible angle when he fell.

Nicole's chest felt like a pincushion pierced by a thousand burning needles. She tried to run to her husband, but another warrior held her back. She flew into a black rage now, screaming and kicking, but the Indian who held her remained impassive and restrained her with little effort.

"Witt!"

The professor's mule kept running, petrified, and skidded to a halt near the Indians' horses and the Lowsleys' other mule.

Bone Necklace loped his spotted horse to Witt's prone body and took another shot at point blank range. The Indian's face was expressionless, as if he were putting down a dog.

When the bullet smashed into Witt's skull, spraying Bone Necklace's leg with blood and bone, Nicole had the sensation she was falling. Her body grew numb, her senses shutting down one by one like candles flickering out. A coldness moved through her veins as she buckled to her knees. Her face went ice-white and dead-eyed.

I will cry for him one day, she thought. But for the moment, she couldn't quite comprehend it.

Some of the Armagnac had spilled beneath the wagon and now exploded into flames. Nicole felt a whoosh of hot air and a burning sensation on her hands and face.

The Indian who'd been holding her finally released his grip. She broke into a run and fell on Witt's body, blood pooling beneath his oddly angled neck. She took the handkerchief from her sleeve and covered what was left of his face.

Bone Necklace pulled her up behind him on his spotted horse and tied her to him with a leather cord. She'd seen a cowboy rope a bleating calf in four seconds flat at an exposition once; it felt like that.

Nicole arched her back and gripped the back of the saddle, putting as much distance between herself and the Indian as she could. The sour scent of his sweat, the blood spatter on his skin, the red stripes painted on his face, the vacant stare, vapid as a cow's—everything about him repelled her to the core.

"What am I?" she asked. "A prisoner? A slave?"

"A guest," he said, with no apparent sense of irony. "The cord will keep you from coming off the horse if you fall asleep. We'll ride all night."

"A guest?"

"All I can promise is that you won't starve, which you would do if I left you here."

Nicole was incredulous. The man who'd just murdered her husband and beaten her hired man senseless wanted her to believe he'd take care of her. She wanted to curse him. If she could have killed him with her bare hands, she would have done it then and there without the least regard for the condition of her soul. And yet, she didn't dare upset him.

"I just want to go home," she said.

"I do too," he said.

Chapter 22

Running Bird delivered the captives to the chiefs, mutely accepted a scolding for killing the artist's husband, and went looking for Prairie Dove. Most of the Indians' lodges had been burned or abandoned at the Big Hole, which meant that the people had to sleep out in the open or huddled in crude shelters, which in some cases consisted of nothing more than broken branches stuck into the ground to support an awning of filthy rags. Running Bird stepped over and around exhausted families and hungry dogs until he finally found Prairie Dove asleep in the shrubbery with her mouth agape.

Prairie Dove's surgery two nights before had been ghastly. The bullet was deeply embedded in her shoulder blade and wouldn't budge. Cedar Smoke finally extracted it in three separate pieces, each one requiring a deep plunge and searching probe with a sharp knife. Two strong women held Prairie Dove down, leaving white fingermarks on her skin. She'd bitten a hole through the leather strap they'd wedged between her teeth, and had lain insensible ever since.

Running Bird removed her filthy flannel shirt and the blood-soaked bandage. The wound had turned an awful green-gray color, surrounded by swollen red flesh with the putrid smell of infected meat. He filled a copper kettle with water and crushed elderberries and poured the concoction over Prairie Dove's injury, then sat down and held her hand, not knowing what else to do. Her lips were the pale color of a mud puddle that had dried and cracked in the sun.

They'd known each other all their lives, but it wasn't until last summer that they'd become a couple, at the harvest dance. Running Bird had tied hoof rattles to his ankles and wrists and was circling the fire, bent at the waist, stomping his feet, when he'd noticed Prairie Dove. He couldn't articulate what was different about her dance, but he'd found himself looking for her on every rotation. Finally, he'd caught her eyes. Then he'd caught her waist and together they'd spun, faster and faster until her feet lifted up off the ground and her arms stretched out like wings, the pull of each the only thing keeping the other from toppling into the flame.

Now she was fighting for her life.

Cedar Smoke shuffled toward them, glassy-eyed. Running Bird studied the medicine man's haggard face, which had aged a thousand years since the disaster at the Big Hole. Every time another Nez Perce died, Cedar Smoke added another ornament to his white felt hat—a feather or a flower or a piece of bone or wood. It was a wonder he could still balance the whole contraption on top of his head.

Running Bird didn't dare ask if the medicine man thought Prairie Dove would die. He didn't want to hear the answer.

"I wish I'd gotten that bullet out sooner," Cedar Smoke said.

"*Isquel*," Running Bird said. "So many things I wish."

"It's not your fault," Cedar Smoke said.

Running Bird said nothing.

"It's not your fault," Cedar Smoke said again, touching Running Bird's shoulder.

Running Bird felt the sting of tears, then the medicine man's warm embrace.

If Running Bird had to identify the exact moment when his life had spun out of control, it was the day he saw his father falling backward with a bullet in his chest. Ever since that moment, he'd made every possible wrong decision. He might have gotten away with drowning Grooms, who had no friends, but setting the sheriff's house on fire—*yahahiya*. Why hadn't he given Black Hoof a chance to talk him out of it?

If Running Bird hadn't killed the sheriff's wife, maybe Black Hoof and his family would still be alive. Maybe Prairie Dove wouldn't have been shot. Maybe there wouldn't have been a war at all. Or maybe there would have been a war (Thin Ice had cut a baby's tongue out, so yes, there would still have been a war), but different people would have been killed. Was it wicked of him to wish for that?

Running Bird considered it one of the great mysteries of this war that he—who had offered to surrender to save his people from this war, who had gone into battle at White Bird Canyon wearing a red shirt, practically begging the Big Hats to take him down, who had raced up and down the Big Hole River killing soldiers and swearing at them—had sustained no serious injuries, while better warriors, like Black Hoof, lay dead. It seemed that he, like Sheriff Peniel, had not yet suffered enough to die.

"You need to get some sleep," Cedar Smoke said.

"I can't," Running Bird said.

"I'll call you if there's any change," Cedar Smoke said. "Listen for the pronghorn. *Fweeeewwww!* If you hear that, it's me, calling you back. Come right away."

Chapter 23

The medicine man had urged Running Bird to get some sleep, but sleep was a waste of time, a luxury the warrior couldn't afford with General Howard just two days behind. He still had to find wood for arrow shafts and feathers to fletch them and flint or obsidian for the points. He had to sharpen his knife and mend his tack and find a new water carrier because somewhere along the way he'd lost his canteen, an idiotic mistake. He had to tend the horses, who were so spooked by the geysers they wouldn't hardly drink for fear that the water would grab them. He had to keep moving or else he'd curl up in a ball and weep.

Running Bird was tired of fighting. Tired of feeling trapped. Tired of watching people suffer. Tired of the guilt. Tired of being tired. He felt like he'd been swimming against a powerful current and had stopped to catch his breath on a tiny island whose sand was washing away beneath his feet. He could rest for a short time, but he still had a long way to go, and exhaustion was setting in. His body felt like a sack of sand, heavy and difficult to move.

He lay on the hard earth and closed his eyes, but it was no good. His mind was frenzied. His muscles twitched and spasmed. When sleep finally came, the nightmares began, bloody images that made him bolt upright, sweating and breathless. He dreamed of Peniel, ducking out of the red lodge with blood and bone spattered on his clothes, and of Black Hoof, walking into the Big Hat fusillade, and of Prairie Dove, biting a hole through a leather strap wedged between her teeth. He dreamed of skeletons, smiling at him from a small round boat. He dreamed of Scott Grooms, emptying his blood into the water, and of Sally Peniel, screaming as the fire claimed the space around her, and of Witt Lowsley, looking up at him with terrified hazel eyes the moment before Running Bird shot him in the head. He felt the widow's animosity hovering about him in the camp, tightening its cold, oily fingers around his throat. Her skin was the color of milk, but her cheeks flushed crimson and her back arched like an angry cat's whenever she caught sight of Running Bird. Who could blame her?

He got up. He swallowed some soup the women had prepared, boiled roots and a few bony fish in a watery broth. It didn't satisfy.

He went to tend the horses, grazing along a moonlit ribbon of water with strange orange foam along the edges. He pried small stones away from the tender frogs of their feet and curried their bony withers with a dried corncob, drawing comfort from their soft nickers. He looked around to see which ones had fallen behind that day, unable to keep up with the brutal pace of the march. Even the strongest animals were beginning to fail, with cracked hooves and swollen legs and festering saddle sores. Black Hoof's rose gold filly was among the fittest in the bunch, but she still wouldn't let anyone else ride her. Running Bird loved her for that.

The Nez Perce had journeyed almost eight hundred miles since the war had begun. Every day, the families traveled from dawn to dusk, while warriors like Running Bird covered twice or three times the distance, setting fires to mark the positions of the oncoming soldiers, stealing as many fresh horses as they could, and bringing in barely enough meat to keep seven hundred starving people alive. If anybody got in Running Bird's way, he shot them down with so little regard he could hardly remember all the faces of his victims.

War wasn't the adventure he'd expected. It wasn't a journey and a return. It was a closed circle of grief and suffering. It poisoned the soul.

War had changed him in ways he didn't like to admit. In the beginning, when he'd pushed Scott Grooms's hideous face underwater, it had felt like an ugly job that the sheriff should have done himself. When he heard Sally Peniel screaming from the dormer window, clutching her white nightgown, he was horrified by what he'd done. When the Big Hats fired on the chiefs' white flags at White Bird Canyon, he felt overwhelmed with fear for his people, and fought with a sense of desperation. But by the time he shot Witt Lowsley right in front of the poor man's wife, he hadn't felt anything at all. It was as if he'd jumped off a cliff and was gaining appalling momentum as he surrendered moral height.

Running Bird imagined defending himself before an imaginary judge. All he could say was that, in other circumstances, he might have lived an honorable life. He might never have harmed another person. He might have raced his Appaloosa stallion against Black Hoof's rose gold filly for years and years, trading victories. He might have married Prairie Dove and planted his seed in her belly. He might have been a loving husband, father, and uncle. Instead, violence had entered his heart like a chilling rain, drip by drop, washing away what was good in him.

He was disconcerted by what he'd become, and yet he could be nothing else, now. Everything he did was because he could think of no other way to protect his people from the next disaster. His body had been given over entirely to the needs of the families, as the grass gives itself over to those who depend upon it, and yet it was a futile gesture. Every soldier he killed was replaced by at least ten more. There was only one way this war could end. Black Hoof had been right about that.

All his life, Black Hoof had guided him, often annoyed him, always protected him. When Running Bird turned twelve, his parents had sent him into the mountains for three days and three nights to fast and pray. He'd been terrified that first night and had nearly crept home in ignominy. Then he'd heard his brother's call piercing the dark—*Hoo-h'HOO-hoo-hoo!* It might have been a real owl, but Running Bird had been convinced, at the time, that it was Black Hoof, watching out for him from the trees. It had gotten him through the ordeal. Now when he listened for his brother's voice, all he heard was silence.

Black Hoof would have loved Yellowstone, with its vibrant colors and its tranquil waters that sometimes erupted into a boil, hotter and more violent until the entire surface domed upward, lifting the startled birds. But Black Hoof didn't live long enough to see it, and Running Bird was too hard-pressed to enjoy it.

Running Bird saw a steamy pool at the top of a purple butte and wondered if it had healing powers like the hot springs back in Idaho Territory. He was willing to give anything a try.

It was an easy vertical ascent to the pool, fifteen or twenty feet of soft, uneven rock that bit into Running Bird's fingers and toes as he climbed. When he reached the pool, he stripped off his clothes and was surprised to find a piece of fine swan's down wrapped around his head. He held the soft down in his hands, trying to remember where he'd gotten it. More images flashed through his mind: the hapless guide, the burning wagon, the painter snatching back her canvas. Her husband must have been insensible when he came around the bend, ready for his tea, and saw the mayhem Running Bird and his warmates had unleashed. The professor's final charge was as suicidal as Black Hoof's, and as understandable, and as tragic.

All his life, Running Bird had imagined himself as a person who could handle whatever life threw at him. *I'm fine*, he said when his father was murdered, when his mother stopped eating and drinking to hasten her own demise, when General Howard hauled out his Gatling gun at Fort Lapwai. Now the self that he'd constructed over so many years and with such determination turned out to be nothing but tattered red threads, out of which nothing new could be assembled. He wanted to be the man he used to think he was, but the war had blown that chimera all to bits. He was not fine. He was a very long way from fine.

Running Bird lowered himself into the steamy pool and felt its stillness where it touched his skin. He held his breath and looked up through the lambent water at the rising moon; the pure beauty of it quieted his soul, if only for a little while. He imagined the coldness seeping out of his heart, burying itself in the sediment at the bottom of the pool, lying dormant like the mammoth bones at the bottom of Split Rocks Lake. When he came up for air, he listened to his own breath, in and out like a great, internal sea.

He warmed some resin from a Douglas fir and spread the balm on his various scrapes and wounds. The woody fragrance of the balm, the heat from the underground spring, and the broth he'd swallowed so ungratefully took the hardest edge off his sense of mounting desperation. He felt the muscles in his shoulders and back begin to relax a little. He untied his hair and untangled the knots with his fingers.

Memories came flooding back, comforting Running Bird like an old, worn blanket. A blue mountain lake, reflecting the snow-capped mountains. A familiar nook in the rocks where he used to hide things, knowing they would stay exactly as he left them. His father teaching him to swim, holding him steady against the river's muscular undertow. His mother teaching him how to spot a kill-deer's nest so he wouldn't accidentally step on the fragile eggs, camouflaged among the rocks. Black Hoof diving from a jagged ledge, bringing his outstretched arms together just at the moment of impact, the water gently splitting and then rolling over him. Prairie Dove sitting beside him in a log canoe, watching the pelicans circle high and then dive, head-first, into the water for a fish.

What would his father say to him now? He'd say that a man became a chief by touching an enemy *without* killing him. By exercising the kind of restraint that a fool might interpret as weakness, but a warrior ought to recognize as its opposite.

Life wasn't hammers and nails. It was people who took care of each other and people who didn't. It was looking into your brother's bowl to make sure he had enough, not to see if he had something you could take. It was feeling everything too much, not letting yourself go numb.

Running Bird thought about the day Black Hoof's son had been born, how powerless he'd felt, how hard it had been to surrender to whatever *Peyewit*, Death Spirit, decided to throw at them. He experienced the same fear now, the same heaviness in his limbs, when he heard Cedar Smoke's ear-splitting call. *Fweeeewwww! Fwew! Fwew!*

Chapter 24

Scouting for General Howard proved grueling. Jack spent his days tracking the Nez Perce families and his nights riding back to the general's camp to report the Indians' position, leaving almost no time to eat or sleep or even take a shit. Add to that the familiar misery of acute alcohol withdrawal—vomiting, nausea, anxiety, heart palpitations, dry heaves, fatigue, fever, throbbing headache, uncontrollable tremors, irrepressible craving, soul-crushing malaise—and he'd call it two of the cruelest weeks since God's torment of Job.

Finally, though, Howard was within striking distance of the Indians, trailing them by just ten miles in Yellowstone's rugged terrain. The general's plan was to capture and slaughter the Nez Perce horse herd, forcing the Indians to surrender without much of a fight, but Howard's prediction of a quick surrender sounded an awful lot like Gibbon's, and could be just as wide of the mark. Jack worried it could turn into another bloody massacre: more women and children killed, more survivors haunted by guilt and shame, more graves dug up and desecrated.

Jack had told Howard he wouldn't do any more killing, but when the next battle came, what was he supposed to do? Hide in the shrubbery again? He'd feel the pressure to fight and probably give in to it. In every interaction with his fellow soldiers, he felt himself being scrutinized and tried too hard to gain approval.

Somehow, he'd been convinced that it was in the Indians' best interests to be captured by General Howard rather than some other ambitious officer, but the Nez Perce themselves clearly disagreed, and the seed of Jack's own doubt had grown large enough for hawks to come and build their nests in its branches. When General Howard had asked whether Jack had friends among the Indians, Jack hadn't been entirely honest. He didn't have any Nez Perce friends; that much had been true. But he was pretty sure he had Nez Perce blood.

Jack couldn't point to any single moment when he'd realized his mother must have been Nez Perce. It had been instead an accumulation of small intimations over a period of many years. Rooms going silent when Jack walked in. People studying his dark features, then glancing away when he caught them. Friends eyeing each other every time Jack's father told the preposterous tale of the French beauty he'd married in his youth, who'd supposedly died when Jack was very young. Sometimes it felt like Jack's entire life had been an unfunny practical joke, played upon him by his father.

The whole unfortunate stack of lies left Jack feeling vulnerable. Dependent upon his father and others to keep up the charade. He lived in constant fear of the day when bigotry finally caught up with him and struck him from behind like a white-hot whip, bringing him to his knees. It made him do stupid things to prove his whiteness, like joining this low-down war. It made him want a drink so much he could weep.

If Jack really wanted the truth about his mother, all he had to do was to ask the Nez Perce. Peniel was their missionary at the time Jack was born. Surely there were plenty of Indians who still remembered Peniel's first wife and could say whether she was French or Indian. There might even be a tintype of her somewhere.

Jack had thought about approaching the famed Chief Joseph many times, but in the end, he'd opted for deliberate ignorance.

When the Indians had come to Lewiston to trade, he had avoided them with a determination that would have done an ostrich credit.

As a scout, Jack had been able to observe the Nez Perce more closely than he'd ever dared before. He found that he enjoyed watching them, so much that he sometimes had difficulty tearing himself away.

Their skin was darkened by sun and veiled in dust so that sometimes they looked like beings provoked right out of the volcanic rock. They traveled in rag-tag groups of ten or twenty, past boiling lakes and stands of sunflowers that sometimes reached their horses' withers, determined to the ends of the earth to be who they were and not who others wished to make them. Their expressions were tense and fragile, reminding Jack of a three-dimensional puzzle he'd once seen where each piece depended upon the placement of the other, and removing any one of them would bring the entire structure down. They were always reaching out and touching one another on the shoulder or the sleeve, as if they were afraid a loved one might suddenly disappear.

Chief Joseph ran up and down the line all day, shouting "Don't cry; hurry!" and "It's better to sweat than to bleed!" They carried their children on their backs and tied their sick and wounded to saddles with high pommels and cantles cinched to gentle geldings. When they quarreled, their voices jangled like church bells, and yet Jack never saw them turn their backs on one another. He never saw a Nez Perce traveling alone, except the ones who stayed back deliberately to die.

Over the years, so many people had moved in and out of Jack's life, and yet he had not one single person to walk beside. Even Hammertoe and Chocolate Bar had left him.

He wondered where he'd be right now if he'd walked into Chief

Joseph's camp when he'd first had a mind to do it. He'd probably be running for his life, but maybe it would have been a life worth living. A song echoed from some closeted place in his memory, *Hmmmmmm-Ah-Ah. Hmmmmmm-Ah-Ah.*

Jack staked a borrowed mule named Frying Pan in a copse of trees and crept through a thorn thicket on his belly, close enough to hear a young mother quieting her child as the Indians passed by him on their horses. A shale slide slipped like broken glass as the travelers passed over it, undone by the unremitting thrum of footfalls. A dog pulled a heavy travois filled with copper pots wrapped in blankets to mute the clatter and clang.

The woman whose daughter Jack had killed jostled along woodenly, leading a gentle roan with a small, empty saddle. The shining man rode beside her, talking in a whispery church voice. They were surrounded by steepled mountains, straining toward a blue dome of sky that looked thin and frail as silk, so that a bird could tear right through it and fly off to some other world altogether.

Watching the grieving mother, Jack felt his cheeks flush again with shame. He wanted to tell her that he'd buried her daughter deeper, just a little deeper, after the soldiers had dug her up. He wanted to tell her that he'd go back in the spring to plant flowers on the child's grave. He wanted to ask what kind of flowers the girl had liked best. Honeysuckle, perhaps, for its sweet scent, or violets, for their bright, cheerful color.

Warriors rode up and down the families' path with their eyes cutting through the trees and their long hair feathered and braided with beaded hair pipes. Old men carried long poles, fluttering with fur and beads and trinkets, held aloft as if they were flags. Young girls cut the inner bark from ponderosa pines, collecting the humble food in woven grass baskets. The old trees carried the scent of vanilla and molasses, but Jack knew from recent experience that the fragrance oversold the taste. Tree bark tasted like tree bark—no disguise could make it otherwise—but the sugary sap would keep them going.

He felt the drumbeat of hooves and watched in confusion, then astonishment, as a few dozen warriors drove what appeared to be General Howard's entire mule train around a bend in the Yellowstone River, throwing up an enormous cloud of dust. Jack couldn't quite believe what he was seeing, and yet he recognized the mules, and the longer he watched, the more certain he became that they were, in fact, General Howard's.

He'd visited Howard's bivouac the night before and seen for himself the extraordinary measures that the general had taken to protect the mule train from Nez Perce raiders. The warriors must have ridden into Howard's fortress-like encampment and stolen two hundred animals—including the bell mares—right out from under the general's nose.

Jack couldn't help laughing. God Almighty. They'd stolen General Howard's mule train. Wait until General Sherman found out about it. Wait until the press got hold of it. "Uh-Oh" Howard would have some explaining to do, that much was clear. At this very moment, Howard was probably screaming in an apoplectic rage. All the sentries would be punished, for all the good it would do.

Jack had lost another nickel, this time on a wager that they'd all be home in time for the potato harvest. Howard would be stopped in his tracks for two weeks or more while new mules were brought in from Virginia City. What if the Indians turned north, toward Canada, in the meantime? They might just make it. It would be a humiliating defeat for the U.S. Army if the Nez Perce received political asylum there, like Sitting Bull's Sioux. *Imagine*, Jack thought. *A few hundred hungry and exhausted Indians, evading the U.S. Army for an entire summer, then slipping across the border to safety as winter set in.* It would be David beating Goliath all over again. It would be the stuff of legends.

Jack had been watching the Nez Perce since the early days of the war. He'd seen them cross dangerous white water with women, children, and invalids in tow, in conditions that most strong men couldn't have survived. He'd seen them carry clubs to a gunfight and not only win, but win decisively. He'd seen them repel Gibbon's attack at the Big Hole, despite being caught completely by surprise after Captain Rawn's promise of safe passage. He'd experienced first-hand the near impossibility of keeping up with them in the mountains, though they had many wounded to tend to, plus children and elders who required extra care. He'd seen them stop for half an hour, though their very lives were at stake, to admire a pair of trumpeter swans stretching out their necks with a loud *oh-OH! oh-OH!*

Things had been done on both sides that couldn't be defended. The Indians' circumstances were desperate. But the audacity. The tenaciousness. The indomitable will. Jack knew he was witnessing greatness. Knew it as surely as he knew the blood-beat of his own heart.

"Find the beauty in it," Motsqueh had said.

Jack was a loner, an alcoholic, a mercenary. The Nez Perce represented everything his life lacked. Community. The will to live. The capacity to hope.

All those years, Jack had rolled with his father's ridiculous story about the French beauty. He'd signed up for this damnable war. He'd fired low into the teepees. Like all weak things, he'd looked for a stronger counterpart, finding ready accomplices in the church, the law, the military, and his father, who represented all those things.

He had tried to be white because it just didn't pay to be half Indian, knowing the Indians were doomed. Well. The Nez Perce had proved him wrong, hadn't they? They weren't destined for destruction. They were destined to survive.

The Nez Perce families stopped to cheer the returning warriors, emerging victorious like apparitions from the dust thrown up by hoof-beats. A bare-chested warrior raised his arm and his voice to keep Howard's mule train moving forward, "Whoop! Whoop! Whoop!" The young man was breathing hard, glistening with sweat, almost naked but for an unusual bone necklace.

Jack watched the young warrior for some minutes, riding a spotted horse like the reincarnation of some winged hussar. It was almost as if Jack had come around a corner and bumped into a version of himself that he'd always hoped might exist somewhere. He felt a sudden and inexplicable bond to the bare-chested horseman that was so strong, so irresistible, he couldn't imagine the warrior wouldn't feel it too if their eyes could but meet.

Jack rose up to his full height and emerged from the cover of the thorn bushes. He stood out in plain sight of the warriors, cheering with the families, laughing out loud. He understood the idiocy of it. He was still wearing pieces of his army uniform. He would surely be recognized as one of General Howard's scouts. And yet the war that had raged within him for so long finally seemed to have tipped. These were his people, even if he didn't know them. When they suffered, he suffered. When they rejoiced, he did too.

The warrior with the bone necklace drew his shoulders back, every line on him as taut as a bow. He aimed his rifle at Jack and fingered the trigger, but he didn't shoot. He stared directly into

Jack's eyes, as if trying to read his heart. His expression deepened. Overhead, broken clouds swirled.

Jack made no move to defend himself. He felt pried open for all the world to see. He held the younger man's gaze, determined to wrest something beautiful from this war, even if it was only this flashing connection. They'd never met, and yet in that moment, Jack would not have refused a bullet if he'd thought it might help the younger man escape.

The Indian lowered his gun. His warmates, seeing that he'd reached some kind of decision about Jack, seemed to accept it. They moved on.

Jack smiled as he watched them go.

Howard had ridiculed Jack's naiveté. He'd insisted that the Indians were irrevocably doomed either to slaughter or to confinement. The Nez Perce were just then surrounded by four converging armies. All of their friends, even the Flathead and the Crow, had been bought off by the government, and turned against them. They were hundreds of miles from Canada, and they were still headed east, not north. And yet Jack couldn't give up hope for them, not anymore.

He shouted at the top of his voice. He didn't care who heard him, so long as the warrior with the bone necklace did. "Go to Canada! For the love of God! Turn north!"

Chapter 25

Nicole was furious at Witt for dying. Maybe it wasn't fair to blame a man for getting shot by an Indian, but rage was the only emotion she had that didn't make her weep. Mark Twain famously said, "Anger is an acid that can do more harm to the vessel in which it is stored than to anything on which it is poured," but the American humorist never saw his spouse gunned down, did he? Never got kidnapped by Indians either, did he? So he could keep his platitudes.

She still found it hard to believe that Witt had tried to save her with a mule and a bird gun, with such utterly predictable results, leaving her stranded in this blasted topography of boiling mud and noxious steam and naked savages. The landscape that seemed so exquisite when her husband was alive looked preternaturally fiendish now. The whole place smelled like rotten eggs.

What were you thinking? she asked Witt over and over.

I wasn't thinking, my dear. But really, what else could I do?

Nicole worried she was going mad, having conversations in her head with her dead husband, and yet the fact that she worried about it implied that perhaps she still retained some reason, and that her husband was, in fact, as flippant in death as he had been in life.

Chief Joseph had said he was sorry about Witt's murder, but words wouldn't bring Nicole's husband back or get her home, would they? Joseph said that for her own safety she must stay with the Indians a little while longer, yet she wouldn't have been stranded in the burned-out floor of Hell if the Nez Perce hadn't murdered her husband, destroyed her wagon, stolen her mules and all her supplies, and kidnapped her guide. Not even Joseph could talk his way out of that.

Nicole had always been told that Indians had an intimate relationship with the land, as if it were a relative or a living mother, but the Nez Perce didn't seem to know where they were or where they were going. Sometimes Nicole swore they were moving in circles while Chief Joseph ran up and down the line with his many wampum necklaces, shouting, "Hurry! Hurry!" He reminded her of the Red Queen from Lewis Carroll's book, who explained to Alice: "Here, you see, it takes all the running you can do, to keep in the same place. If you want to get somewhere else, you must run at least twice as fast as that!"

Yellowstone was even more bizarre than she and Witt had imagined, with mounds of earth that were scarlet and violet and golden-green, and wet clay shimmering with striations of ochre and orange, and white rocks in the midst of a desert embedded with images of the sea, and dead trees whistling like songbirds, their resin scented like cinnamon, their branches clawing at the sky like bony fingers, and the sky like a silver colander, leaking rain. Geysers spewed, mud boiled, pools steamed. Earth's fury, like that of the Indians, simmered just beneath its surface.

The Indians conducted experiments with the geysers, which Nicole couldn't help thinking her husband would have enjoyed. A group of young men threw a thirty-foot log into a boiling mud pot and shrieked with delight when it came flying back out. A woman dropped some clothes into a crater and waited for the geyser to deliver them back, boiled clean. An old man caught a fish in the river and then walked a few steps to cook the meal, still dangling from the gaff, in a boiling pool. Every night when the Indians stopped to camp, young boys built cairns out of horse dung—contemptuous trail markers for General Howard, whom they called General Day-After-Tomorrow, on account of him being almost perpetually two days behind.

Nicole's erstwhile guide, Mr. Ford, spent most of his time with the Indian scouts, helping them find places to hunt and camp. He had contusions in every hue of purple, blue, green, and yellow from his beating, but the colors had started to fade. He'd "traded" away his own fine clothes and accepted in return a pile of rags that would have been comical under other circumstances. At least they'd given him pants, which were patched with calico, out at the knees, fringed at the bottom, and too short. A tattered shirt fluttered at his back. His wreck of a hat had lost its crown and fallen down around his neck, where he wore it like a scarf.

The Indians had "asked" Mr. Ford to guide them to the Great Plains and promised to release the two captives after that. Perhaps the Indians would keep their word, but how could she trust such volatile people in such desperate conditions with anything as fragile as her hope?

The families traveled at a slow trot all day, from dawn until dusk. The pace was brutal for a sedentary and some might say slightly overweight painter. Her body had never been pushed so hard, yet the physical exertion helped her through the waves of grief that made it hard to breathe sometimes.

The Indians let her ride a lame gelding with a bullet in his shoulder. Even if she'd been given a healthy horse and could somehow break away, it wouldn't have helped. According to Mr. Ford, they were at least a thousand miles from the nearest train. She doubted she could find civilization on her own, or survive the coming winter in the wilderness.

Nicole could feel the changing weather in the contrast between the sun-drenched afternoons and the freezing temperatures at night. Yellow-headed blackbirds, black-necked stilts, and white-faced ibises flocked and departed to the south. Clusters of trembling aspen dropped their heart-shaped leaves, which drifted away with the unceasing wind.

She'd cut her satin skirt and petticoat from the hip to the hem so that she could ride without a sidesaddle. Joseph's oldest wife gave her strips of leather to cover her legs. At first, she resisted wearing the oily buckskin garments, but she couldn't have her legs obscenely exposed for all to see, nor did she like the scratchy feel of horsehair against her skin. Besides, the leggings kept her warm at night. She put them on.

Her kidskin boots were in tatters, the heels broken off, the satin buttons long since lost. The remnants were held together with strips of rawhide wrapped and tied around the soles of her feet.

I told you to pack a pair of sturdy laborer's boots, Witt said.

Nicole fumed that he should try to shift the blame for this cataclysm to her. He was the one who had wanted to see Yellowstone Park. He was the one who had spent a year planning the trip, poring over maps and surveys, writing to other geologists. He was the one who'd died, leaving her in this bloody, Godforsaken place.

At the eastern edge of Yellowstone Park, the Nez Perce reached the snow-capped Absaroka Mountains, which seemed to go on endlessly to the horizon, jagged and steep, with nothing remotely resembling a road in sight. The horses slipped down precipitous hills as if on sleds, but somehow always recovered their footing. Nicole felt like she'd fallen into unmapped territory that ancient cartographers would have labeled simply, "Here be dragons." She focused on the march, the relentlessness, the grueling unremittingness.

The Indians traveled in small groups, four or five people abreast, spread out over two or three miles, with an enormous herd of unruly horses, warriors roving in and out pell-mell, women stopping to collect roots and seeds, little girls cuddling cornhusk dolls, boys throwing mud balls at each other, dogs getting stuck with their heavy travois, barking in frustration. All day long, Chief Joseph ran up and down the line, yelling "Hurry! Hurry!" Some of the people retorted, "Don't tell us what to do," but then they picked up the pace, as if they had been about to do it anyway.

Somehow the whole collective—seven hundred people—managed to find each other every night in some remote corner of the wilderness, with grass, water, wood, and just enough food to get them through another day. They reminded her of a starling murmuration, hundreds of individuals, iridescent with speckled breasts, swooping left and then right, poised to tip, wheeling and turning, splitting into separate formations and then joining together again. To the outsider, the formation looked completely disorganized, but the individuals shared such a mysterious and perfect connection with each other that they moved as one loosely composed whole.

Nicole recognized odd pieces of her clothing among the flock, as if the Indians had taken ownership of some part of her. A girl wore one of Nicole's skirts around her neck like a cloak. The medicine man wore one of Witt's expensive shirts buttoned up the back instead of the front. A tiny child, barely old enough to walk, wore a scrap of Nicole's pink mosquito netting.

They've taken all your shirts, she told her husband.

I have no need of them now, my dear, he said.

Most of the tourists' clothing had been torn into strips and applied as bandages, scraps of gorgeous fabric wrapped around devastating wounds. Nicole saw a young girl with broken teeth whose gums would not stop bleeding. A little boy with a bayonet wound in his side who would not stop crying. A warrior with a bullet in his belly, silently clenching and unclenching his jaw. Some of the Indians looked as if they'd been tossed from their very graves, with tangled hair and long fingernails and blood pooled beneath their eyes.

Nicole struggled to keep up with even the weakest members of the tribe. Her mouth was dry, her stomach empty, her eyes red from weeping and dust. Her legs throbbed after an hour or two in the saddle, then cramped excruciatingly, and finally went numb, so that she had to be helped off her horse every night. Joseph's oldest wife told her to relax her legs and move her hips with the rhythm of her mount, but who could relax in the circumstances she faced? Even her teeth were tense. She thought about the tree in the Firehole River, the one she was trying to paint the day Witt died. What would the tree say to her now? *Sink your feet into Dante's fifth circle if you must. Stretch your arms to the sky if you dare. Endure! Survive!* She made it her mantra.

Most days, the Indians didn't have enough food, and what they had was mostly inedible. Usually, they cooked just a thin broth, flavored with roots and small game. By the time they entered the Absaroka Mountains, Nicole's whalebone corset slipped loosely around her shrinking frame.

You must eat, my dear, Witt said, though he'd never eaten such unpalatable fare in his own life, and so was in no position to criticize.

The children and elders ate first, then the warriors. The women shared what remained out of a common pot. Nicole noticed that the men took the stringiest meat, which meant that the women ate better but not as much. They chewed on willow sticks to clean their teeth and draped their babies with wild roses and goldenseal to keep the biting insects off.

When it got too dark to travel any farther, the Indians stopped to rest. Nicole slept in Chief Joseph's lodge, which was constructed with tall poles and pliant hides. Her bed was a buffalo robe topped with deerskin and a wool blanket. Joseph's wives and teenage daughter slept in a circle around her, so she didn't feel unsafe.

"Sleep fast," the chief's oldest wife would tell her every night.

Despite this excellent advice, sleep proved elusive and often unachievable. The camp was noisy at night with the cries of the children and the moans of the wounded and the ethereal calls of male snipes, which sounded like flying ghosts. When Nicole did manage to doze off, she had surreal dreams and often awoke with a start. One night she dreamed that Witt lay beside her. She straddled his hips and pressed her hands against his chest which was soft and spongey like peat. When she bore down, his ribs collapsed beneath her weight, opening up a yawning hole from which a rat jumped out. She woke up screaming, too horrified to fall asleep again.

If only she could have buried him properly. She remembered being pulled away from his body, which was probably unrecognizable by now, the limbs carried off by wolves. Exposed to the elements, his remains would begin to liquefy, and—

No. She mustn't draw the picture with her artist's eye for detail.

People died in the Indian camp every night or stayed behind to die the next day. Some of the dead had impossible names like Tahwistokaitat, Watyetmestahmoe, and Tipyahlanah Kapskaps. Others had Christian names like Timothy, Reuben, and James. Many had taken new names after the Big Hole: Shot in Belly, Shot in Head, Shot in Bicep, Shot in Mouth, Shot in Eye, Two Wounds,

Five Wounds, Many Wounds. After each death, Cedar Smoke rang a bell, after which the name was not to be spoken again.

An old woman named Mimilu paced in the dark, searching for her husband, who'd been killed in battle. Mimilu had painted a second set of eyebrows on top of the original pair, making her look perpetually surprised. Every few hours, someone had to tell her, again, "You mustn't speak his name," whereupon she'd suffer the loss anew, and throw dirt on her head, and tear out handfuls of her hair. Nicole couldn't decide which was worse: knowing that your husband was dead or learning it again every few hours. She thought the hours of forgetfulness might be well worth the terrible price, and almost envied Mimilu's amnesia.

In the mornings, they'd break the shoreline ice to ford the creeks and watch for moose with green moss hanging off their antlers, and coffee-colored grizzly bears that left long-clawed prints on the muddy trails, and musky-smelling wallows where the grass had been trampled flat. They traveled on narrow goat paths, gaining elevation every day, expanding their view of the surrounding snow-capped peaks.

Cedar Smoke became, for her, like a guy rope on a storm-tossed ship. There was nothing extraordinary in his appearance except for his face, which had an inexplicable glow, like fired clay. It was his gentle voice that drew her in, his quiet presence, his small acts of kindness which couldn't stem the tide of grief but seemed to imply some capacity to rise above it. Who were they, after all, but Hobbes's brutes if they didn't treat each other with kindness? She helped the medicine man tear her stolen clothes into bandages, and wash the blood-stained clothing of the wounded, and gather willow bark for painkilling tea, drawing far more comfort from the work than she gave.

The medicine man fell off his horse almost every day, crumpling to the ground as if he were asleep. The horse would drop his head and stand there, waiting patiently. After a few minutes, Cedar Smoke would mount up again, seemingly refreshed.

"He walks in his sleep," Joseph's oldest wife explained.

"Is he asleep right now?"

"Nightmares keep some of us awake. Life keeps Cedar Smoke asleep."

The women in the camp were gentle with Nicole, but they lived a brutal existence. They did all the packing and unpacking and had to make at least one meal a day out of practically nothing. The oldest ones had leathery skin, few teeth, hunched backs, hands nearly crippled by work, and Chief Joseph constantly yelling at them, "Move! Move! Move!"

"Why do men persist in making war when they can see how the women and children suffer?" Nicole said.

Why did I charge twelve mounted Indians with a mule and a bird gun? Witt answered.

Because you're foolhardy, temerarious, senseless—

What else could I do?

They robbed us, so you shot at them (and missed), so they shot you (and did not miss), so General Howard will fire his Gatling gun at them (and perhaps kill me accidentally). Where does it end?

"Forgiveness," Cedar Smoke said.

She blinked at him. She hadn't realized she'd been speaking out loud. "I thought I was talking to Witt," she said.

The medicine man trotted away, glassy-eyed.

Chapter 26

Fergus Dewsnap, "General Sherman Flees The Nez Perce," *Lewiston Telegraph* (August 22, 1877)

General Sherman skedaddled when he found out Chief Joseph was in the same neighborhood. The commanding general of the army was vacationing in Yellowstone Park. After assuring other tourists they would be perfectly safe, Sherman cut his own trip short. Days later, a tourist named Witt Lowsley was murdered. His wife, Nicole, is still missing, along with the couple's guide, David Ford.

Howard is gallantly pressing the Indians from the rear, with the hope of coming in sight of the fugitives before Christmas, assuming the Indians don't get disgusted and turn the chase around. Referring to the cloudy way in which a recent raid on Howard's camp was reported, and the suggestive indications of another disaster involving the loss of Howard's entire mule train, Sherman said only that "accounts from the field are too confused to make anything out." The Montana volunteers are returning home in disarray, many of them putting leather to the test on foot.

Whatever may have been the merits of the cause in which this expedition began, the Indians have done much to enforce a favorable consideration of their claims by their successful resistance to compulsion. If we really cannot subdue these Indians, the government should address their legitimate grievances, if not as a matter of justice, then to secure the safety of our white settlements and bring this embarrassing war to an honorable close.

«———»

August 24, 1877

From General Oliver O. Howard, Commander, Department of the Columbia

To General William T. Sherman, Commanding General of the Army

My command is so much worn by over-fatigue and used-up animals that I cannot push it much farther.

«———»

August 24, 1877

From General William T. Sherman, Commanding General of the Army

To General Oliver O. Howard, Commander, Department of the Columbia

General Sheridan has three large forces to receive the Nez Perce east of the Absaroka Mountains. Yours, as the pursuing force, requires great patience, but has not much chance of a fight. It has simply been a race, and in a race for life, the fellow being pursued can always go a little faster.

There are many things in your department about

which I would like to consult you, and I feel your absence much. Really, I do not see any reason for you to stay in the field after having driven the hostile Indians out of your department and into General Sheridan's hands. I don't want to order you back to Oregon, but I do say that you can, with perfect propriety and without a bit of shame, transfer command of your troops in the field to some young, energetic officer, leaving him to continue until the Nez Perce have been destroyed.

«———»

August 27, 1877

From General Oliver O. Howard, Commander, Department of the Columbia

To General William T. Sherman, Commanding General of the Army

You misunderstand me. I never flag. It is the command, including the most energetic young officers, who are worn out and weary by a most extraordinary march. You need not fear for the campaign. We move in the morning and will continue to the end.

«———»

August 30, 1877

From Major H. Henry Clay Wood, Assistant Adjutant General

To General Oliver O. Howard, Commander, Department of the Columbia

Having heard from you on other matters, which I presented in subsequent dispatches, but not on the matter of Red Heart, I am embarrassed to raise the subject again. The Indians are forlorn, not least because of the sickness and death in captivity of a two-year-old child named Little Bear. Those who are able to work, including women, have been put to forced labor. They have done no wrong to merit such injustice. It blights the honor and reputation of the U.S. Army. Can we please release these peaceful Indians from the prison in Fort Vancouver and send them back to their reservation in Idaho?

❮━ ━ ━❯

September 6, 1877

From General Oliver O. Howard, Commander, Department of the Columbia

To General William T. Sherman, Commanding General of the Army

> The hostile Indians are between my command and that of Colonel Sturgis, and one day in advance of me. Our animals have recuperated on the good grass, and the command is in excellent health. It seems hardly possible they can escape this time.

Chapter 27

After a two-day scouting mission, Running Bird found Prairie Dove on a grassy hillside, collecting wild strawberries in her tightly woven cap. She was still weak from her injury and the brutal pace of travel, but her strength seemed to increase every day.

She smiled when Running Bird called her name, and gave him a strawberry, which he popped into his mouth. Her fingers and lips were stained with sweet, sticky juice.

"Have you eaten anything today?" she asked.

"A strawberry," he said.

She handed him her upturned cap, which was filled with bright red fruit. There would be fresh meat that night, too. Looking Glass had killed some antelope, which the women were turning on spits above an open flame. The scent and sound of sizzling fat teased Running Bird's empty belly.

"Watch this," Prairie Dove said.

She still wore a sling to immobilize her right arm while they traveled during the day, but she took it off when they stopped at night to exercise the shoulder. Now she straightened the arm and held it out at her side, palm up, almost level with her waist. She grimaced and smiled all at once, bursting with pride.

Running Bird picked her up and twirled her around, laughing and whooping. His eyes were playful at first but grew more serious as he put her down.

"What's wrong?" she asked.

He held her gaze. He'd wanted to marry her for more than a

year, but things kept getting in their way. First, they'd agreed to wait until she turned fifteen. Then the war came. Now time was their enemy. They didn't have much of it left.

Running Bird knew from his scouting mission that the Nez Perce had two days, three if they were lucky, before the final battle, which they couldn't possibly win. The Indians were too exhausted, their animals too used up, the numbers consolidated against them too appalling. Their only hope was to evade capture again, but there didn't seem to be any way to do it with the mountains hemming them in, Howard pushing them from behind, and multiple armies converging to block every possible outlet.

Running Bird had spent many hours thinking about the final, hopeless battle. He didn't know what death would be like and he didn't listen to anyone who claimed they did. Maybe it would be better than anyone supposed. His parents and his brother hadn't been afraid of it. Running Bird hoped the dying itself wouldn't take too long, or hurt too much, and that death itself would be very quiet and still.

How he lived these final days was all he had, now. Like a spawning salmon, he was fighting against the current, starving and exhausted, driven to one final act. He had two or three days. Two or three sunsets. Two or three chances to hold the woman he loved.

"Marry me," he said. "Tonight."

Prairie Dove didn't say anything at first. She studied his face in a way he recognized, trying to read his thoughts. Her mouth began to form the obvious question: *Why now?*

He didn't want to frighten her. Even if he said what he was thinking—*We don't have much time*—she wouldn't admit to herself, or anyone, that they were beaten. It simply wasn't in her nature.

Impatience swelled. Running Bird didn't want to explain himself or debate the finer points of acceptance versus despair. He didn't want to talk about where and how it all would end. He only wanted her to feel what he was feeling. He kissed her long and hard and whispered in her ear, "Marry me."

«———»

There was no wedding ceremony—it was neither necessary nor practical—but people brought them little gifts after the evening meal. A bundle of dried syringa still clinging to the scent of spring. A parfleche bag filled with sausages that could be eaten on the run, a priceless commodity. A small brass pot filled with stew. A scrap of honeycomb.

Running Bird constructed a small shelter, humble even by the camp's reduced standards, but comfortable enough for the newlyweds. It was just a few hides stitched together and draped over short poles on one end to create a sort of lean-to. There was no room to stand up or even sit up except on the end with the poles. Looking Glass gave them a thick buffalo robe and two beaver pelts—extravagant luxuries.

The tiny space was warmed by a fire near the opening. The northern lights on the horizon colored the sky lime green and fuchsia pink marbling to purple. Prairie Dove said that she felt safe inside their little cocoon for the first time since the war began, and that in the morning they'd fly away like butterflies.

"You're a dreamer," he said.

"Sometimes, dreaming is the only sensible thing to do," she said.

He sat in perfect awe while she undressed. Her nervous fingers fumbled with the layers of elkskin and calico. Finally, she stood before him. She could have been made of glass, the way she dazzled.

"*Icwewlcicqiy*," he said, beckoning her to him.

The September air was cold. Their frozen breath swirled and twined. Firelight flickered on her skin. She lay on her side, looking at him. She smelled like a forest after it's rained.

His eyes followed the curve of her shoulder, the bow of her waist, the rise of her hip, the bend of her leg. He ran his hand down her spine and rolled her over on her back. He whispered her name. He kissed the nape of her neck. He caressed and gently pinched her breasts. He spread her legs and gently stroked with his tongue, gradually increasing pressure and tempo until she trembled and moaned.

He felt her fingernails digging into his back. Deep inside her he rose and stilled, rose and stilled, releasing when he felt her body shudder.

He held her in his arms, breathing hard, and felt the pain and hurt and fear of the past four months float off into the eccentric sky. He stared into the stillness of the deep, dark pools that were her eyes. She quieted his soul.

The sun rose too soon, tinting scattered clouds pastel shades of ginger and gold. Jagged pinnacles of rock stretched to the horizon in every direction. The water in the creek drifted lazily toward the sea, muting the sounds of the camp coming awake. The small, yellowing leaves of an aspen tree swished and rattled like miniature paper fans. Horses stamped and whinnied in the semi-dark.

Confetti Cloud was staked nearby. The stallion nickered when he heard their voices. Running Bird held a piece of the sweet honeycomb in the flat palm of his hand. The horse licked up every sticky drib with his soft, wet tongue. Running Bird stroked the stallion's shoulders and flank. The horse stretched out his neck in quiet contentment.

Running Bird wrapped his arms around his bride while they waited for the stew in the little brass pot to warm. He thought about all the pain he'd caused and endured in this war and found it nothing short of miraculous that a feeling so transcendent was still possible. He hadn't lived the life he would have chosen, yet there had been moments of perfection in it, moments that made the rest endurable. This was one of them.

"I didn't think I would ever be happy again," he said.

"I didn't think you'd give yourself the chance," she said.

If Running Bird could go back and do one thing differently, what would it be? He wouldn't go looking for revenge. He'd let Scott Grooms finish out his miserable life. He'd leave the sheriff's fine house standing. Maybe Black Hoof and his family would still be alive. Maybe he and Prairie Dove would be living on the reservation, poor but safe. She'd always said she didn't care if they were poor. Why hadn't he believed her? Pride. Idiocy. Recklessness.

He buried his face in her long, loose hair. He wished he could hold back the sun, to make the morning last. He felt greedy for time, knowing they had so little of it.

"I'm afraid to let you out of my sight," he said.

"Then find a way for us," she said.

"*Sikstiwa*," he said. "Dearest one. There's no—"

Prairie Dove put two fingers on his lips to stop the words. Her voice was fierce now. "You're my husband! You find a way for us!"

Running Bird closed his eyes. After everything they'd endured, there it was. The same unflappable optimism. The same refusal to dignify real obstacles by deigning to acknowledge them. Even now, she couldn't conceive that they were surrounded and hopelessly outnumbered.

"I'll try," Running Bird promised. He would, too, with every ounce of his being. But in his heart, he knew their song was coming to an end.

Chapter 28

Running Bird had never traveled in terrain with such poor footing. Unlike the mostly granite Bitterroot Mountains he'd left behind in Montana or even the basaltic Blue Mountains in Idaho, the Absaroka Mountains were made of soft, vulnerable stone that crumbled away beneath the weight of a horse and rider. Black Hoof had always warned Running Bird not to imagine his own death, but it was hard to think of anything else as his sure-footed stallion lost his confidence in the very ground. It was like teetering on a precipice of sand. Wind-swept pines and parched brooms of sage clutched desperately at toeholds of dry earth, waiting for the inevitable collapse.

With his field glass pressed to one eye, Running Bird strained to see, through the morning haze, where the eastern edge of the Absaroka Mountains flattened out into the Great Plains, a high plateau of undulating hills covered with citrus-colored grass. The Crow chiefs had sent word that the Nez Perce were not welcome in their country—a heartbreaking but unsurprising development— but if the fleeing families could somehow reach the plains, they might still make a final dash for Canada. The problem was that there was no way to get from where they were to the plateau.

There were two narrow passageways through the Absaroka Mountains. To the northeast, through the valley of the Clark's Fork of the Yellowstone River, there was a path barely wide enough for two horses breast to breast, hemmed in on both sides by impassable rock walls four hundred to twelve hundred feet in height.

To the southeast, there was an equally formidable path along the North Fork of the Stinking Water River. Roughly halfway between the two outlets, Running Bird counted about six hundred Big Hats, bitter remnants of Custer's command flying a Seventh Cavalry flag, lying in wait to block whichever route the fleeing Indians took. Other Nez Perce scouts had reported two more armies converging to reinforce the Seventh Cavalry—about two hundred fifty Big Hats from a fort on the Bighorn River, and five hundred more from a fort on the Wind River. In addition, General Howard was still pushing the Nez Perce from behind, with six hundred men.

Running Bird's people had begun the war with fewer than two hundred warriors. They'd lost some of their very best at the Big Hole and in smaller skirmishes since. If the odds against the Indians were merely two or three to one, and if their best warriors were still alive, the Nez Perce might still have had a fighting chance. But with nearly two thousand soldiers arrayed against an already diminished and exhausted Nez Perce force, the warriors would be outnumbered by twelve or thirteen to one. The battle would be ridiculously lopsided, no matter how poorly the Big Hats fought.

"You find a way for us," Prairie Dove had demanded, but how? As soon as the Nez Perce dropped into one of the two valleys leading out of the Absaroka Mountains, they'd be plainly visible to army scouts from the high ridgelines. The Seventh Cavalry would move to block whichever route they took, with reinforcements just a day or two behind, and General Howard blocking the Indians' retreat.

There was no way out.

Running Bird noticed a killdeer on a bare branch with two dark slashes on its face like a warrior. He remembered the first time he'd seen one running across the ground, dragging her wing as if it were broken but somehow managing to stay just ahead of him when he tried to catch her to help. Finally, he'd realized that the bird wasn't really injured, only trying to lure him away from the fragile eggs she'd deposited in a pile of rocks.

What the Nez Perce needed now was a killdeer, he thought. A broken-winged decoy to lure the soldiers away from the families' path.

He put the field glass to one eye and studied the two narrow paths through the mountains again. One for the families, one for the decoy. Was it possible?

Running Bird could almost hear Black Hoof chiding him, insisting the idea was further evidence of his fundamental recklessness. "There's brave and there's reckless, and you're not always on the right side of that line," Black Hoof had once said.

Running Bird couldn't deny that the idea seemed crazy. The odds that it would work were staggeringly small. Everything was stacked against them. But at least it wasn't giving up.

He imagined what the soldiers might to do to Prairie Dove if the families got caught again. Reckless or not, he had to try.

«———»

Running Bird asked to speak at the war council later that night. It was almost unheard of for a warrior so young to make such a request. He felt nervous as he sat with the chiefs around the fire, with older and more experienced warriors forming concentric rings around them. Women and children huddled at the outer edges, straining to hear.

The chiefs passed a long-stemmed pipe from one to another, ending with Running Bird. He breathed in the smoke, filling his lungs with the taste of willow bark and mint, releasing the smoke in a series of perfect rings.

When called upon to speak, he used a broken pine branch, sticky with sap, to draw two lines in the gravelly loam—one representing the Clark's Fork of the Yellowstone River, the other representing the Stinking Water River. He marked the approximate positions of the Big Hats and planted the stick in the ground to mark the approximate location of the Indians' camp. There was much discussion about the map. After a few adjustments, the Nez Perce scouts all agreed it was reasonably accurate.

Running Bird explained the broad outlines of his proposal, pausing now and then for discussion. The chiefs listened grimly, sometimes skeptically, but they listened to the end. The longer they let him talk, the more he gained confidence in the plan, so that by the end, he'd almost convinced even himself that it would work.

He explained that if the families moved fast—faster than they'd ever moved before—they might be able to reach one of the two gateways to the Great Plains before the Big Hats from the Bighorn River or the Wind River could block their exit. Nobody was sure whether the families, traveling with infants and children and elders and many wounded, could move fast enough, but that was the least of their challenges. The chiefs were willing to assume that if speed was all they required, it could be delivered.

The bigger problem was the Seventh Cavalry, with six hundred soldiers already in position to block whichever path the Nez Perce chose, and General Howard, with six hundred more fighters, pushing them from behind.

Running Bird proposed that the families hide themselves in the trees while a small decoy force dropped down the Stinking Water. When the Seventh Cavalry moved to intercept the decoy, they would leave the Clark's Fork of the Yellowstone River open.

The families could escape by that route.

Everything depended on the Seventh Cavalry falling for the ruse completely. If they left even a small force guarding the route the families would take, there would be a bloody and disastrous fight. Once the Nez Perce reached the Great Plains, the families would have to keep moving fast enough to evade the other two armies converging on their position.

The chiefs talked for many hours. How would they make the decoy look convincing enough that the Seventh Cavalry would send its entire force to the Stinking Water? How would they hide seven hundred people and almost two thousand horses in broad daylight, something they had never even attempted to do previously?

It was a long shot, Running Bird acknowledged. It would require perfect execution and immense physical exertion from an already hungry, fatigued, and distraught people. It depended, in large measure, on pure luck. Yet it was the only plan they had.

Running Bird volunteered to lead the decoy horses down the Stinking Water. He would become the killdeer, luring the enemy away from his relatives. If the ruse worked, he would be caught between the Seventh Cavalry and Howard's pursuing force. The only way out would be straight up a sheer wall of rock, steeper and more difficult than anything he'd previously attempted to climb. He doubted he had the skill to climb that wall without Black Hoof there to guide him, not to mention his weakened physical condition after four months of constant strain. Nevertheless, there were no other options.

After much debate, the chiefs agreed.

Chapter 29

Nobody slept in the Nez Perce camp that night.

Running Bird culled five hundred of the weakest horses from the herd. These were the decoy animals that would go with him to the Stinking Water and, if the plan worked, fall into the enemy's hands. It was hard to give up so many animals, especially knowing they'd likely be slaughtered by the Big Hats, but there was nothing for it. Running Bird tried to choose the orneriest, laziest, most worn-out mounts, but with each painful selection, he felt the accumulating weight of treachery. Each one trusted him in a way that only a horse ever could. Now he was throwing them away.

Women and children tied sagebrush brooms to the decoy animals' legs and tails, so that every step they took would throw up enough dust that Army scouts looking down from the high ridgetops would think they were seeing the entire Nez Perce horse herd on the move. They also tied travois weighed down with rocks behind General Howard's stolen pack train, to leave the expected deep ruts along the trail.

The warriors drove the rest of the animals into a copse of lodge-pole pines mixed with more substantial spruce and juniper, tall, old souls that had seen much and maybe knew how this fight would end. The warriors hobbled the stallions and the dominant mares so the herd wouldn't wander out of the trees and risk being spotted by army scouts. Clothes, pots, pans, food, and other treasures that had survived the fight thus far were loaded onto packhorses so the families would be ready to move as soon as the chiefs gave the word.

Running Bird wandered through the trees, stroking his favorite horses one last time. Fear had a distinctive smell, like sweat but more pungent, and the horses seemed to sense it on his skin. It was a peculiar quality of horses that they could sense fear in a man and taste it in the grass and inhale it from the air. Horses fed on fear, helping it multiply and build. They snorted and stamped their feet.

When Running Bird came to Confetti Cloud, he slid his hand along the Appaloosa's muscular shoulder. As a boy, his greatest hope, his only ambition, was to ride a horse like this one. For some reason, his father had given him the stallion. Confetti Cloud had taught Running Bird patience, balance, and courage, as well as submission. The bond between them was so strong that Running Bird needed only to think right or left, fast or slow, and the horse would respond. He'd never gone into battle without Confetti Cloud and wondered if he'd have the courage to do what was needed now without the stallion's speed, agility, and sharp hooves beneath him. Nevertheless, he couldn't bear to let Confetti Cloud fall into the enemy's hands, and decided to leave him behind. He wrapped his arms around the horse's neck and buried his face in the thick, rose-colored mane. He heard the horse nicker as he walked away.

He found Prairie Dove struggling with her one good arm to take down their humble lean-to. He didn't know what to say or how to say it. He pressed into her hard and deep, not tentative or gentle as he had on their wedding night but hungry and almost desperate, she standing on one leg with the other crooked around his waist, her back pressed against the thick trunk of a tree, her teeth breaking the skin on his shoulder. He looked into her eyes, afraid that if he blinked it would break the spell that caused each to put every hope in the other. There was no word for "goodbye" in their language, so they said *qo'c 'ee hexnu.* "Until I see you again."

←————→

Dawn broke gray with a thin layer of mist just below the tree line. The decoy animals moved slowly toward the Stinking Water, throwing up great clouds of dust with their sagebrush brooms. Some of the animals didn't like the brooms and pawed the ground in protest, whinnying and braying loudly, but eventually Running Bird got them moving forward in a long, thin line. They would have to walk almost single file to pass through the narrowest parts of the canyon, but it was still the easier of the two available routes, and therefore the passage the soldiers probably expected the families to take.

When the sun was almost directly overhead, the grullo Running Bird was riding started to buck. Other horses, startled by the grullo, skittered sideways across the rocks. A few of the animals turned around and started running the wrong direction, back toward the families and the rest of the herd. A mule got tangled up in her heavy travois, panicked, and broke her own leg.

The problem was a rattlesnake, almost invisible among the white pebbles with its oyster-colored skin, holding its rattle erect and shaking it hard and fast. It seemed astonishing that a plan upon which so much depended could unravel so quickly because of one tightly coiled rattlesnake, and not a very big one. It was a stark reminder of how precarious Running Bird's plan actually was, and how many different ways it could go wrong.

Running Bird jumped off the bucking grullo, pinned the snake's head to the ground with a stick, and chopped it off with his Bowie knife. The decapitated head snapped its teeth while the headless body writhed and thrashed. The grullo kept bucking and rolling its whited eyes. Running Bird dropped a heavy rock on the snake's decapitated head and threw the lashing body high up over the river. A black crow caught the snake mid-air and carried it off with a *caw!* that sounded like laughter echoing against the rocks.

Running Bird mounted the grullo and managed to get all the decoy horses under control and moving in the right direction again, but the incident had unnerved him, especially being mocked by the crow. Running Bird had hated crows ever since he'd seen one pecking the eyes out of a baby seal. They were bad medicine.

He worried that he'd overestimated his own importance and put the tribe in tremendous danger by persuading the chiefs to follow such a risky plan. Given an audience, he tended to improve upon the facts, a tendency that the war had exacerbated. He'd escaped *Peyewit*, Death Spirit, so many times in the past few months, and so unexpectedly, that perhaps he'd grown too bold. He wondered if he should have accepted the offers of some of the other warriors to join him, risking their own lives, and yet it still seemed better to have as many fighting men as possible traveling with the families.

Running Bird halted the grullo on a gravel bar and dropped his head to think. Perhaps there was still time to turn around and surrender to General Howard.

But as risky as Running Bird's plan was, surrendering made even less sense. Hadn't General Howard's men fired on the chiefs' white flags at White Bird Canyon? Hadn't they murdered women and children at the Big Hole River? No. The Nez Perce had to make the killdeer ruse work.

Running Bird thought he saw the sun glinting off a field glass on the ridgeline up above, but he couldn't be sure with the lingering dust thrown up by the sagebrush brooms and the commotion with the snake. Sand and sweat caked his skin and stung his eyes.

He pushed the decoy horses forward, wondering if the cloudy sky and poor visibility would work for or against the Nez Perce that day. Maybe the Seventh Cavalry would fall for the trick and move their entire force to the Stinking Water. Maybe, in the face of uncertainty, they would split their force and try to block both exits. If they left even a small force in the families' path, there would be another bloody massacre.

When sunset came, tinting the sky red and gold, Running Bird hobbled the stallions and dominant mares so the decoy horses would stay where he left them, in the narrow canyon, pinched between two converging armies. By morning, the Seventh Cavalry would arrive. If Running Bird still hoped to escape the Stinking Water before the soldiers caught him, it was time for him to start his climb.

The families would be headed down the Yellowstone soon, under cover of darkness. He'd helped them all he could. They'd escape or they wouldn't. What an irony if Running Bird, who'd dreamed up this suicide mission, survived, while the families he was trying to save got slaughtered. He pushed the image from his mind.

He stretched his arms and legs and drank some water. He walked to the base of the canyon wall, which rose up vertically and disappeared into the clouds. He smelled the broken rock and the rotten egg odor of the fumarole that gave the Stinking Water its name.

Running Bird had been climbing mountains all his life, but never anything as steep or as high as the Stinking Water gorge, and never in a state of such utter mental and physical exhaustion. It didn't help that he'd be doing it by moonlight.

Climbing required strategy, technique, endurance, and extreme mental focus. It required strength and flexibility in every part of his body including his fingers and toes. Every movement had to be efficient, balanced, and correctly sequenced. Staring at that wall, Running Bird didn't know if he could climb the first twenty feet, let alone touch the sky.

He wondered if his spirit would stay in that canyon if he died there, or if it would travel back to the Big Hole, looking for Black Hoof, or to the Clearwater, looking for his parents. He hoped there would be some way for his family to touch each other again when he died, maybe through the rain or the rivers or the grass.

Qo'c 'ee hexnu, Prairie Dove had said. *Until I see you again.* She wouldn't even consider the possibility that he might fail.

War had taught them both the absolute necessity to dig deeper, go farther, try harder, never-endingly. Prairie Dove had endured her surgery. Running Bird would find a way to climb out of this trap.

He took a deep breath, hugged the deeply cracked and folded rock, and started his ascent. The volcanic stone was porous and rough against his skin but easier to grip than other surfaces he'd climbed, like granite, which could cut like a knife. He jammed his hands into cracks and divots created by wind and water and time. His legs and feet straddled vertical grooves to create additional tension points. The canyon wall became deeply red, almost purple against the darkening sky.

The sound of the decoy horses' hooves clacking on the canyon floor faded as Running Bird gained height. There was no stopping to rest, no intermission, not even when his muscles cramped and seized. The rock face rose straight up from the river, with cracks and grooves and ledges just big enough for a hand or a foot, and no room to sit or even stand without three pressure points.

In places, the wall proved unreliable, crumbling beneath his weight. Several times, he had to backtrack and find another line when the one he was following ended unexpectedly, leaving him stranded. He took one final look into the abyss that had opened up beneath him as darkness swallowed the scene.

All through the night he ascended, found himself trapped, moved down and sideways to find another line, then ascended a few feet more. Climbing wasn't normally a competition or a race against others—it was more a battle against the climber's own limits and fears—but Running Bird didn't feel alone in the gorge that night. He sensed Long Walker's calloused hands and his mother's soothing song holding him up, *Hmmmmmm-Ah-Ah, Hmmmmmmm-Ah-Ah.* He imagined Black Hoof talking him through every move, telling him exactly what to do and precisely how to do it. *Push with your legs; balance with your hands. Don't just hang there, wasting your strength. Push with your legs; push with your legs; again, again.*

Running Bird felt the strange presence of Prairie Dove and the families who, at that very moment, were racing for their lives through a dark canyon more suited to mountain goats than horses carrying invalids and children. He imagined himself traveling with them, hurrying them along, urging them to move faster and harder over impossible footing. He imagined Joseph's booming voice, "Hurry! Hurry!" He imagined the children crying, and the wounded and elderly begging to be left behind, and himself pressing them forward, mercilessly, yelling "Forward! Forward!" He thought about Confetti Cloud, who would run until his heart burst if Running Bird asked him to do it.

The river pulsed below him, so full of fish in the narrowest parts it might have been made of solid muscle. Running Bird imagined the sturgeon thumping against each other in the silent depths, and the horses jostling in the gorge, pressed together beneath the giant blue moon. On top of the ridgeline, two wolves howled harmonically. The sound was hauntingly beautiful, like the songs his father used to play on an elderberry flute. The mournful notes echoed off the canyon walls and somehow kept Running Bird grappling, clutching, scrabbling up, fighting for every inch.

He pushed his body well beyond what seemed plausible in the thin air. Every muscle burned as if he'd been set aflame like Sally Peniel and the children at the Big Hole. He imagined that his pain might somehow absorb theirs and embraced it.

By morning, he didn't know if he was sleeping or awake, dead or alive, man or spirit. It seemed possible that he'd already died, and that it was only his spirit still working to ascend that wall. *I am flying up*, were his father's last words.

As Running Bird neared the top, soldiers' voices drifted up from the canyon floor ("Bet you a nickel they make it to Canada") but he couldn't think about that now, couldn't worry that they'd look up and notice him there, clinging to the wall like a spider, easy target practice. He couldn't lose his focus on the rock, the cracks, the seemingly endless ascent toward a brightening sky.

Chapter 30

When the Nez Perce reached the Great Plains, they left Nicole and Mr. Ford behind with a handful of boiled roots, the matched pair of chocolate-colored mules (which, according to the aggrieved guide, had been reduced to "shambling bone-boxes"), and a promise that General Howard would be along soon to help them. Mr. Ford wanted to take the two mules and start out right away for a small outpost called Fort Smith, about two hundred miles distant, but Nicole was too exhausted, and decided to wait for General Howard, who might be persuaded to spare them a wagon and some supplies.

She wept with relief as the Nez Perce disappeared across the graceful folds of grass, toward a flat expanse where trees dispersed into solitaries and then mostly disappeared. She hadn't expected to feel so conflicted as she watched them go. They'd murdered her husband, after all, and held her hostage for nearly a month.

Nicole remembered the day Running Bird had dragged her away from Witt's body, pulled her up behind him on his spotted horse, and tied them together with a leather cord. She'd nearly toppled them both off the horse, half-crazed with grief and fear. She didn't know where Running Bird was taking her. She didn't know what the Indians would do to her. A few days later, she was one of them, dressed in rags, running for her life, terrified General Howard would kill her with his Gatling gun. It was as if she'd been plucked from the quiet pool of her own life and dropped into the swirling torrent of someone else's brutish existence.

Before Witt died, she'd never really wanted for anything except maybe a dollop of cream for her tea. Life with Witt was a kiss whenever she wanted one, a perennial garden near Piccadilly Circus, mint juleps served on a pretty silver tray. Tragedy, privation, hunger, exhaustion, desolation, anguish, despair—those were things that happened to other people. Things she read about in novels while she sat in her rocking chair with the tri-colored tabby purring on her lap.

Nicole didn't just mourn Witt. She mourned the person she was before she lost Witt. The person who still thought life was gentle and easy. She felt like Orpheus, who'd followed his love to the netherworld and returned broken-hearted and alone.

She realized now that people were much the same, though their circumstances might be vastly different. Everybody made mistakes. Desperate people made more and bigger mistakes. Young men who'd seen their families bayonetted? Who'd seen children burned alive? Well. Stay out of their way. That's what General Sherman should have said when he passed the Lowsleys on his way out of Yellowstone Park. Turn around. Go home. It isn't safe, and it isn't going to be safe for a very long time. Not with so much blood crying out from the ground.

Part of Nicole still wanted it to be somebody's fault. General Sherman, for claiming the Indians wouldn't go near the geysers. Mr. Ford, for igniting the Indians' smoldering anger by offering them crumbs. Witt, for charging them with a mule and a bird gun. Running Bird, for being the better marksman. God Almighty, for not stopping this cursed war. But in the end, Nicole found that anger required too much effort. It flattened out into Thoreau's quiet desperation.

She flipped through the sketchbook she'd kept throughout

her ordeal. The Nez Perce stared back at her from the pages: Peopeo Tholekt, wounded in the right leg and again in the head; Chellooyeen, shot in the right side of his waist; Espowyes, with a bayonet wound in the abdomen; Temme Ilppilp, with a gunshot in the right thigh; Tahkoopen, also shot in the leg; Yellow Wolf, wounded five times, most recently by a bullet to his head; and Inwholise, who used to be called White Feather, whose new name meant "Broken Teeth," who could hardly eat, who had no mother and no sister now. There were gentler drawings too: Prairie Dove collecting strawberries in a tightly woven basket; Cedar Smoke with his extravagant hat; Joseph helping his daughter, Sound of Running Feet, with a horse; White Bird holding an eagle's wing in front of his face; young boys building their contemptuous dung cairns for General Howard; a snowy owl, almost invisible in a white-barked aspen.

Nicole already missed the medicine man's shining face, and Joseph's oldest wife, holding a child on each hip, and the chief himself, running through the camp, shouting "Hurry! Hurry!" She worried about Silooyelam's broken ankle and Eeahlokoon's torn-up leg and Elaskolatat's strained back. Now that Nicole was gone, who would collect yarrow for Inwholise's infected teeth and willow bark for painkilling tea?

She realized she was crying, but she didn't bother to wipe the tears. She looked out over the plains, at the grass fading and stiffening, the spent flowers crumbling on broken stalks, the bright sun reflecting off chalky alkali fields. She felt the pull of exhaustion, a heaviness in her eyelids and limbs.

She recalled the time she'd gone to see the Severn River bore at Minsterworth, how the river had surged toward the sea until high tide, then buckled back upon itself in a wave, six or seven feet high, heaving and swelling and breaking in the wrong direction before turning back toward the sea again. She felt like that river now, flowing in two directions at once, her sympathies aligned with both sides of this war.

Still, Nicole doubted she could have survived with the Indians for much longer. She was too exhausted, too cold and hungry, too unaccustomed, by birth and experience, to the hard way that they lived. She was well-educated and well-traveled, but it turned out she was helpless in the wilderness, having acquired not one single useful skill through all those years of boarding school. She knew how to plant a flower garden, but she didn't know which flowers she could eat. She knew the difference between a fish knife and a butter knife, but she didn't know how to use a knife to gut a gopher or a squirrel. She could embroider a handkerchief, but she couldn't patch a moccasin. She could select the silver, but she couldn't cook the meal. The Indians must have found her ridiculous.

She supposed they were no better suited to life on a reservation than she was to life in the high, cold mountains. She tried to imagine Running Bird wearing farmer's coveralls and laughed out loud at the absurdity of it. The government might just as well tell a fish not to swim or a peacock not to preen.

"I can't imagine what you find so funny," Mr. Ford said, as if she owed him an explanation.

"I can't imagine you finding anything funny," she said.

Nicole folded her arms, conserving warmth, and tried to ignore the gloomy guide, against whom her resentment had softened, but only a little bit. A brisk wind gripped from the north, scattering leaves, which caught in the riotous curls tumbling down her back. Her hair, which hadn't seen a comb in weeks, was tangled like a sticker vine hanging down from a dried-out tree. She'd traded her impractical skirts and petticoats for Indian garb and lost her wide-brimmed hat. Her face, hands, and arms were sunburned and scratched with angry lines. Her lips were chapped and cracked.

The dour guide made a fire the laborious way, rubbing two sticks together to produce a wisp of smoke, coaxing the wood into flames which flickered in the wind as he added tinder. Nicole huddled near the warmth and thought about home, and the long distance she'd have to travel to get there, and the many months it would take.

According to Mr. Ford, she had two options. She could travel a thousand miles west, back over much of the same treacherous ground she'd just covered, and catch a boat out of Portland, which would take her around Cape Horn. Alternatively, she could travel a thousand miles east, catch the Union Pacific Railroad to New York, and book a steamer across the Atlantic. Either way, the trip would be long, tiring, lonesome, and sad.

Perhaps she'd spend the winter at Fort Smith, recovering her strength, and then go back to Yellowstone Park in the spring to look for Witt's body. There wasn't much waiting for her in London anyway. The home she yearned for was a home that had Witt in it, which wasn't the one she'd be returning to at all. She'd gone away a wife and would return a widow. The life she'd had was over now. The life she faced was a footnote at the end of a story whose best parts were already finished.

Witt's voice stayed strong in her head while she traveled with the Indians, but she was half delirious then. Once she was warm and plump again, sleeping on a feather bed instead of a buffalo robe, she knew that her husband would become more memory than presence, and that even his memory, in time, would start to fade. His leather chair, his piles of books, his dresser filled with collars and cuffs, the mattress hollowed out on one side by the vestige of his shape—every empty room would evoke a longing for the past, a nostalgia for trivial things from a life that had come unspooled.

Nicole worried that people would treat her differently, now. Assume that she'd been raped and whisper behind her back. Unpack her words, looking for evidence of lingering trauma. Avoid her altogether, for fear of not knowing what to say. Treat her like damaged goods. She'd be the carriage accident that people craned their necks to see without bothering to stop and help.

With physical effort, she threw back her shoulders and tossed her hair. Her life might not be as easy as it was before, but it wasn't a scrap to be thrown away, either. She'd learn to live around the grief, like a tree root encircling a boulder, pressing through the crevices and the gaps.

What else can I do?

Exactly, my dear, Witt said.

←———→

"Someone's coming," Mr. Ford said, nudging Nicole awake.

She followed the guide's line of sight and saw a lone rider approaching on a big-eared mule. She guessed he was one of General Howard's men. He was coming from the right direction, wearing an army slouch hat and a blue neckerchief.

"Hide behind those boulders until we're sure he's friendly," Mr. Ford said.

"He's already seen me," Nicole said, and stayed where she was.

Mr. Ford crunched across the frost-tipped grass to meet the stranger, who introduced himself as Jack Peniel and confirmed he was one of General Howard's scouts.

"We'd almost given up on finding you alive," Jack said. "Is either one of you hurt?"

"I can't speak for Mr. Ford," Nicole said, still staring into the fire. "I'm fine."

"I won't bore you with my complaints," Mr. Ford said. "It wouldn't do any good anyway."

Jack removed his hat and crumpled it between his hands. "I'm sorry to inform you that Mr. Lowsley is dead," he said. "We buried his remains."

"We saw it happen," Mr. Ford said.

"We had to leave him there," Nicole said. "No coffin, no preacher, no funeral procession." She felt her eyes well with tears again. Wind whipped a solitary white pine, showering her with needles.

"The ground claims all of us back just the same," Mr. Ford said.

Had there ever been such a cold fish? Why did Witt hire him? Who recommended him? She threw a pinecone into the campfire and watched the flames reduce the wood to sooty ash.

"General Howard should arrive in a day or two with wagons and supplies," Jack said. "He'll see to it that you receive your husband's watch and wedding ring."

"I'd like to bring him home," Nicole said. "Bury him properly."

"I'll speak to the general," Jack said, replacing his hat on his head.

Jack untied a blanket tightly rolled behind the cantle of his saddle and draped it around Nicole's shoulders. She clutched the soft fleece in one tight fist. It smelled like leather and horse and grass.

"Were there any other hostages?" Jack said.

"Just us two," Mr. Ford said.

"We're looking for a woman named Sally," Jack said. "Early forties, proud bearing, elegant hands—"

"It was just us two," Mr. Ford repeated.

Jack unsaddled his mule, hobbled her two front legs, and let her join the guide's chocolate colored pair, crunching the rimy grass between square white teeth.

"You must be hungry," Jack said.

"Indians didn't feed us much," Mr. Ford said, as if they were beggars.

Jack reached into his saddlebag and produced stale biscuits and condensed milk, sweet heaven in a can. He warmed the milk, poured it over the biscuits, and served Nicole in a hammered tin bowl. The men ate hardtack and jerky.

"The crème brulèe at Harrods never tasted better," Nicole said.

"Harrods must have gone downhill a ways," Mr. Ford said.

He was the most unimaginative man Nicole had ever met. She doubted he could put red and blue together to come up with purple.

When she finished eating, Mr. Ford picked up the empty bowl and spoon and walked to the creek to wash them, cracking the thin ice at the edge with his boot.

"I still hear Witt's voice sometimes," she confessed to Jack.

"My best friend died when I was eight," Jack said. "I still talk to him sometimes."

"It's normal, then?"

"It might be the only normal thing about me."

Nicole opened her sketchpad to a charcoal drawing of Running Bird. "This is the man who shot him," she said.

It was only a few lines and a little dab of paint on the Indian's unusual bone necklace, but Jack studied it with an intensity that surprised her. When he finally spoke, his voice was barely a whisper. "You've forgiven him," he said. "I can see it in the way you've drawn his face. I wouldn't have thought it was possible."

Nicole told him how the medicine man had urged her to forgive, how he'd refused to wake up to all the ugliness in the world, how she'd imagined him as Jesus in disguise, how she'd always been taught that if a man's regret was equal in depth and sincerity to the sorrow he had caused, then it was incumbent upon a Christian to forgive. Otherwise, what was the point of all that piety?

"You're looking at me as if I were mad, Jack."

"'I'll tell you a secret,'" he said, quoting Lewis Carroll's Alice. "'The best people usually are.'"

"'Mad, bonkers, completely round the bend,'" she said, giving him the rest of the quote.

"I think they'll make it to Canada," Jack said, smiling for the first time.

Nicole still had a hard time picturing her new life without Witt, but maybe there would be people like Jack in it, people who were kind and interesting, who didn't know her before and would be pleasantly surprised if she managed just to comb her hair.

She leaned in as if they were co-conspirators. "Please," she said. "You must help them."

Chapter 31

Fergus Dewsnap, "UNEXPECTED MERCY," *Lewiston Telegraph* (September 10, 1877)

The Nez Perce released Nicole Lowsley and her guide, David Ford, unhurt. The two traveled with the Nez Perce for nearly a month after Professor Lowsley charged twelve warriors with a mule and a bird gun, with inevitable results. "Mr. Ford and I were never in real danger," Mrs. Lowsley said. "My husband was killed in a dreadful misunderstanding."

After Mrs. Lowsley and Mr. Ford were released by the Indians, they suffered some from cold and hunger, but they soon met up with one of General Howard's brave militiamen, Mr. Jack Peniel, and were saved. Mrs. Lowsley expressed her deepest gratitude for Mr. Peniel's gallantry and solicitude in their rescue. The Ladies Auxiliary of Lewiston will hold a luncheon in Mr. Peniel's honor, at a date and time to be announced in the spring.

«———»

September 10, 1877

From General Oliver O. Howard, Commander, Department of the Columbia

To General William T. Sherman, Commanding General of the Army

The Indians slipped between four converging armies in the Absaroka Mountains. It is as if Moses himself parted the mountains to let them through. I assure you we are doing all that human endurance can possibly accomplish to circumvent them yet.

«———»

September 13, 1877
From General Oliver O. Howard, Commander, Department of the Columbia
To General William T. Sherman, Commanding General of the Army

The Indians stopped at the freight yard at Cow Island to buy food. When our patriots refused their money, they took what they wanted and burned the rest, killing five men. I think they will reach Canada.

«———»

September 14, 1877
From General William T. Sherman, Commanding General of the Army
To Colonel Nelson A. Miles, Commander, Military Division of the Missouri

Four days ago, I wouldn't have given a dollar to have had Joseph's capture insured. Now it seems almost certain that the army will be humiliated by the Indians' escape to Canada. If Joseph unites with Sitting Bull in Saskatchewan, there is no end to the mayhem that could follow. They could wipe out the entire garrison at Tongue River and all the surrounding settlements in an afternoon. At a minimum, they will embolden our tame Indians and remain an annoyance and an open threat for the indefinite future. Every available force in your command should be dispatched at once to intercept the Nez Perce before they join forces with the hostile Sioux.

«———»

September 17, 1877

From Colonel Nelson A. Miles, Commander, Military Division of the Missouri

To General William T. Sherman, Commanding General of the Army

I fear I have received your request for additional troops too late. Our telegraph line was down, apparently cut by the fleeing Indians. We will depart the garrison at Tongue River within the hour with three companies of Seventh Cavalry, three companies of Second Cavalry, five companies from Fifth Infantry, thirty tame Cheyenne, and a wagon train, totaling five hundred thirty men.

«———»

September 25, 1877

From Colonel Nelson A. Miles, Commander, Military Division of the Missouri

To General William T. Sherman, Commanding General of the Army

We had hoped to catch the Nez Perce on the south side of the Missouri River, but they crossed ahead of us. As a matter of pure luck, by firing our guns into the air, we were able to gain the attention of a passing steamship. The captain turned around and ferried all our men and equipment across; otherwise, our cause would have been lost. We are headed northwest with some hope of stopping the Nez Perce before they reach the Canadian border.

Part Four

Chapter 32

Running Bird and Prairie Dove awoke in the shrubbery about thirty miles south of Canada, in a crescent-shaped hollow at the foot of the Bear Paw Mountains. Dawn was a luminescent ball rising behind thick gray clouds that had dropped five inches of powdery snow overnight. Nothing moved in the sleepy Indian camp except the gusty wind, which lifted the snow in great white swirls, and a sage grouse with yellow patches around his eyes, strutting along the frozen creek.

The couple lay beneath two stitched hides draped over willow branches. Near the opening of the simple lean-to, dried buffalo chips burned orange around the edges, producing a curl of blue smoke that smelled mostly like burning grass. They lingered beneath the blanket with their bodies fitted together like two stacked spoons.

The Nez Perce were well ahead of General Howard and had stopped to rest for a few days, to wash their clothes and hunt for meat so they wouldn't show up in Sitting Bull's camp looking like beggars. Running Bird wondered what Canada would be like, and when he would be able to give his wife a proper home. He imagined a day when they might wake, not in the shrubbery, but in a sturdy lodge, covered with buffalo hides dyed a buttery yellow, with a fur lining to hold in the heat. They'd have a stone fire pit and the shiny copper pot and bundles of dried syringa and pine tied to the lodgepoles to sweeten the air. Just outside, they'd have a field of winter wheat, a cache of salmon smoked over cedar and sage, and a sturgeon nose canoe tied to a tree on the shore of an alpine lake.

"What kind of pictures will we paint on our lodge?" Running Bird asked.

Prairie Dove rolled over on her back and stared into his eyes. She didn't point out the obvious—that they didn't have a lodge or even paint. "Only happy things," she said. "Nothing sad."

"No battle scenes," he agreed.

"You and Confetti Cloud," she said.

"You and the children," he said, moving his body on top of hers.

She stroked his back. "We don't need a lodge, Running Bird. We're happy as we are."

They did need a lodge, but he didn't press the point. He was leaning in for a kiss when he heard a low, rumbling sound. At first, he thought it was buffalo stampeding across the frozen turf, pursued by Nez Perce hunters, but then he heard a bugler trumpeting *Double quick!* and realized it was cavalry.

"No, no, no—"

"Not again—"

Running Bird ran outside. A warrior on the hillside was riding in circles, waving a red blanket, signaling, "Soldiers right on us!"

Running Bird saw the Big Hats charging toward the Indian camp from the south and the east with bayonets drawn. In addition, a party of reservation Indians—Cheyenne from the looks of their dome-shaped, black-feathered caps—was thundering toward the Nez Perce horse herd, grazing on a hillside nearby.

Chief Joseph raced through the camp, rousing the people. "Move! Move! Move!"

Running Bird grabbed his weapons, trying to think what to do. "Hide in the willows by the creek," he told Prairie Dove. "Hurry!"

He ran to catch a horse, slicing his bare feet on broken ice and prickly pear. Stupidly, he'd let Confetti Cloud graze overnight rather than tethering his war horse close to camp. The Nez Perce horses had gotten wise to the sounds of battle and were already terrified, snorting and stamping and tossing their heads.

Running Bird caught the first horse he could, a high-headed white gelding. He'd barely mounted up when the Cheyenne crashed into the herd, triggering a stampede. Running Bird tried to get outside and to the front of the herd in order to gain control, but it was no good. The white gelding stumbled, nearly tossing Running Bird to the ground, then came up lame.

Running Bird watched the Cheyenne run the Nez Perce herd over a ridgeline and disappear toward the west. He could still hear the pounding hooves and the Cheyenne whistling and whooping to keep the animals moving forward, but there was no hope of catching up with them now. Running Bird's mount was too worn out after so many miles on the run, and too lame in the hind end after stumbling on the ice.

Running Bird understood that, without horses, the war was already lost, even if the Nez Perce managed to repel the cavalry assault on their camp. Without horses, the Nez Perce couldn't move their young, old, sick, and injured the final thirty miles across the medicine line. Without horses, Running Bird's people were trapped, caught in winter conditions with no food, no shelter, no way out. It was Running Bird's worst nightmare, the fanged fear that had been his constant companion since the Big Hats had fired on the chiefs' white flags in White Bird Canyon.

He felt a bullet whiz by his head and realized that cavalrymen had encircled him and the other warriors who, while trying to save the herd, had been cut off from the rest of the Indian camp. Still astride the now-lame gelding, Running Bird took cover in a tumble of sandstone boulders, surrounded by a murderous fire. Bullets ricocheted off the stone, sending razor-sharp shards of broken rock slicing into his bare skin.

He felt his mind freezing up, like the day at the Big Hole battlefield, but this time Black Hoof wasn't there to talk him through it. He felt a shock of pain and saw that a bullet had removed one finger and part of another. The next bullet barely missed his head, slamming into the rock behind him. His position was untenable.

He attempted a wild dash toward the camp, which looked to be holding for now. The white gelding was hard to see in the snowstorm, which gave Running Bird a fighting chance, but the used-up animal wasn't accustomed to being ridden like a war horse and became difficult to control.

A bullet slammed into Running Bird's right leg and buried itself deep in his calf like a red-hot poker. He lost his balance just long enough for the gelding to buck him off. He fell to the ground like a sack of sand. An image of Witt Lowsley flashed through his mind, injured and prone in the dirt.

"Get up and run! Come on! I'll cover you! Don't quit now! Get up!"

The voice belonged to White Bird, who delivered a withering suppressive fire while Running Bird half ran, half crawled behind a bluff protecting the besieged Indian camp. Someone carried him to Cedar Smoke, who was setting up a hospital at the relatively secure northern end of the battlefield. A moment later Prairie Dove was there, pressing painfully against his calf to stop the bleeding.

Cedar Smoke's face looked almost incandescent with sweat and steam from boiling medicine pots. Many people had suffered in this war on both sides, but Running Bird thought the medicine man had suffered the most, sharing the pain of every wound and every loss, trying to press little bits of broken rubble into a dam that would never be able to hold the great tide of grief arrayed against it. Yet his expression was much the same as always, a refuge of calm amidst the chaos.

"Get me back into the fight," Running Bird said.

"You're done fighting for today," Cedar Smoke said.

In the distance, Running Bird could hear the captured Nez Perce horses being slaughtered, screaming in terror. With each loud gunshot, he wondered which piece of his soul had just been snubbed out. The Appaloosa stallion? The rose gold filly? The fancy paint colt with the gorgeous, delicate neck? His tongue felt thick with the taste of blood and mud.

Fast-moving clouds distorted the light so that the sky looked almost like a river running overhead. Running Bird imagined he was looking up from the bottom of an ice-cold creek. Maybe this was how the sky looked to Scott Grooms while Running Bird was killing him.

The medicine man cauterized Running Bird's amputated fingers with heated stones, removed the bullet from his calf, plucked shards of rock and prickly pear from his flesh, and disinfected the whole mess with whiskey.

Running Bird tried not to think about the pain, tried to imagine he was back in Idaho Territory, learning to swim in the Clearwater River, looking for killdeer nests along the gravelly shoreline, racing his spotted horse against Black Hoof's rose gold filly. He let his mind sink deeper and deeper into the comfort of the past before finally, mercifully, passing out.

Chapter 33

With extraordinary effort, Running Bird opened his eyes, lifting his good hand to touch Prairie Dove's hair. The night was sepulchral gray fading to black, filled with moving shadows and muffled sounds.

"How many days since the siege began?" he said.

"Three," she said.

"If you said three hundred, I'd believe you."

The Indians had repelled three major assaults so far, but at a terrible cost. Half the Nez Perce warriors were dead or wounded. Everyone else was frantically digging trenches with knives and captured bayonets, throwing out snow and frozen soil with tin pans and chapped hands, piling rocks in front of crude shelters with cracks just big enough to poke a gun barrel through. Gunfire was sporadic now, just enough to keep the soldiers outside the Indian camp and the Indians trapped inside it, but Running Bird suspected there would be another attack at dawn. The smell of gunpowder and lead gripped the slushy ground.

His body felt unfamiliar, like it belonged to someone much older and enfeebled. He'd never fully recovered his strength after the escape from the Absaroka Mountains, and with his injured leg and mutilated hand, he felt nearly helpless now. The mere act of crawling into a trench with a rifle and an ammunition belt was almost more than he could do. When the weapon recoiled against his shoulder, it felt like his brittle bones would shatter.

Running Bird felt the same annihilating despair Black Hoof

must have experienced on the day he'd died. He yearned for some invisible door to swing open on its hinges so his spirit could fly free, and yet his beating heart clung stubbornly to life, like a tree that wouldn't let go its frost-burnt leaves. He looked across the battlefield, blurred by heavy snow and sleet, and thought about his brother, reloading his rifle with powder-blackened fingers after bullets had slammed into his leg, hip, arm, and head. Running Bird, too, would fight to the death.

He flinched when Prairie Dove pulled an ice- and mud-caked bandage off his ruined hand. It felt like the missing fingers were trapped in a painful, twisted position, crushed between heavy stones.

"I'm sorry," she said.

"The cold numbs it," he said, and jammed the raw finger stumps into the fresh snow. He couldn't bear to look at them.

It hardly seemed worth the trouble to dress his wounds—the new bandages would be just as filthy as the old ones in the time it took him to sneeze—but Prairie Dove seemed determined to make the effort. His eyes watched her, but his body felt gelatinous with fatigue. His bones were pin-thin, the marrow leaking out. His spine was a frayed rope. He felt tired in a way that no amount of rest could ever satisfy. He had an unquenchable thirst for sleep.

He hadn't eaten in two days. Before the war, it wasn't unusual for him to fast for a day or two, but food was always available, so it never felt like he was starving. Now, with no food and no prospect of food, he felt a new desperation. Hunger stooped at his elbow, waking him from fitful dreams, tormenting his insides which were hollow as a gourd.

He thought about Scott Grooms, how much he must have

wanted those apples. He thought he understood, now, how a man might kill for an apple.

If Running Bird had an apple, what would he do with it? He'd give it to Prairie Dove, who'd give it to the boy who brought him water every few hours. Maybe he'd take one bite and let her give the boy the rest. Two bites. Half. Didn't Running Bird need the apple more than the boy, in order to fight for the boy?

Nothing compared with hunger in its power to corrupt, he realized. If his soul could still be saved, it wouldn't be done by courage or fulfillment of duty but by the solitary fact that there wasn't any apple for him to steal from a child.

When Prairie Dove cut the bandage from his leg, he knew without looking, knew from the stench of rotting meat and the way she drew in her breath, that the wound was infected.

"We're almost out of ammunition," he said.

"We still have these," she said, picking up a handful of stones.

His mind groped for words. "Listen to me," he said. "You're still strong. You can slip through the siege line and walk to Canada. You can practically see the medicine line from here, just beyond those hills."

Prairie Dove's eyes welled up with tears, but she quickly blinked them away. She finished wrapping the torn end of a threadbare blanket around his useless leg, then tipped her head back and straightened her shoulders, looking him in the eyes.

"I'm pregnant."

Running Bird stared at her, dumbstruck. His heart felt like a gloved fist, beating against his ribs. Then his face cracked into a grin from ear to ear, so wide he couldn't speak.

Prairie Dove grinned too, but her face was etched with grief and worry, too. He realized she'd already decided to leave him, to save the life of their child. He saw it clearly now, in the small quaver of her lips, and the fact that she didn't trust her voice to speak.

"It's all right," he said, which opened the dam of tears streaming down her cheeks, glazing her face.

He reached for her, but she was determined to finish dressing his wounds. Her hands fumbled with the bandages. It was a useless exercise, like scattering fragrant petals on the floor of a burning house, but it seemed to be of great importance to her, so he gritted his teeth and endured it.

A baby. It was extraordinary. Sublime. Humbling. Despite his wounds, despite cold and hunger, despite ineffable weariness, there was still this sweetness in life. It was even better than surviving the war himself because a baby could carry forward a better version of him, one that hadn't been sullied by violence.

Prairie Dove finished with his bandages and curled up beside him. He wrapped his arms around her and felt her body go limp.

"Be strong," he whispered.

"I'm tired of being strong," she said.

"I can't walk—"

"Don't."

"If there was any way I could—but the leg—it's useless."

She put two fingers to his lips. "Rest, now."

He heard her snuffling in the hollow of his throat. He imagined taking her tears into himself, her tears and all the other tears cried during this war, along with the slushy rain and snow, and pouring it all back out in a soothing stream. He imagined drifting in a well-made canoe, coming to no shore, and drifting some more. What a relief it would be to disappear, with no further aspirations.

His mind turned and turned like an animal in its burrow, preparing a place to sleep. He felt his bones softening into wet sand, his body going slack as a jellyfish. There were no edges between his body and hers, now. No boundaries between him and the undulating hills, the trees clustered like guests at a funeral, the mountains looming invisibly, the darkness swallowing him up. He felt his spirit drift away from his body, flying high and free and breathless.

Clouds rushed overhead like a river. Running Bird imagined Long Walker's hands holding him steady against the pull, then releasing him. He felt himself being swept away by the rush of the water, cold and bottomless. He fell into the kind of black, dreamless sleep where the drop rolls into the ocean and becomes the ocean, defying all attempts to shackle it.

Chapter 34

On the fourth day of the siege, General Howard arrived with reinforcements and sent Jack to carry a message to Chief Joseph. Jack had imagined meeting the chief so many times—to ask about his mother, to rescue Sally, to reclaim Hammertoe and Chocolate Bar, to apologize for killing the little girl—that as he crossed into the siege area, he had to keep reminding himself that this was no dream, that the rifles aimed at him were real, that maybe he was about to die. He carried a white flag and prayed the Indians wouldn't shoot, despite the example set by the army at White Bird Canyon.

The Nez Perce had come so close to freedom, only to be ensnared at the very last moment by Colonel Miles, who was now so puffed up with pride he could hardly button his showy bearskin coat. The Indians had traveled almost twelve hundred miles, only to be captured just thirty miles from the Canadian border and safety. They were so close to Canadian soil they could almost taste their hard-earned victory, like a dog balancing a biscuit on his nose.

There were few trees on the snow-covered ridges, only thorny shrubs encased in ice, which meant that his approach was through an open field, an easy target for Nez Perce sharpshooters. Two lumbering shadow-shapes slowly emerged from the Indian camp and walked toward him with rounded shoulders bent into the wind.

"I'm Jack Peniel," he said when he and the two Indians stood toe to toe. "I have a message from General Howard."

"I'm Hinmahtooyahlatkekt," one of the Indians said. "You can call me Joseph. This is White Bird. All the other chiefs are dead."

Unlike Joseph, White Bird didn't extend his hand, but only regarded Jack with wary eyes, hiding the rest of his face behind an eagle's wing.

The chiefs guided Jack into a bowl-shaped hollow surrounded by low bluffs. They squatted around a small dung fire and smoked willow bark from a red clay pipe, a ceremony the Indians apparently deemed indispensable before Howard's message could be delivered or received.

Children emerged from underground shelter pits and crowded around, touching the men on the shoulders with tentative, tiny fingers, eager for the fire's warmth. Jack could feel their wispy breath and dark eyes on the back of his neck. Some of the smallest ones whimpered, but most of the children stood silently with vacant expressions.

"General Howard arrived with reinforcements today," Jack said. "I'm sure you saw."

Joseph crossed his arms across his chest.

"He'll promise whatever it takes to get you to surrender," Jack continued, "but the final decisions will be made in Washington, D.C. Howard said that if you surrender, nobody will be hanged, and your people will be returned to the reservation in Idaho Territory. I think he'll do what he can to make it come out that way, but like I said, the final decision doesn't belong to him."

Joseph frowned. "Why does Washington, D.C. send a man into a battlefield to negotiate with us if he can't agree to anything?"

"This isn't a negotiation."

Joseph and White Bird whispered in their language. Other voices drifted out from dark shelter pits, speaking a language that Jack no longer understood.

"When do you need an answer?" Joseph asked.

"Sunrise," Jack said. "If I haven't returned by then, they'll start the final assault. They've got two Howitzers and men who know how to aim them this time."

Joseph stared blankly into the fire, watching orange sparks drift sideways in the wind. White Bird twitched.

"There's something else," Jack said. "The warrior you call Running Bird. Is he still alive?"

Joseph whispered something to a boy, who ran to a rifle pit in one of the surrounding bluffs. Jack nearly wept with relief when he saw the young warrior with the bone necklace limp out of the hole, using his rifle as a crutch. He remembered how Running Bird had looked on the day he stole Howard's mule train—nearly invincible on his showy Appaloosa stallion—but cold, hunger, fatigue, and bullets had done their awful work. Running Bird moved like an old man now, shivering, hunched, and sluggish, as if every bone, every muscle, every nerve and sinew hurt. He had dark half-moons beneath his eyes and mud-caked bandages on his left hand and his right leg. His lips were purple with cold and curled in an expression that seemed to hold deep disappointment in the entire cosmic plan that had delivered him to this moment. Nevertheless, he didn't refuse Jack's hand when it was offered.

"I'm Jack Peniel."

"I know who you are," Running Bird said.

Jack thought about the day Running Bird had stolen General Howard's mules, how the other warriors had waited for Running Bird to make the decision after Jack exposed himself so recklessly. There was only one plausible explanation why all those warriors would defer to a man as young as Running Bird.

"We're brothers," Jack guessed.

"I thought you knew," Running Bird said.

"My father is an eel-skinned liar."

"If his hair caught fire, I wouldn't piss on him to put it out."

Jack had always imagined that if he went looking for his Nez Perce relatives, they'd welcome him like the prodigal son, but of course it was more complicated than that, even before he showed up wearing pieces and parts of a blue army uniform. He wanted to gain Running Bird's trust, but how?

"I bought ten of your horses from the army before the slaughter," Jack said.

"Congratulations," Running Bird said.

"They're staked in a copse of cottonwoods about a mile from here." He handed Running Bird a scrap of paper. "I drew you a map."

Running Bird looked at Jack, then at the map. "Why would you help me now?"

"We don't have much time," Jack said. "All I can say is, I've made a lot of bad decisions. I want to make something come out right for once. If not for me, then for someone else. Maybe this will give me peace. I want you to take those horses and get out of here. I want you to make it to Canada."

Running Bird's eyes softened. He handed the map back to Jack. "I can't walk a hundred feet, let alone a mile."

"I'll carry you," White Bird said. He wasn't a young man, but he looked like he could carry half a moose.

"You've done all you can here," Joseph said, placing a giant hand on Running Bird's hunched back. "Go with White Bird. See if you can find your wife."

"The Appaloosa stallion's there," Jack said, stabbing his finger at the map. "The rose gold filly. The bay mare with the fancy paint colt, plus some others I thought you'd want."

"How did you know which ones?"

"I've been following you since the Big Hole."

Running Bird looked at Jack the same way he did the first time they'd seen each other, as if trying to read his heart.

Jack held the younger man's gaze, still determined to wrest something beautiful from this war.

"Come with me," Running Bird said.

It was so unexpected, Jack thought he might have misunderstood. "To Canada?"

"Yes."

Jack's heart skipped a beat. All those visions he had about some other, unlived life—now was his chance.

He remembered the first time he'd seen Running Bird, covered with white dust and blackening blood, riding a spotted horse like a mythical centaur, whooping and waving his arms to keep two hundred stolen army mules moving forward. The mules were slicked with salt and sweat, tearing up the grass with sharp, powerful hooves, and it seemed like Running Bird was one of them, flying across the yellow grass.

If Jack could have switched places with Running Bird in that very moment, he would have done it, even though, at the time, he still believed Running Bird was doomed. Sometimes in Jack's dreams, he was Running Bird, or else he was himself, living the Indian's improbable life. It was always a disappointment and a relief when he woke up and discovered that he was still just himself, still stumbling through the same wilderness between the life he had and the one he wanted.

"I have a son," Jack said. "In Idaho Territory. My life is there, now."

Running Bird smiled. "What's his name?"

"Charlie. He's six."

"He thinks he's white," Running Bird guessed.

"It's complicated."

Running Bird grimaced when he stood up. The two men embraced. Then Jack watched his brother limp away, one arm draped across White Bird's shoulder.

"Wait!"

Running Bird turned around.

"My father. I need to know. What did he do to you?"

A storm flashed across the younger man's face. Then it was gone.

"He sent you," Running Bird said. "Which means he saved my life."

It was, of course, the last thing on earth Robert Peniel had intended when he'd pressured Jack to join the militia, and yet Running Bird had a point. Jack laughed.

"Give him my regards," Running Bird said.

"I will," Jack said.

Chapter 35

From the darkness of the shelter pits, Jack could hear the families murmuring among themselves. He couldn't hear or comprehend exactly what was being said, but he understood that the Nez Perce were separating themselves into two groups—those who were still strong enough to slip through the siege line and follow White Bird to Canada, and those who were too weak to travel any farther, and would stay behind with Joseph, who planned to surrender the following day with the sick and injured. Jack pictured the Nez Perce scattering across the map like bits of broken pottery, mastering new languages and geographies, enduring the same loneliness and isolation he'd suffered for so many years. When their children met, and their children's children, would they sense the old connections, like he and Running Bird had? Or would they only see the differences that had arisen among them?

Jack wished that all the people on that battlefield could put on clean clothes and sit together in perfect stillness. Not in a tight crouch but in a comfortable position with their arms and legs outstretched. Not trying to figure anything out or make any decisions. Just sitting quietly, with no more running to do. He thought that if they could do that, it might end this misery.

Joseph remained seated at the fire, across from Jack, while White Bird's contingent slipped away in twos and threes. The warmth of the flames slowly flickered out.

"I was at the Big Hole," Jack said, watching his breath freeze and swirl. "I acted not against my will but against my common sense and my conscience. I knew it was a damnable business and that the Nez Perce were peaceably inclined, and yet I fired low into a teepee and I killed a little girl."

Joseph rested his eyes on Jack's, level as a string. There was a risk, of course, that the chief would have Jack killed for his crime. But when the old man finally spoke, it was with a voice that had reassurance in it. A voice that said he understood Jack's need to unburden himself.

"The Nez Perce are an old people," Joseph said. "We try to love each other just exactly as the creative power made each one, which is to say, with many imperfections. We've all made terrible mistakes in this war."

"I want to apologize to the mother."

"She'd kill you if she got the chance," Joseph said. "Afterward, she'd regret it, and be even more miserable." His voice wasn't harsh. It was more like that of a father, speaking to a child who'd misunderstood something very basic.

Jack's heart sank. If he was to have any hope of future happiness, it seemed essential that he receive the young mother's forgiveness, and yet he knew the chief was right. He recalled the conversation with his father when he'd tried to apologize for Sally's death. It had not gone well.

"I don't want to cause her any more pain than I already have," Jack said, embarrassed by the quaver in his voice. He wanted a drink. God almighty, he wanted a drink.

Joseph's eyes had more sympathy than judgment in them. He sat very still. "By the time a man has reached our age," he said, "he's made mistakes. He's endured storms, withstood attacks, known sickness and misery. He's regretted the bad things he's done and the good things he hasn't done. His heart is scarred and has pieces missing. The yearning for redemption, the effort to prove, to our-selves and to others, that we're worthy, is what pushes us toward the second attempt, and the third, and the fourth, each one kinder, more empathetic, more generous than the one before. If you want that little girl's death to mean something, become a better man. Leave the grieving mother out of it."

Jack's eyes drifted beyond the burning dung, beyond the shad-owy rifle pits, beyond the rolling hills, to the mountains looming in the south, receding into the infinite distance.

"I can't stop thinking about how different things might have been," he said.

"Your mother was the same," Joseph said.

The chief dropped the reference so casually, so unexpectedly, Jack could have just left it there, but he didn't. All the questions he'd imagined asking so many times came tumbling out. What was her name? What was she like? How did she die? And when?

Joseph explained that it wasn't proper to speak the names of the dead, but he thought Jack's mother would want to be awak-ened, even from the grave, to see that he'd finally come looking for her. The chief spoke her name just once. "Blue Mountain Woman." Then he enjoined Jack, very solemnly, to never speak it again.

"She spent two years looking for you after Peniel carried you off," Joseph said. "She traveled the Columbia River corridor all the way to Astoria, stopping at every trading post, every homestead, and every campsite, showing people a tintype. When she finally found your father, he told her you were dead."

"He'd left me in an orphanage," Jack said. "He called it a board-ing school, but I knew what it was."

"A few years ago, she went to Lewiston to sell some of her crafts on the corner of Second and C Streets. That was when she saw you, walking down the street with an armload of buckets."

"She came into my studio," Jack said. "I'm sure it was her, now. I sold her a bone necklace. Charged her full price, which she paid from a buckskin pouch filled with gold. Running Bird was wearing it."

"She wore it until she died," Joseph said.

"It was just a simple piece of bone plucked from a carrion pile," Jack said. "I liked the idea of turning it into something beautiful. I didn't even ask her name."

"You weren't ready," Joseph said. "It doesn't matter. You're here now."

It wasn't the forgiveness Jack had been hoping for, but there was compassion in the old man's voice. Acceptance notwithstanding Jack's devastating flaws. A sense of belonging that he'd never known before. It was enough.

Chapter 36

Jack returned to General Howard's camp with news that Joseph intended to surrender at noon. With luck, Running Bird would reach the Killdeer Badlands in Saskatchewan by then.

General Howard and Colonel Miles waited all morning for Joseph's arrival. Miles strode through the camp wearing high boots and a showy bearskin coat, which rolled down his back like a cape. General Howard padded around inside his tent wearing sheepskin slippers, dictating a report and sneezing into a handkerchief. An orderly emptied a wheelbarrow of amputated limbs next to a field of slaughtered horses swarming with vultures and crows.

Jack had already mustered out and was loading his saddlebags for the long trip home when he heard the bugler blast a few quick notes to rally the men around the guidon, signaling that Joseph was finally on his way. He secured his bedroll behind the cantle of his saddle, then joined the others beneath the colors. A puppy that looked almost exactly like Chocolate Bar had followed him back from the Indians' camp and was nipping at his shoelace. Jack picked up the dog, who nestled in the crook of his arm.

Howard and Miles stood side by side beneath the flag, grim-faced.

Joseph walked toward them slowly, holding a white flag, looking neither left nor right as he left the protection of his camp and crossed the field still slick with battle gore. Tall wisps of yellow grass poked through fading pink slush, inviting a fresh blanket of forgetful snow from the dull gray clouds. Gunfire had been sporadic the past few days, and the birds, foxes, deer, and coyotes had mostly returned.

Joseph's face showed outward calm and composure; only his eyes betrayed how hard he was working to hold himself together. His lips were tight, like a fish pulling against a barbed hook. In the bright sunlight, Jack could see where the chief's forehead and wrist had been scratched by bullets.

When Joseph reached the guidon, he held out his Winchester rifle to General Howard, who motioned him to give the weapon to Colonel Miles. A barely suppressed smile played across Miles's thin lips as he accepted the gun. He would display the trophy over his hearth, Jack predicted, and regale every future guest with the story of his improbable victory over the famous Nez Perce chief. His wife would grow tired of the story and leave the room when he repeated it for the umpteenth time. His children would roll their marbles across the carpet and yawn.

"I am tired of fighting," Joseph said. "Our chiefs are killed. Our old men are all dead. It is cold, and we have no blankets. The little children are freezing to death. My people, some of them, have run away to the hills, and have no blankets, no food. No one knows where they are. Perhaps they are freezing to death. I want to have time to look for my children and see how many of them I can find. Maybe I will find them among the dead. Hear me, my chiefs! I am tired. My heart is sick and sad. From where the sun now stands, I will fight no more forever."

After a moment of stillness, Joseph drew a thin gray blanket over his head. For a while, nobody spoke. Then a soldier broke the spell, asking if he could have the blanket as a souvenir. The chief obliged and was left shivering in the cold.

Joseph could have escaped to Canada. He was still strong and healthy. Instead, he chose to stay behind with those too weak or sick to escape. He was the mountain lion bedded down on a cactus, that others might sleep more comfortably on his broad back. He had more dignity in defeat than Howard or Miles did in victory. His Indian name was Hinmahtooyahlatkekt, which meant Thunder Rolling in the Mountains. It was a grand name, Jack thought. The kind of name it took a lifetime to earn.

A straggling procession of Indians followed Joseph, cold, wounded, sick, and starving. Jack retrieved his old Hawken rifle from a pile of surrendered weapons. He left behind the Springfield rifle he'd carried at the Big Hole. He wanted no mementos from that slaughter.

Howard sent stretchers to carry the weakest prisoners to the hospital tent. Some arrived in desperate condition, with wounds wrapped in filthy bandages and nothing to appease their pain but their medicine man's soothing voice. The fighting may have stopped but the dying would continue. Dr. Graham distributed opium and cocaine and whiskey.

Outside the hospital tent, children with bare heads and gloveless hands gathered around a soup pot suspended above blue-orange flames. Snowflakes swirled and floated, down from the sky or up from the ground, Jack couldn't tell which. He was just about to mount up on old Hammertoe when Howard and Miles stopped him.

"You bought ten horses yesterday, in addition to that mule," Miles said. "Where are they?"

A small group of men seemed to sense that some disgrace was brewing and stopped to watch.

"I staked those horses about a mile from here," Jack said. "This morning, they were gone."

"There are about three hundred Indians here," Miles told

Howard, looking around. "There should be at least twice that many."

Howard glared at Jack. "You helped them, didn't you? Gibbon tried to warn me."

"Arrest him," Miles snapped at a sergeant. "Joseph too."

Jack wasn't overly concerned for himself. It wasn't a crime to lose ten horses, and nobody could prove he'd conspired with the Indians.

Joseph, however, was another matter. It never occurred to Jack that the chief might be punished just because Miles's siege line proved so leaky.

"You promised the chief wouldn't hang!" Jack said as a sergeant pinned his arms.

"That was before I knew about this treachery," Miles said, red-faced with anger. "That bag of nails kept us waiting all morning, hoping to give his friends more time to escape!"

"Take a hundred cavalry," Howard told Miles. "See how many of them you can catch."

Jack felt the press of a gathering crowd, murmuring words like "half-breed" and "traitor," words they wouldn't dare to say to his face, and was surprised to discover he didn't care. Why should he worry about the opinions of people who'd never cared about him?

Miles stomped off, spewing obscenities. A bugler blasted *To horse!* The ground rumbled as cavalrymen moved out. With any luck, Running Bird and his wife were in Canada by now, but it would be close. Too close.

Jack and Joseph were rolled in blankets so they couldn't move their arms or legs, then tied up and thrown on the muddy ground in a stockade with the mules. The two men lay side by side in the wet, windy cold. Hammertoe was still saddled and tied to a hitching post. Jack guessed that she would have liked to kick him in the face again, but she couldn't quite reach.

Jack saw General Howard's polished boots standing before him in the mud. "You still want to wear the white hat, don't you?" Howard asked.

"I'm lying in a pile of frozen manure," Jack said. "I just had my reputation, such as it was, knocked down another few pegs. I can almost hear the blistering tirade from my father when he hears about this from his friends. He has nothing to do, now, except think up new ways to insult me. I suddenly need to take a piss, which, as you can see, is quite impossible in my current predicament. I can't really express to you how much I want a drink right now. I haven't had one since the Big Hole, which ought to count among the great historical examples of personal stoicism. And yet I'd rather be here, wondering how you tie your shoelaces one-handed, than celebrating this damnable business with those other men. If I ever happen to catch that mumblecrust who begged Chief Joseph's last bullet-riddled blanket, I'll strand him naked and barefoot in a god-damned blizzard."

"You've changed, Jack. You've stopped walking away from all the ugliness in the world and started trying to fix it. I doubt you'll succeed, but I hope you prove me wrong. I'll be the first to congratulate you if you do."

"Thank you, sir."

"Untie him," Howard told the sergeant, overruling the absent Colonel Miles.

Jack was anxious to get out of there, but he was still worried about Joseph. "What's going to happen to the chief?"

Howard stiffened. "You're still as impudent as ever," he said, turning to go.

While the sergeant untied the ropes binding Jack, he sang the chorus of a popular new show tune:

Not for Joe, Not for Joe,
If he knows it, oh, dear, no,
No, no, Not for Joe,
Not for Joseph, oh, dear, no.

Howard turned back around. "You find this amusing?"

"No, sir," the sergeant said, straightening his back.

Howard's eyes drilled into the sergeant. "Untie the chief, too," he said. "Give him a blanket and something to eat."

"Yes, sir," the sergeant said.

Jack smiled, glad that he hadn't misjudged the one-armed general. He stood up and brushed himself off. There was wet green dung on his ear, where he'd been tossed to the ground, but he didn't care.

"They're already in Canada, aren't they?" Howard said.

"I hope so, sir," Jack said.

Chapter 37

Jack untied Hammertoe's lead line from the hitching post and picked up the puppy who'd followed him back from the Indians' camp. He was about to put his foot into the stirrup when he saw Dr. Graham walking toward him. He wondered if the doctor had seen Jack's latest humiliation and changed his mind about letting Jack meet Charlie.

"I knew you'd gone looking for a sapphire," Graham said, shoving his hands into his pockets.

"You're the only person I told before I left," Jack said.

"I knew the Sapphire Mountains were three hundred miles away and that it was the kind of thing you wouldn't rush. Still, I convinced myself that something must have happened to you, and that you weren't coming back."

"I wanted to knock out your teeth when I found out you'd married Jessica," Jack said. "But I can't say for certain I wouldn't have done the same thing if I'd been walking in your shoes. If you want my forgiveness, you have it. I just want to meet my son."

"On your way back to Lewiston, maybe you could stop by Mount Idaho for supper," Graham said.

Jack smiled. "I wouldn't miss it for anything," he said.

Chapter 38

Fergus Dewsnap, "THE RED NAPOLEON SURRENDERS," *Lewiston Telegraph* (October 6, 1877)

Colonel Nelson Miles has at last accomplished what his superior officer, General Howard, could not. Ending one of the most stubborn and gallant running fights known in history, Miles has compelled Chief Joseph and the remnant of his band, harassed and worn out, to surrender. Miles's telegraph to General Sherman was subdued, noting simply, "we have had our usual success." General Howard arrived at the field too late to render assistance and made no attempt to assume command.

The Nez Perce crowned their last struggle with striking examples of generosity and humanity. All along they have refused to scalp or mutilate our dead soldiers, or to kill the wounded who fell into their hands, even though our own men have desecrated Indian graves for souvenirs. They have released captive women, including the artist Nicole Lowsley, who has become one of their strongest advocates.

Soldiers now relate that the Indians not only spared but cared for wounded Americans throughout Miles's battle. They roamed the battlefield late at night while our wounded lay helpless behind the Nez

Perce line and assured them that "it would be shameful for us to shoot men who can no longer fight." In one case, a blanket was placed under the head of a wounded soldier. In at least seven cases, the Indians delivered water to our helpless men. Lieutenant Jerome, who was captured and held prisoner for one day, said the Indians put him in an ingeniously constructed rifle pit so that he might be protected from the bullets of his friends. These are the people we have called savages. Meanwhile, there are reports that the City of Deadwood is offering $250 for the scalp of any Indian of any sex or age.

Colonel Miles promised Joseph that the Nez Perce would be returned to their reservation in Idaho if they surrendered, but after Joseph accepted the terms and gave up his weapons, General Sherman countermanded Miles, and ordered the captives, including women and children, sent to Fort Leavenworth instead. "Every assurance and promise made to them on the battlefield has been disregarded," Miles said. "Such is the justice of our government."

Joseph was a foe worthy of any fighter's steel. Cunning, bold, brave, and resourceful, his campaign has been one of splendid dash and pertinacity. He surrendered in the Bear Paw Mountains with about three hundred of his followers, stoic and dignified to the end. While fighting stubbornly and for as long as they could, the Indians acted, on the whole, in a manner which entitles them to be treated with the dignity of warriors rather than criminals.

Joseph crossed the Missouri River four or five days ahead of Colonel Miles, and why he permitted the latter to overtake him is perhaps the most singular part of the whole affair, as he could have kept on one or two days longer and been out of harm's way. But for that final, fatal mistake, General Sherman said that the Indians "fought with almost scientific skill," and "displayed a courage and ability that elicited universal praise." These facts only make harder the fate that awaits them, for it shows that no forbearance, bravery, or competence can win justice for the Indians.

We freely express the opinion that the war was, on the part of our government, an unpardonable and gigantic blunder—a crime whose victims are alike the gallant officers and men who fell prey to Nez Perce bullets and the peaceful bands who were goaded into taking the war path. It is greatly to be regretted that the immediate responsibility for this war is so obscurely distributed that it is difficult to bring anybody to account. It is our sincere hope that, in the future, our troops will be used in a more honorable exploit than hunting down men, women, and children with whom the nation has broken a solemn compact.

«———»

October 6, 1877

From General William T. Sherman, Commanding General of the Army

To General Oliver O. Howard, Commander, Department of the Columbia

If I had my choice, I would kill every reporter in the world, but I am sure we would be getting dispatches from Hell before breakfast. *Vox populi, vox humbug.*

❮————❯

October 7, 1877

From General Oliver O. Howard, Commander, Department of the Columbia

To General William T. Sherman, Commanding General of the Army

It is natural for reporters to follow the crowd, but the Lord calls upon each of us to sacrifice such easy gains on the altar of truth.

Noah built and voyaged alone. His neighbors laughed at his strangeness and perished in style.

Abraham wandered and worshipped alone. Sodomites smiled at the simple shepherd, followed the world's fashion, and fed the flames.

Daniel dined and prayed alone.

Elijah sacrificed and witnessed alone.

Jeremiah prophesied and wept alone.

Jesus lived and died alone. And of the lonely way His disciples should walk, He said, "Straight is the gate, and narrow is the way, which leadeth unto life, and few there be that find it."

❮————❯

October 8, 1877
From General William T. Sherman, Commanding General of
the Army
To General Oliver O. Howard, Commander, Department of the
Columbia

If you ever preach to me again, I shall have you ca-
shiered.

I am glad you were there at the end. Public opinion
has tipped so strongly in favor of the "Red Napoleon"
that if Miles had dared to hang the chief, he would
never get his star. Is it true Miles held your arm, in the
secession war, while the doctor sawed it off?

«———»

October 9, 1877
From General Oliver O. Howard, Commander, Department of
the Columbia
To General William T. Sherman, Commanding General of the
Army

I can still feel the arm and Miles's firm grip, though
it's been fifteen years. I am weary, I admit. I do not
know whether it is because I captured Joseph or because I failed to do so. Sometimes I feel like Ahab, ensnared in his own hemp.

«———»

October 9, 1877
From General Oliver O. Howard, Commander, Department of
the Columbia
To Major H. Henry Clay Wood, Assistant Adjutant General

Red Heart and his people may be returned to Idaho, but do it quietly, and wait until spring. The reporters will be crowing about something else by then.

«———»

October 10, 1877
From Major H. Henry Clay Wood, Assistant Adjutant General
To General Oliver O. Howard, Commander, Department of the Columbia

I fear they've beaten you, sir. (The reporters, I mean.)

Epilogue
Alberta, Canada

Running Bird placed his hand beneath a frozen waterfall, feeling the suppressed power. He imagined the roaring sound of the water before it was subdued by winter's cold grip. He picked up handfuls of earth and stone lying quiescent beneath the giant icicles, nearly washed away but not quite.

Greens, blues, and purples traveled over and through the opalescent ice but never lingered long, shifting with the angle of the sun and the position of the scattered clouds. The surface of the ice was smooth in some places, crystalline in others, fractured, cracked, and faulted throughout. At lower elevations, the ice had started to weep in the relative warmth of spring. The oldest glaciers looked like blocks of colored glass.

Running Bird strapped axes to his wrists and metal spikes to the front of each boot and started to climb the ice. He swung an axe and then thrust with the spikes, using the axes for balance and his legs to gain altitude. *Axe, spike, spike. Axe, spike, spike.* He held the axes with just enough power to keep his center of gravity balanced. He kicked his feet with just enough force to embed the spikes into the ice without shattering it. He used the minimum effort needed to stay attached, just like climbing rocks.

He kept his heels down and pushed his hips toward the ice to weight the spikes. He heard the axes and spikes *thunk* into the cold, dense surface. He felt the tiny vibrations of each solid, precise placement. He pushed with his legs, pushed with his legs, up and up. His right calf still pained him, but not unbearably. He wondered if it always would.

Running Bird and Prairie Dove had spent the first part of the winter on the northern plains with the Sioux. When Running Bird's leg had gotten strong enough, they'd gravitated west to the jagged, snow-capped Canadian Rockies. Running Bird had taken a job training horses for the Mounties and leased a piece of land with a fenced pasture and a little creek. For the first time in his life, no white man could wave a piece of paper from the federal land office and order his family to move.

Prairie Dove would begin her confinement in the red lodge soon. Running Bird couldn't stop hearing the sounds of Corn Tassel's ear-splitting screams, but for Prairie Dove's sake he knew he must be brave. Soon a child conceived in war would be running around, telling them they were wrong about this and that, showing them things they'd never noticed about the world. The child would be hurt, bruised, heartbroken. There would be ups and downs, a depth of emotion that would shake the new parents as if they were dried leaves. Life would go on.

The war hadn't broken Running Bird, but the scars ran deep. The nightmares. The numbness. The continuous replaying and second guessing of every split-second battlefield decision. The naked fear that gripped him every time he let Prairie Dove out of his sight, even for a short time. The time spent wondering, pointlessly, endlessly, what he might have done differently. How he could have stopped it all.

If Black Hoof had lived, the two brothers might have ascended this massive ice field together. Black Hoof would have gone first, testing the ice. He would have been opinionated and loud, telling Running Bird to do exactly this and precisely that. He would have pressed forward at a pace that no man, certainly not Running Bird, could match. His ascent would have been steady, confident, technically flawless.

Running Bird tried to imagine his brother climbing beside him, encouraging him, loving him. He hadn't properly mourned the loss. During the war, he didn't have the chance. Afterward, he was too numb. This journey was his good-bye.

With each step of the climb, Running Bird imagined himself leaving the burden of the war behind him, becoming lighter in spirit, mind, heart, and body, retaining only what was essential, only what he really needed: to love, to forgive, to survive.

He reached the lonely summit near sunset. Colossal mountains stretched to the horizon in every direction. He looked at the sky, the mountains, the rugged peaks of ancient rock, the curtains of gleaming ice, the talus and scree scrambles giving way to thickly timbered slopes and turquoise lakes. He sensed the creative power embracing him, restoring him, cloaking him with compassion and grace. He recalled his mother's voice, *Hmmmmmm-Ah-Ah, Hmmmmmmm-Ah-Ah,* and Cedar Smoke's psalm, *we are not crushed.* He began to think his soul could heal.

He stretched out his arms and spun in circles, looking skyward. In that grand, vast expanse, alone on top of the shining mountain, he felt impossibly small.

He shouted to be heard. "Do you hear me, brother?" His voice echoed off the stones and through the canyons, reverberating back to him. He shouted again, louder still. "Do you see me, brother?"

A snowy owl circled in the azure sky. The bird beat its powerful wings to gain height, then soared with unerring grace, tipping its heart-shaped face toward the solitary man. *Hoo-h'HOO-hoo-hoo!*

Running Bird watched the bird in awe. He laughed and cried

simultaneously. He fell to his knees. He answered the call. *Hoo-h'HOO-hoo-hoo!*

The bird answered back, loud and insistent. *Hoo-н'HOO-нoo-нoo!*

The owl spiraled down and around the icy summit to Running Bird's eye level. Its wings were feathered so softly that its flight was soundless, ghost-like, circling so close that Running Bird could feel the ruffled air sweep across his skin. Intense, jasper-colored eyes stared at him unblinking as the raptor circled once, twice, three times. On the third sweep, a white feather tipped with black floated down and was swept away by wind. Then the great white owl—the mystic bird patiently waiting in that sweeping space where earth touched sky—moved on.

Running Bird watched it go.

He didn't know if his brother's spirit found him on the solitary mountaintop that day. He didn't know if men were meant to know such things. All he knew was that, for the first time in a very long time, he danced.

Author's Note

Bone Necklace was inspired by the Nez Perce War of 1877, which contemporaneous newspapers described as "a gigantic blunder and a crime," a "fraud and downright robbery," and a product of the government's "rascally representatives." The simple words of Chief Joseph's surrender speech—"from where the sun now stands, I will fight no more forever"—struck a chord with a war-weary nation and gained the chief national prominence, which he used effectively in subsequent years to secure better conditions for his people. The tribe's forbearance before the war, their bravery and humanity during the conflict, their dignity through years of exile and injustice, and their eloquence and artistry earned them a place among America's icons.

Some of the historical figures who shaped the events of 1877 and inspired portions of the novel are briefly introduced below.

Chief Joseph

After the war, Chief Joseph became a prominent advocate for Native American rights. With plainspoken eloquence, the Nez Perce chief talked about equal protection and non-violent resistance in a way that would not be accepted by mainstream America for almost a century. He was granted interviews with President Hayes in 1879, President McKinley in 1897, and President Roosevelt in 1903. On at least one of these trips, he delivered a lecture at Lincoln Hall in Washington, D.C. His portrait was engraved on the great bronze doors of the Library of Congress in 1897.

After seven long years of exile in Leavenworth, Kansas, and the Indian Territory in Oklahoma, the captive Nez Perce were returned to the reservation in Lapwai, Idaho, if they agreed to become Christians, or to a reservation in Colville, Washington, if they did not. Chief Joseph went to Colville, where he died and was buried in 1904.

Chief Sitting Bull

Chief Sitting Bull was a Hunkpapa Lakota chief who became famous for his role in the June 25-26, 1876 battle in which General George Armstrong Custer and the Seventh Cavalry were destroyed. In May 1877, Chief Sitting Bull led his band into Canada to escape retaliation and was granted political asylum.

Chief Sitting Bull welcomed Chief White Bird and hundreds of other Nez Perce refugees into his camp when they arrived in Canada in October 1877. According to some accounts, Chief Sitting Bull sent a war party to rescue the Nez Perce when he learned about the siege at the Bear Paw battlefield, but by then Chief Joseph had surrendered. Chief Sitting Bull was lured back to the U.S. in 1880 and was murdered in the custody of police in 1890.

Chief White Bird

Chief White Bird escaped the Bear Paw battlefield and crossed the "medicine line" into Canada. On October 22, 1877, North-West Mounted Police Superintendent James Walsh met with White Bird and other Nez Perce refugees in Sitting Bull's camp in Saskatchewan. Walsh counted two hundred and ninety Nez Perce refugees living among the Sioux. All were given political asylum. White Bird lived the rest of his life in Canada, where he died in 1892.

Chief Looking Glass

Chief Looking Glass and all his people were peacefully camped on the Nez Perce reservation in Idaho when the army preemptively attacked to keep them out of the war. Five Nez Perce were badly wounded, one fatally. In addition, a woman and her child drowned while trying to escape the soldiers. Seven hundred and fifty of Looking Glass's horses were confiscated by the government.

After his camp was attacked, Looking Glass and his people joined the fight. Some accounts later blamed the famous buffalo hunter for two great mistakes: the decision to rest at the Big Hole River, and the decision to rest in the Bear Paw Mountains. Looking Glass lost his life at the Bear Paw battlefield when he stood up from his rifle pit to get a better view of what he thought were Sioux warriors coming to rescue the Nez Perce. In fact, it was only a herd of buffalo.

Chief Red Heart

On July 16, 1877, Chief Red Heart and thirty-nine members of his band surrendered to General Howard. They had just returned from a hunting trip in Montana and by all accounts were determined to stay out of the war. Although the band had committed no crimes, they were held prisoner at Fort Vancouver through the winter of 1877-78 without a trial. A woman and an infant died during this imprisonment.

Chief Yellow Wolf

Chief Yellow Wolf was a Nez Perce warrior who survived the war and escaped to Canada. During the war, he was wounded five times. He principally served as a scout and a rear guard to protect his people from unexpected attack. A year after the war, he voluntarily returned to the U.S. and was sent into exile with the other

Nez Perce who had surrendered to Colonel Miles. He died in 1935 and was buried next to his uncle, Chief Joseph.

Chief Yellow Wolf was interviewed at length by historian Lucullus McWhorter, who recorded his story. Chief Yellow Wolf was concerned that the next generation of Native Americans would continue to suffer under white oppression. "I want the next generation of whites to know and treat the Indian as themselves."

The fictional character Running Bird was inspired in part by Chief Yellow Wolf.

Chief Ollikut

Chief Joseph's brother, Ollikut, was described as tall, graceful, intelligent, fun-loving, and daring. He was a hunter and warrior who was also experienced in diplomacy, accompanying his father and older brother to treaty negotiations between the U.S. and Nez Perce in 1855, 1863, and 1877. General Howard believed that Ollikut "would rather than not have a fight." After Ollikut's wife was killed at the Big Hole battlefield, Ollikut went silent. He died at the Bear Paw battlefield.

The fictional character Black Hoof was inspired in part by Ollikut.

Wahlitits

A miner named Larry Ott asked Wahlitits's father, Eagle Robe, for permission to build a house on the family's land. Eagle Robe agreed. Later, Ott asked for another piece of ground to make a garden. Eagle Robe agreed. After that, Ott asked for more land to plant an orchard and vineyard. When Eagle Robe objected, Ott gunned him down.

The Indian agent bound Ott over to the grand jury. The grand jury refused to hear testimony from the Nez Perce witnesses and released the murderer. Some reports say the Nez Perce witnesses refused to take the oath on a Christian Bible. Another explanation is that Oregon had a statute prohibiting Indians and Negroes from testifying against whites.

After Howard ordered the Nez Perce to report to the reservation, Wahlitits decided to kill his father's murderer. When he couldn't find Ott, he targeted others who had wronged the Nez Perce over the years. Thus began the Nez Perce War of 1877.

Wahlitits was killed at the Big Hole battlefield. His pregnant wife picked up his gun and shot down the soldier who'd made her a widow, after which she, too, was killed.

Some accounts say Ott eluded Wahlitits by disguising himself as either a woman or a Chinese miner. Others say Ott fought in the war as a civilian volunteer. Both accounts could be true.

The fictional murder of Long Walker by Scott Grooms, Sheriff Peniel's failure to prosecute the murderer, and Running Bird's quest for revenge were inspired in part by these events.

General William T. Sherman

Sherman served as Commanding General of the U.S. Army during the Nez Perce War of 1877, which he described as "one of the most extraordinary Indian Wars of which there is any record." During the hostilities, he happened to be vacationing in Yellowstone Park. He assured other tourists that they would be perfectly safe, then cut his own visit short. Days later, two parties of tourists were attacked. One tourist was forced to act as a guide for the fleeing Nez Perce while his sisters were taken captive. One of the sisters, who thought her husband had been killed, learned when she was released that he had survived the ordeal.

Historian Elliot West described the grimly comic reunion of the kidnapped woman and her grievously wounded husband:

"Once [Mr. and Mrs. Cowan] were reunited, exactly a month after she had last seen him, shot in the head and presumably dead, they quickly set off for medical treatment in Bozeman. On the way, the wagon flipped over a precipice, tossing [Mr.] Cowan and the others onto the road. In town, he was taken to a hotel, where, as a friend worked on his wounds, his bed collapsed with a great crash. This 'nearly finished him,' [Mrs. Cowan] recalled, and [Mr.] Cowan reportedly called for an artillery strike to end his misery, but he was seemingly indestructible, and after some recuperation the couple made their way home to Radersburg. Thus ended what was surely the worst vacation in American history."

This story was the inspiration for the fictional kidnapping of Nicole Lowsley and her guide, David Ford.

General Oliver O. Howard

Howard commanded the U.S. Army's Department of the Columbia during the Nez Perce War of 1877. Before the war, he urged civilian authorities to bring indictments against settlers, including Larry Ott, who had murdered innocent Nez Perce. Instead, the government ordered Howard to confine the Nez Perce to a reservation in Idaho Territory, using force if necessary.

Howard was deeply religious and promoted prayer meetings and temperance among his command to such an extent that he became known as "the Christian General." He believed that the Indians should be dealt with through peaceful means and only lastly through force—a belief most other officers on the frontier thought naïve. During the war, when he learned that one of his scouting parties had scalped a Nez Perce woman, he was furious.

Twenty-seven years after the war, Howard appeared on a stage with Chief Joseph at the Carlisle Indian Industrial School, where he said:

> There are no people we honor more than we do the Indians. You will say, 'But didn't you fight the Indians?' Yes. I am an army officer. I would fight you if you rose up against the flag. I want it understood that when I fought with Joseph, I was ordered by the government at Washington to take Joseph and his Indians to the reservation that was set aside for them. . . . I could not do otherwise. I did my best to perform the duty.

The fictional dialogue between Howard and Jack is informed by Howard's generally sympathetic attitude toward the Nez Perce. The dispatches between Howard and General William T. Sherman are based in part on actual telegraphs from the field. In some cases, I have ascribed to Sherman statements that were made by others who reported to him. Some of the dispatches in the novel are entirely fictional, such as Sherman's derisive offer to catch the Nez Perce himself.

Newspaper coverage of the war was harshly critical of Howard. The novel's fictional *Lewiston Telegraph* was inspired in part by actual stories published by dozens of different newspapers during the war. A sampling of the contemporaneous coverage is included in the Appendix.

Howard attained the rank of Major General. He died in October 1909.

Colonel John Gibbon

During the war, Gibbon commanded the U.S. Army's Seventh Infantry in Montana Territory. When the Nez Perce fled Idaho

Territory in July 1877, General Howard telegraphed Gibbon with instructions to intercept them.

The Nez Perce entered Montana Territory on July 26, 1877. Some reports suggest that the Nez Perce entered the territory by sneaking around the army breastworks on the Lolo Trail, which were later dubbed Fort Fizzle. Chief Joseph offered a different account:

> We retreated to Bitter Root Valley. Here another body of soldiers came upon us and demanded our surrender. We refused. They said, 'You cannot get by us.' We answered, 'We are going by you without fighting if you will let us, but we are going by you anyhow.' We then made a treaty with these soldiers. We agreed not to molest anyone, and they agreed that we might pass through the Bitter Root country in peace. We bought provisions and traded stock with white men there. We understood that there was to be no more war. We intended to go peaceably to the buffalo country.

The Nez Perce were attacked at the Big Hole battlefield on August 9. Heavy casualties were inflicted by both sides. Most of the Nez Perce casualties were women and children. In one lodge, two women were killed, and a newborn baby's head was smashed on his mother's breast. In another lodge, five children were shot at point blank range. In another, a whole family was burned alive. A little girl had her teeth knocked out with the stock of a rifle. Some of the Nez Perce women, seeing their husbands and children killed, joined the fight. These events inspired the description of the battle in the novel.

In an award-winning essay written in 1880, Gibbon described his philosophy regarding Native Americans, which perhaps explains his order to shoot low into the teepees:

> Philanthropists and visionary speculators may theorize as they please about preserving the Indians as a race. But it cannot be done. Whenever two races come in contact, the weaker one must give way, and disappear. To deny this is to deny the evidence of our own senses, and to shut our eyes to the facts of history.

Gibbon attained the rank of Major General.

Colonel Nelson A. Miles

During the war, Miles commanded the U.S. Army's Fifth Infantry Regiment in Montana Territory. He intercepted the Nez Perce at the Bear Paw battlefield and held them there until Howard arrived. Miles and Howard told Chief Joseph that if he surrendered, the captured Nez Perce would be returned to their reservation in Idaho Territory. Instead, Sherman ordered them sent to a malarial swamp in Leavenworth, Kansas. Howard accepted Sherman's decision, but Miles never did. "Every assurance and promise made to them by you or me has been disregarded," Miles would later complain to Howard. "Such is the justice of our government." For years, Miles persistently pressed for the return of the prisoners to Idaho, even petitioning President Hayes.

Miles attained the rank of Lieutenant General. From 1895 to 1903, he served as the last Commanding General of the U.S. Army before the office was abolished.

Major Henry Clay Wood

During the war, Major Henry Clay Wood served as Howard's Assistant Adjutant General. A lawyer by training, he openly disagreed with the U.S. Departments of Interior and War about their Native American policies. He attained the rank of Brigadier General.

Lieutenant Charles Erskine Scott Wood

Charles Erskine Scott Wood was General Howard's aide-de-camp throughout the war. He took personal custody of Chief Joseph after the chief surrendered at the Bear Paw battlefield. In 1892—at a time when the U.S. government was forcibly removing Native American children from their homes and sending them to the Carlisle Indian Industrial School—Lieutenant Wood sent his twelve-year-old son to live with Chief Joseph for six months at a reservation in Nespelem, Washington. Wood's son returned to Chief Joseph's lodge the following year, this time for four months. At their final departure, Joseph told the boy, "Be brave and tell the truth."

«———»

Bone Necklace features poems and songs reproduced with attribution from the U.S. public domain: Alfred Lord Tennyson, "Maud" (1855); Walt Whitman, "Leaves of Grass" (1855); Arthur Lloyd, "Not for Joseph" (1867); Anonymous, "I Doubt It" Yale Literary Magazine (1906); *Nez Perce Presbyterian Hymn Book* (Caxton Printers 1967); Mark Twain, "The War Prayer" (1910).

Chief Joseph, 1877, Bismarck, Dakota Territory, courtesy of National Park Service

Chief Ollikut (center), circa 1877, U.S. public domain

Chief White Bird, undated, courtesy of Idaho Historical
Society

Chief Looking Glass, undated, courtesy of National
Park Service

Peopeo Tholekt (Bird Alighting), photographed in 1900, courtesy of Smithsonian Institution Collection, Nez Perce National Historical Park, photographer Delancey L. Gill. Peopeo Tholekt was with Looking Glass on July 1, 1877, and provided an account of the Army's attack on the chief's peaceful camp.

Chief Yellow Wolf, undated, taken by or for Lucullus Virgil McWhorter, during the course of their friendship and collaboration on Yellow Wolf: His Own Story (Caxton Press 1940)

General William T. Sherman, circa 1888, photograph by Napoleon Sarony used in the second edition of Sherman's Memoirs (Appleton 1886)

General Oliver O. Howard, circa 1908, courtesy of Library of Congress

Chief Joseph with General Howard, circa 1904, from Howard's Famous Indian Chiefs I Have Known (The Century Co. 1908)

Colonel John Gibbon, circa 1860-1865, courtesy of Library of Congress

Chief Joseph with Colonel Gibbon, undated,
courtesy of Newberry Library

Colonel Nelson A. Miles, circa 1894,
courtesy of Library of Congress

Appendix

Excerpt From *The Tennessean*
(Nashville, Tennessee), June 20, 1877

The whole country is wild with alarm. The Indians are massacring men women and children in Camas prairie country, and settlers are fleeing in all directions for safety. Gen. Howard is now at Lewiston, but is powerless, owing to inadequate military forces.

Excerpt from *The New Northwest*
(Portland, Oregon), June 22, 1877

When we contemplate the repeated horrors that have been perpetrated upon pioneer settlers on this continent from the Atlantic to the Pacific, we are almost ready to advocate extermination, as the only safe and permanent treaty that can be concluded with treachery.

Excerpt from *The Ouachita Telegraph*
(Monroe, Louisiana), June 29, 1877

Of course there is no military force in the neighborhood adequate to the task of chastising the murderous bands, who are butchering the settlers and laying waste the whole region around them. General Howard, who is in command, is gathering all the available troops from various posts in the department, and will probably be in a position for effective operations by the time the savages have wiped out the settlements. The disturbance seems to have arisen from the murder of some Indians by whites, the savages retaliating with a general massacre of settlers.

— *Chicago Times.*

Excerpt from *The New Northwest* (Portland, Oregon),
June 29, 1877

THE INDIAN WAR IN IDAHO

The outbreak of a portion of the Nez Perces tribe in Idaho is emphatically declared to be without the slightest provocation on the part of settlers. It grew out of the order commanding these roving renegades to repair to the reservations designated by treaty, and the method taken to compel them to comply with such requirement.

General Howard has been by many in the region of hostilities severely blamed for his course, but without reasonable foundation. His only error in the premises seems to have been the failure to have troops in readiness to enforce his commands to the Indians. If, however, he expected to control these Indians by moral suasion or any of the mistaken methods denominated "peace policy," he is now thoroughly aware of his mistake, and will not hesitate to supersede moral suasion with ordinance which Indians are calculated to comprehend.

The details of the massacre of settlers about Mount Idaho are given, and the savage atrocity which accompanies it shows conclusively that in spite of the teachings of Christianity and the humanizing influences of the peace policy, Indians will be true to their savage instincts. They have been long preparing for the onslaught, and the wonder of the whole affair is that settlers have slept so securely for months past, while these Indians have been gathering arms and ammunition and laying plans for the onset.

Excerpt from *The Saint Louis Dispatch* (St. Louis, Missouri), July 5, 1877

The new Indian war inaugurated by the Nez Perces of Idaho seems to have been unprovoked by the whites or any ill treatment of the savages, and they have gone into the matter in a spirit of pure deviltry. In their mountain fast-nesses they are in a position to do us much damage with little injury to themselves. But Gen. Sherman is on his way to that neighborhood, and as he is not a man to recommend soothing syrup to convert savages into Christians, these bareheaded gentlemen of the Idaho hills had just as well re-turn to their wigwams while their top knots are still grow-ing.

Excerpt from *The Saint Louis Dispatch* (St. Louis, Missouri), July 5, 1877

"BUFFALO BILL"

His Ideas About the New Indian War.

He is Anxious to Take a Hand in it –
He Expects Graver Trouble Still –
Something About Indian Wars.

To "Buffalo Bill," Idaho, as he understands it, is a field full of promise for a long and disastrous Indian war if the aborigines choose to make it such. He arrives at this con-clusion from the fact that the whole country is sparsely set-tled, miners, herders, woodmen and farmers being in small groups and scattered all over the territory. This manner of settling up has been brought about by a long season of peace, which has engendered a feeling of security that has exceeded common precaution.

Excerpt from *The Inter Ocean* (Chicago, Illinois), July 10, 1877

From the home of the settler in Idaho comes a wail of anguish, and dreadful news of savage slaughter of the sturdy men, who, with their brave wives and children, have been forced to die at the hands of the Nez Perce savage, alone, unprotected, unwarned of the danger. The blood of the massacred settlers is upon the government, and its peace policy.

Excerpt from *The Times* (Philadelphia, Pennsylvania), July 14, 1877

THE INDIAN CAMPAIGN.

No one who has been a careful observer of Indian campaigns during the last few years, will be surprised that General Howard has made another bloody failure in attempting to bring the Nez Perces to peace by war. We have had the usual bombastic bulletins from military officers, and graphic descriptions of the strategy that was to bring the wily Chief Joseph to battle and exterminate his warriors. Day after day, General Howard has telegraphed how he had crossed the Salmon river, then how he had crossed it again; then how Joseph had crossed it somewhere; then how regular troops were expected soon to complete the marvelous strategical movements of Howard, and then how he would be "concentrated" when all his troops got together in one place; but Joseph scattered as Howard concentrated, swooped down on isolated commands now and then by way of airing his strategy, and finally concentrated his dusky warriors so suddenly and in such numbers as to make the country await in painful suspense for the news of another massacre.

It is the old, old story of military tomfoolery against the cunning of the savage, and it will be told and told again, and told ever until Indian wars are conducted with some little regard for common sense.

Excerpt from *The Tennessean* (Nashville, Tennessee), July 14, 1877

In Administration and army circles Joseph's outbreak is regarded in a most serious light. The greater part of the Cabinet session yesterday was devoted to its consideration, and the indications are that a more stringent Indian policy will be inaugurated. Joseph will be treated in a manner that the hostiles will remember for all time to come. The Government will take care that the troublesome tribes hereafter do no harm, in case they fail to learn from the fate of the Nez Perces. Howard has been authorized to raise volunteers, and probably Joseph's band will soon join the Modocs, though, it is to be hoped, not after as long a fight as that in the lava beds.

Excerpt from *The Vancouver Independent* (Vancouver, Washington), July 26, 1877

The Idaho Indian War.

On the 16th, Red Heart, a Nez Perce chief, with sixteen warriors from Joseph's and Looking Glass' bands, with 23 women and children, surrendered themselves to General Howard. They were made prisoners and told that they would be tried; that the murderers of white men and outragers of women must be punished.

Excerpt from *The Times* (Philadelphia, Pennsylvania), July 28, 1877

The Nez Perces Indians, who were so badly whipped by General Howard – by telegraph – a short time ago, appear to have kept their spirits up in the midst of the disaster, and just as soon as Howard ceased to telegraph accounts of his success in breaking up the hostile band, Joseph began to re-organize, and in addition to getting a pretty formidable band together in an unusually formidable position, has captured some stragglers who belonged to Howard's command. Joseph does not have the free use of the telegraph as Howard does, but he seems to have some other advantages which, to one in his line of business, are really worth a great deal more.

Excerpt from *The Tennessean* (Nashville, Tennessee), August 2, 1877

The strike disturbance is subsiding, but there are three other chronic bores that seem immortal. They are the Turks, the Russians and the Nez Perces.

Excerpt from *The Junction City Weekly Union* (Junction City, Kansas), August 4, 1877

THE RED DEVILS IN MONTANA.

While Gen. Howard is congratulating his troops who did not whip the Nez Perces, the Montana people are in a fever of excitement and apprehension on account of the march of the savages through their settlements. Dispatches from special correspondents detail the mustering of the Montana militia at exposed points. Severe fighting is expected. The Indians appear to be well armed, and determine [sic] to fight their way to the buffalo range; and unless the territorial volunteers are more successful than regulars were in crippling them, that purpose is likely to be accomplished. There appear to be no United States troops anywhere in the neighborhood.

Excerpt from *The Atchison Daily Champion* (Atchison, Kansas), August 12, 1877

A Terrible Battle Between General Gibbon's Command and the Nez Perces.

The Heroic Conduct of the United States Troops and Citizen Volunteers.

Eighty Out of One Hundred Men Either Killed or Wounded.

Captain Logan and Lieutenant Bradley Among the Killed.

One of the Fiercest Indian Fights Ever Recorded.

THE INDIAN WAR.

HELENA, M.T., August 11. – The following was received this morning:

"Big Hole, M.T., Aug. 9.

To Gov. Potts – Had a hard fight with the Nez Perces, killing a number and losing a number of officers and men. We need a doctor and everything. Send us such relief as you can.

[Signed]

JOHN GIBBON

Colonel Commanding

Excerpt from *The Times* (Philadelphia, Pennsylvania), August 14, 1877

It is high time, if the campaign—which should never have been begun—against the Nez Perces is to be carried on, that the incompetent Howard were removed and an officer who knows how to win success in Indian warfare were appointed in his place. He has already been responsible for too much useless bloodshed and too many disgraceful defeats.

Excerpt from *The New York Times* (New York, New York), August 14, 1877

The remarkable feature of the war with the Nez Perces is the skill with which the Indians have fought. We do not now refer to simple feats of valor, but to the actual tactical conduct of battle; for they have in every respect proved themselves as thorough soldiers as any of our trained veterans. In the affairs on Camas Prairie their celerity and boldness were conspicuous. In Howard's battle on the Clearwater, there is little doubt that he outnumbered the hostiles, and he had the advantage of artillery; yet, despite his Gatling guns and his howitzers, the Nez Perces got on his line of supplies and for twenty-four hours threatened to destroy him. Their manoeuvres have been in every way skillful. Whether the demand is for selection of the battleground, for skirmishing, for flanking, for threatening communications, for attack in mass, for intrenching with rifle-pits, for detaching sharp-shooters "to command a spring of water," as in Howard's fight, or for charging "a high, wooded bluff," which proves to be the strategic key of the position, as in Gibbon's fight, the Indians exhibit instincts and methods as strictly military as if they had been acquired at West Point.

Joseph and his band have been much underrated by the common reports. He is no vagabond, putting on the war-paint from thirst of blood and greed of booty. He has a cause which, we regret to say, is too much founded in justice; he and his tribe have been wronged; and the costly war he is now waging could, with ordinary good sense and a sincere purpose to do him justice, have been prevented. His braves are by no means a gang of besotted brutes, with no instincts above drinking, thieving, and scalping.

Excerpt from *Spirit of the Age* (Woodstock, Vermont), August 15, 1877

It becomes more and more evident that the conduct of this campaign is in incompetent hands. It has been noted only for foolishly sanguine promises and utter failures in performance. Whatever may have been the merits of the cause in which the expedition was made, the Indians have done much to enforce a favorable consideration of their claims by their successful resistance to compulsion.

Excerpt from *The Indiana Democrat* (Indiana, Pennsylvania),
August 16, 1877

THE NEZ PERCES

Ex-Senator Nesmith Points Out the
True Cause of the Present Outbreak.

Salem, Oregon, July 28. – The recent outbreak of the
Nez Perces in Idaho, which has caused such fearful destruction of life and property, and which in its suppression will
cost the Government millions of dollars, is not the result of
sudden impulse. The causes which led to it have been in existence twenty years, and furnish an apt illustration of the
miserable policy of our Government in the management of
its Indian affairs.

I have known the Nez Perces tribe since 1843. They are
[sic] under my charge, as Superintendent of Indian Affairs,
from June, 1857, until July 1859. They are the finest speci-
mens of the aboriginal race upon this continent, and have
been friendly to the whites from the time Lewis and Clark
visited them up to the inauguration of the present outbreak.
From a kind, docile, friendly people, the mismanagement,
frauds, and down right robbery perpetrated by the general
Government and some of its rascally representatives, have
driven them to take up arms, and converted them into a
fierce, dangerous, and relentless enemy.

Excerpt from *The Daily Review* (Wilmington, North Carolina),
August 16, 1877

HOWARD AND HIS INDIANS.

At last advices, "Howard, Brigadier-General" was gallantly pressing forward in the rear of the Nez Perces with the hope and expectation of coming in sight of it before Christmas, provided the Messrs Nez Perces don't get disgusted and turn and show a fighting front, in which case the situation of affairs will probably become slightly reversed and Howard may never find what he is now so eagerly and so confidently looking for. How 'ard it is that the Nez Perces will not stop long enough to enable the panting epaulettes to come within spy-glass distance of them.

Excerpt from *Fort Scott Daily Monitor* (Fort Scott, Kansas),
August 18, 1877

Gen. Crook, a veteran and successful Indian fighter, says that the Indians are now as well armed with breech-loaders as the regular troops, and shoot better. This statement gives pertinency to the recent order of the President forbidding the sale of arms to the savages. The terrible loss suffered by Gen. Gibbon's command in the Big Hole battle, proves that the Nez Perces had excellent weapons and knew how to use them.

— N.Y. Tribune.

Excerpt from *Harrisburg Telegraph* (Harrisburg, Pennsylvania),
August 20, 1877

[T]here is no little alarm felt at headquarters for the safety of General Sherman, who is supposed to be at the present moment in the Yellowstone Park. He has only five

men with him and an escort. The squad is well armed, however, and might worry Joseph and his band fearfully if the
two commands should come together.

Excerpt from *Wichita Eagle* (Wichita, Kansas), August 23, 1877

Lo, the poor Howard, whose untutored mind, permits
the Nez Perces to leave him behind!

Excerpt from *The Galveston Daily News* (Galveston, Texas),
August 23, 1877

THE NEZ PERCES INDIANS.

Howard Ventures too Near the Rear of Joseph – Returning Home Disgusted

Salt Lake, Aug. 22 – Gen. Howard ventured too near the
rear of Chief Joseph. He lost one killed and seven wounded
yesterday. The Indians stole two hundred of Howard's horses night before last.

The Montana volunteers are returning home disgusted
– many of them on foot.

Gen. Sherman is at Helena, Montana.

Excerpt from *The Times* (Philadelphia, Pennsylvania),
August 24, 1877

It is well enough for the fleeing Nez Perces to keep out
of reach of the pursuing Howard – if they can; but when
the fleeing Nez Perces steal the horses belonging to Howard's command it's too mean for the average Indian. No
decent Indian would steal horses from the command of
a general who is in hot pursuit of that Indian, and who is

constantly telegraphing that he can't find him.

Excerpt from *The Junction City Weekly Union* (Junction City, Kansas), August 25, 1877

General Sherman has started from Bozeman for the Yellowstone Park with an escort of four soldiers. In a letter to the war department, he denies the story set afloat by some enthusiastic admirer to the effect that with this force he is on his way to Big Hole, with the intention of capturing Joseph Nez Perces.

Excerpt from *The Times* (Philadelphia, Pennsylvania), August 25, 1877

If Howard were as light in his heels as he appears to be in his head the Nez Perces would have trouble to get away from him.

Excerpt from *Fort Scott Daily Monitor* (Fort Scott, Kansas), August 28, 1877

Howard is a brave man and a Good, straightforward soldier, but one utterly unequal to the direction of hostilities against the wily savages of the Western country; and the exhibition of conspicuous incapacity to wage the kind of warfare that the army must engage in is certainly sufficient ground for the substitution of another commander. It is not Howard, therefore, that should be blamed for future failures, but the Commander-in-Chief, who so little comprehends the material he has to use as to constantly put "round pegs into square holes."

Excerpt from *The Leavenworth Times* (Leavenworth, Kansas),
August 30, 1877

GENERAL HOWARD REPLIES.

General Howard writes a letter defending himself
against those who have been criticizing him in regard to his
management of the present campaign against the Nez Perces, and seems to think he has been unjustly treated. The
following is a portion of the letter:

The effect of this treatment is to create distrust on the
part of your people, with whom I want the heartiest co-op-
eration. I have not rested in the pursuit of these hostile Indians; I have taken the offensive at all times, and never the
defensive; they have run from me again and again, but at
last, by a forced march, I struck them and beat them. Surely
I should not be treated to insult and contumely for which
there is not a shadow of reason. It makes the officers of my
command indignant in the extreme, after having marched
some of them six and others eight hundred miles, and having been pushed almost to the extreme of human endurance, and with real success, to have the grossest falsehoods
sent from localities near the scene of operations broadcast
throughout the land. The anxieties of loved ones at home
are great enough already without having them aggravated
by stories of inefficiency and slowness that are known to be
so palpably false as hardly to need contradiction.

Excerpt from *The Ingelligencer* (Anderson, South Carolina),
August 30, 1877

The country is tired of this bungling warfare. The government ought either to yield to the Indian demands or

force them to come to terms, and it ought to be done at once for the protection of white settlements.

Excerpt from *Goldsboro Messenger* (Goldsboro, North Carolina), August 30, 1877

Gen. Sherman, in a dispatch from Helena, Montana, says: "Accounts from the Indians and Gen. Howard are too confused to make anything out." The general evidently refers to the cloudy way in which the recent raid on Howard was reported, the vague story of a fight and the too suggestive indications of another one of those disastrous victories.

Excerpt from *Harper's Weekly,* September 1, 1877

Our portrait of the redoubtable Indian warrior who, at the head of the disaffected portion of the Nez Perce tribe, is now waging war against the United States forces in the far West, shows him to be a man of intelligence and strength of character. He is certainly a shrewd and active fighter, and his influence over the Indians is very great. …Their mode of fighting, their knowledge of the country, the ease and celerity with which they shift their quarters and attack or retreat, give them a great advantage of the soldiers.

Excerpt from *The Osage County Chronicle* (Burlingame, Kansas), September 6, 1877

If the Nez Perces will kindly spare Gen. Howard, it is probable arrangements will be made to promote him to the position of Associated Press Agent. He has such a cheerful way of transmitting dreary intelligence that his services in such capacity would be invaluable. – *Philadelphia Times*

Excerpt from The Donaldsonville Chief (Donaldsonville, Louisiana), September 8, 1877

The announcement may appear inexplicable to many long-range Indian fighters, that Gen. Howard, despite his failure to send all the Nez Perces to the "happy hunting ground" in the time allotted him, still retains the confidence of the War Department; and to hear the absurd talk made there, one would be almost convinced that he and his little army had done a good deal of hard work in the present campaign, entitling them to credit rather than censure.

Excerpt from *The Times-Picayune* (New Orleans, Louisiana), September 12, 1877

We are afraid that we are too apt to accept the dictum of the fearless "Little Phil [Sheridan]"—that there are no good Indians but dead Indians. The great majority of the American people are ignorant and heedless of the causes of this Nez Perces war. The facts are by no means creditable to the United States Government. The truth is, that the Nez Perces have been conducting an aggressive war in self-defense. In times past they have been the firm allies of the United States, and have only been driven into a hostile attitude by persistent oppression and flagrant injustice.

Excerpt from *The Weekly Arizona Miner* (Prescott, Arizona), September 14, 1877

The Indian war which broke out in Oregon over three months ago, and which General Howard promised to

squelch in a very short time, has turned out as we predicted at the outset. Howard with his spread-eagle flourish
has accomplished literally nothing.

Give us an Indian fighter to command our Army, and let
us have this rabble of Indians annihilated.

Excerpt from *The Wyandott Herald* (Kansas City, Kansas),
September 20, 1877

Which are the Savages?

Gen. Sheridan called Gibbon's fight with Joseph at the
Big Hole a hard blow to the Indians. We are just getting the
mail accounts of this hard blow, and find that of the Indians killed by our troops more than two-thirds of them were
women and children, shot down in their camp, while the
Indians killed or wounded probably double as many of our
men as our troops did of theirs.

How do our readers like the picture? And which is the
more censurable, the way in which the war with Joseph has
been conducted, or the iniquities of our Government out
of which it sprung? The latest development in this shameful business is the transfer of still another full regiment, at
great expense, across the continent, to join its many prede-
cessors employed in trying to conquer the handful of Nez
Perces whom the injustice and imbecility of our Government drove to revolt.

Excerpt from *Janesville Daily Gazette* (Janesville, Wisconsin),
September 21, 1877

If he [Howard] would drink whiskey, swear, tell smutty
stories and disgrace himself in the estimation of decent people, he would at once be taken and accepted as a member of
the "crowd" to be written "up" instead of "down." As it is,
the whole herd of riff raff are yelping at his heels. The drunk-
en, malignant vagabonds some of the papers choose as their
representatives ought to be drafted en masse and sent out to
Howard.

Excerpt from *The Montana Standard* (Butte, Montana), September
25, 1877

If General Howard would do more of his fighting on the
battle field and less of it in the newspapers, he would adopt a
course that would win him a greater share of the respect and
admiration of his fellow countrymen than he now enjoys.

The Weekly Kansas Chief (Troy, Kansas),
September 27, 1877

Select Story.

The Mystery of Chief Joseph.

I.

The Christian soldier sat alone in his guarded tent. He
heeded not the wind, which howled dismally without, and he
paid no attention to the distant yells of the demoniac savages, as they danced around the encampment, vainly attempting with insulting taunts to draw the American Havelock
forth to battle. He heeded naught, for his burning sense of

injustice was taking form in eloquent words. His rapid pen skipped impetuously to and fro over the paper; page after page of manuscript fell fluttering like snow flakes to the ground till the floor of the tent was covered with white. The Christian commander was replying to the newspaper criticisms on his conduct of the campaign.

"If these gentlemen of the press," he wrote, "knew the true character of the foe with whom I have to contend, they would perhaps be slower to ridicule my policy. The Chief Joseph is a wily, audacious, and unscrupulous adversary. He united the comprehensive military genius of a Napoleon with the dash of a Massena. Yet he does not hesitate to employ the most reprehensible methods of annoying me, and eludes pursuit by strategems unknown to civilized warfare. My campaign must not be judged by the ordinary standards, for his activity is superhuman, his resources apparently boundless, and his lack of principle wholly beyond belief."

The progress of the general's composition was interrupted by the entrance of a breathless and agitated orderly.

"Well," said the Christian soldier," after he had punctuated his last sentence.

The orderly touched his hat. "Joseph's forces are advancing on the outposts, yelling and swearing like devils!"

"It is as I have written," remarked Howard sadly. "This totally unprincipled Aborigine does not scruple to attack me even upon the holy Sabbath. Direct the Chaplain to go out and read to the enemy the fifth chapter of Matthew."

"I have conscientiously endeavored," continued the General, resuming his pen, "to bring Joseph to acknowledge the unreasonableness of his attitude toward the United States Government, and toward me, the representative of its military arm. It seems to be a case where argument is unavailing."

The orderly again appeared at the tent flap. "They have scalped the Chaplain and are still advancing," he reported.

"He was a good man," reflected Howard, "and we shall miss him. Try and find some pious private who will volunteer to go out and finish the chapter."

"Newspaper criticism," wrote the General, continuing his letter, "serves not only to encourage the enemy, but to grieve me personally. I am therefore constrained to request that it be suspended, and meanwhile I look to history for the vindication of my – "

Another orderly burst into the tent. "The sentries are shot!" he cried. "What shall we do!"

A patient yet mournful look overspread the Christian soldier's features. "Put the flag at half mast," he replied, "and make the necessary arrangements for the funeral to-morrow."

"But they have hauled down the flag, and are making a bonfire of tracts and hymn books around the pole."

"Summon my officers hither to deliberate on the most prudent course of action to pursue under the circumstances."

"But the red devils are this very minute stealing your tent pins, and the canvas will be down on your head."

"This is too much!" murmured the Christian commander. "Saddle my mule without delay, and order a retreat."

Excerpt from *The Bolivar Bulletin* (Bolivar, Tennessee),
September 27, 1877

It would seem that the Nez Perces demon is hardly of
so somber a hue as he is generally painted: A letter from
Montana gives an unexpected example of their clemency. A
council of five debated for some time on the question of the
release of several prisoners in their possession, and at last,
by a majority of one, decided to let them go. Fearing that
they would regret their decision White Bird, the chief, said
to the trembling captives: "You go quick—go by this trail—
don't stop to camp or eat or water your ponies—don't go
up the river—hurry to the Hot Springs and join your people
there—get away—hurry!" He then gave them some bread
and matches and guided them a mile from the camp.

Excerpt from *The New York Times* (New York, New York),
October 11, 1877

THE SURRENDER OF CHIEF JOSEPH

After one of the most stubborn and gallant running
fights known to Indian warfare, Chief JOSEPH and the remnant of his band, harassed and worn out, have surrendered.

So ends the Nez Perce war—a war gallantly fought, but
a costly and sanguinary blunder. A peaceful, non-treaty
chief, who, after being wronged in other ways, had been
peremptorily ordered to go upon a reservation where
he did not belong, was thus goaded to the war-path. Our
troops have pursued him and his allied chiefs with tireless
energy, and have fought him most gallantly, being met by

an energy as tireless, and a bravery even more desperate, than their own. The skill and courage with which Joseph, White Bird, Looking Glass, and their Nez Perce warriors have conducted this campaign are unsurpassed in our Indian annals.

As to the fate of Joseph, much must depend on the terms of surrender. But even supposing it to be unconditional, he and his men deserve the treatment of foes, not of felons. By refraining from scalping and mutilation, by their frequent release of women and children, and sometimes even of unarmed citizens, they have set an example in Indian warfare which should earn them consideration. If they have inflicted terrible losses on our troops, it was in a war for their homes and what they believed to be their rights. We rejoice that this slaughter is over; but the fate of Joseph and his Nez Perces should not be that of Capt. Jack and his Modocs.

Excerpt from *The Times* (Philadelphia, Pennsylvania), October 11, 1877

Now that the power of the Nez Perces has been broken, the question is, what are we going to do with the remnant of the band?

The policy of the government for the last five years, had its object been extermination, could not have been better conceived or executed, and if, with all our boasts of fair dealing, philanthropy and Christian and peaceful methods of dealing with the Indians, this policy is to be persisted in, the cheapest and the kindest manner of disposing of the rest of the Nez Perces would be to take them out and shoot them. Anything would be preferable to the dishonest policy which combines bayonets and Bibles and mock philanthropy and over-reaching robbery which brought on this last war.

Excerpt from *The Independent Record* (Helena, Montana), October 11, 1877

THE END OF THE MARCH.

The most remarkable of wanderings recorded in modern times has just been ended. We refer to that of Joseph and his band of Nez Perces. After they left the Clearwater, Idaho, and until their capture, they traversed a distance of over twelve hundred miles over the worst country on the continent, and all this time were pursued and harassed by from one to three armies, each of which was larger than their own. The band was hampered with women and children and a very large number of horses, yet notwithstanding all these hindrances they succeeded in eluding their pursuers, and even in outgeneraling those who sought to cut them off. ... Joseph has shown the most remarkable generalship that has been witnessed during the century—save in the last days of his travels, and then his prudence seems to have deserted him. He crossed the Missouri four or five days in advance of General Miles, and why he permitted the latter to overtake him is the most singular part of the whole affair, as he could have kept on three or four days longer and been upon British soil and out of harm's way. This remarkable march will place him among the most notable of the red men, and his deeds will be remembered so long as our history lasts. . . .

What will be done with Joseph and his band is uncertain . . . That he has committed grievous wrongs we know, but certain it is that he has done many things that no other Indian would have done—spared the lives of his captors. His tribe has been severely punished and is now thoroughly subdued, and nothing can be gained by making a frightful example of the noblest warrior the Indian tribes have produced.

Excerpt from *The Tennessean* (Nashville, Tennessee), October 12, 1877

When the history of the unparalleled march of the Nez Perces is written, they will be accredited with great gallantry in the field, and wonderful humanity. Their defense could not have been excelled by any body of men, nor their generosity. Seven wounded men lying under the intrenchments during the entire battle live to corroberate this. They took away the guns and ammunition from the disabled troops, but did not offer to molest them.

Excerpt from *The New York Times* (New York, New York), October 15, 1877

A LESSON FROM THE NEZ PERCES

Now that the Nez Perce war has ended in victory, thanks to the energy and courage of our much-enduring Army, it is worth while, before it passes out of mind, to ask why it was fought. We freely express the opinion that the Nez Perce war was, on the part of our Government, and unpardonable and frightful blunder—a crime, whose victims are alike the hundreds of our gallant officers and men who fell a prey to

Nez Perce bullets and the peaceful bands who were goaded by injustice and wrong to the war-path. It is greatly to be regretted that the immediate responsibility for its occurrence is so obscurely distributed that it is difficult to bring anybody to account for it at the bar of public opinion.

Excerpt from *Vermont Watchman and State Journal* (Montpelier, Vermont), October 17, 1877

It is evident that the wrongs committed by the whites upon these Indians, who had always been friendly until now, had aroused them to a pitch of desperation, and rendered them formidable foes. They were amply prepared, and their splendid fighting proves how rapidly the Indian has progressed in the arts of modern warfare, while the engineering skill and military strategy displayed by these Nez Perces braves elicit our admiration. Surely so brave and heroic a tribe of red men deserves honorable treatment at the hands of the government.

Excerpt from *The Greensboro Patriot* (Greensboro, North Carolina), October 17, 1877

The Nez Perces crowned their last struggle with some striking instances of generosity and humanity which make us ashamed to talk of the superiority of civilized over savage warfare. All along they have refused to scalp or mutilate our dead soldiers, or to kill the wounded who fell into their hands, though our Indian allies have scalped their dead. They have also released women and children. Soldiers now relate that in Mile's last fight the Nez Perces spared the wounded throughout the battle. They roamed over the battlefield at night where our wounded, unrescued, still lay, and told them in broken English to fear nothing—that they never shot men who did not resist. In one case a blanket was put by them, it is said under the wounded lad's head; and Lieut. Jerome, who was captured the first day, says they gave him a deep rifle pit to stay in, so that he might be protected from the bullets of his friends. These are the people we call savages. – *N. Y. Sun.*

Excerpt from *Harrisburg Telegraph* (Harrisburg, Pennsylvania), October 18, 1877

THE NEZ PERCES CHIEF.

A Pen Picture of Chief Joseph When He Surrendered to Gen. Miles.

Montana Special to New York Herald.

As the Indian chief thus stood before his captor a self-acknowledged prisoner he presented the figure and mien of as gallant a warrior chieftain as ever confessed himself fairly beaten at the game of war. About thirty-five years of age, five feet ten inches in height, and clad in a pair of blanket trowsers, leggings and moccasins, he wore none of the war-paint or savage bravery of headdress and feathers which usually adorn an Indian warrior on the war-path. His features, regular and handsome in their outline, were covered by hardly a wrinkle. His eyes, black, brilliant and as piercing as an eagle's, rested on those of Gen. Miles with an expression at once melancholy and reserved. His long black hair was gathered into a loose queue at the back of his head and ornamented with a simple cluster of green feathers. Two long braids descended from his temples and hung down in front of his ears. Such was the man who for so long a time has bade defiance to his pursuers and who had almost gained the refuge he aimed for.

Excerpt from *The State Journal* (Jefferson City, Missouri), October 19, 1877

The chief of the Nez Perces is a savage of splendid bearing in his dress and manner. There is little which resembles that of the ordinary savage of the plains. On the battlefield he wore a pair of moccasins and a pair of buckskin pants, over which was drawn a pair of woolen stockings, which fitted closely to his legs and extended to his knees, showing his great muscularity. A blue woolen shirt covered the upper portion of his body, and over his right shoulder a white blanket was carelessly thrown. His face was free from paint and the only sign of savagery was seen in the few green feathers in his hair at the back of his head.

There was little about the dress of any members of the tribes which would class them with any of the prairie Indians. They wore neither paint nor feathers, and there was a lack of brass work about their hair and necks. The women are better looking than ordinary squaws, and carry a more extensive wardrobe.

Excerpt from *The St. Johnsbury Caledonian* (St. Johnsbury, Vermont), October 19, 1877

But there are two sides to this Indian question. A correspondent writing from Deadwood to the *N. Y. Graphic,* says the City of Deadwood offers $250 for the scalp of an Indian of any sex or age. Five thousand dollars for twenty scalps is good wages. But somehow it happens that scalping is a game that more than one side can play at. The Indians are likely to retaliate in kind, and then they are "savages," "fiends," "red devils," and not Christians, like the civilized, educated and enlightened white men who make this atrocious and nation-disgracing offer.

Excerpt from *The Bismarck Tribune* (Bismarck, Dakota Territory), October 19, 1877

MILES AND THE NEZ PERCES.

His Humanity – Howard on the Field.

Gen. Miles has exhibited the greatest humanity toward the surrendered tribe, and is taking great care of their sick and wounded. He recognizes their valor, and admires their manner of fighting. A great plea can be made for these Indians. The fiendish practices of the Sioux do not extend to them. It is not known that they have scalped or mutilated the bodies of those whom they have killed in battle, and numerous incidents are related where they had saved the lives of a number of people during their march through Idaho and Montana. This was wonderfully exemplified by their treatment of the wounded on the field of battle.

Excerpt from *Marion County Record* (Marion, Kansas), October 26, 1877

INDIAN KINDNESS TO AN ENEMY.

Up to the last hours of the fight the Indians never ceased

to belie all the Stories that have been told of the savage. One Nez Perces Chief approached a wounded soldier at midnight and said in broken English, "Poor boy, you're too young to go to war. I no kill you." Then he put a blanket under his head and left him. Gen. Miles in return ordered all the wounded Indians to be well cared for. His surgeons are as alert with our own brave wounded. One soldier exclaimed on the evening of the 5th, "God – the arm. Let that Chief have his leg off first. He's a boaster." The soldier's wound in his arm proved to be mortal. Gen. Miles intends to start to-day for the Tongue River with the wounded of his command and of Joseph's tribe and prisoners. This ends the most remarkable Indian fight on record.

Excerpt from *The Bismarck Tribune* (Bismarck, Dakota Territory), October 26, 1877

JOSEPH'S SPEECH IN FULL

What the Great Chief Said when he Was Asked to Surrender to Gen. Miles – A remarkably Pathetic and Suggestive Communication – "My Heart is Sick and Sad."

One of the officers of the steamer Silver City, arriving to-day with all the Wounded of Gen. Miles' fight with Joseph, except six of the more serious cases left at Fort Buford, furnishes the Bismarck Tribune the following verbatim copy of Joseph's reply, when he was asked for the last time to surrender to Gen. Miles, through Howard's Nez Perces, sent into Joseph's camp:

"Tell General Howard I know his Heart. What he told me before I have in my heart. I am tired of fighting. Our chiefs are killed. Looking-Glass is dead. Ta-hool-hoolshoot is dead. The old men are all dead. It is the young men who say yes and no. He who leads the young men is dead. It is cold and we have no blankets. The little children are freezing to death. My people, some of them, have run away to the hills and have no blankets, no food; no one knows where they are—may be freezing to death. I want time to look for my children and see how many of them I can find. May be I shall find them among the dead. Hear me my chiefs: I am tired. My heart is sick and sad. From where the sun now stands I will fight no more forever."

Excerpt from *Harrisburg Telegraph* (Harrisburg, Pennsylvania), October 31, 1877

GEN. HOWARD'S COMPLAINT.

Gen. Howard, who is in Chicago, has been interviewed. After giving the story of the Nez Perces campaign he said:

"I have had much to aggrieve me," the tears glistening in his eyes as he spoke; "the Government has seen fit to rob me of a large sum of money, and I have been too poor to prosecute my claims; and my countrymen have seen fit to heap nothing but abuse upon me. They seem to have piled me up before the country as some sort of a politician. The only politics I have is to be loyal to my Government. I have been blamed for writing to the newspapers. I have never written a line for self-laudation or for notoriety. I have written articles for money in order that I might put shoes upon the feet of my children. I don't know why I should be so abused and maligned, but I suppose it will be kept up until I am dead, and after I am gone I hope that my children, at least, if nobody else does, will be able to see what good, if any, there was in me."

Excerpt from *Harper's Weekly*, "End of the Nez Perce War – Bear Paw Battle Field," November 17, 1877

Joseph has a gentle face, somewhat feminine in its beauty, but intensely strong and full of character. A photograph could not do him justice. A bullet scratch has left a slight scar on his forehead. In each shirt sleeve and in the body of the shirt are bullet holes, and there was also a bullet hole in one of his leggings, a bullet scratch on his wrist, and one across the small of his back. Colonel Miles begged his shirt as a curiosity, so full was it of visible evidence that Joseph had been where lead was flying.

Excerpt from Chief Joseph, *An Indian's View of Indian Affairs*, North American Review 412, 432-33 (April 1879)

When I think of our condition my heart is heavy. I see men of my race treated as outlaws and driven from country to country, or shot down like animals.

I know that my race must change. We can not hold our own with the white men as we are. We only ask an even chance to live as other men live. We ask to be recognized as men. We ask that the same law shall work alike on all men. If the Indian breaks the law, punish him by the law. If the white man breaks the law, punish him also.

Let me be a free man – free to travel, free to stop, free to work, free to trade where I choose, free to choose my own teachers, free to follow the religion of my fathers, free to think and talk and act for myself – and I will obey every law, or submit to the penalty.

Whenever the white man treats the Indian as they treat each other, then we will have no more wars. We shall all be alike—brothers of one father and one mother, with one sky above us and one country around us, and one government for all. Then the Great Spirit Chief who rules above will smile upon this land, and send rain to wash out the bloody spots made by brothers' hands from the face of the earth. For this time the Indian race are waiting and praying. I hope that no more groans of wounded men and women will ever go to the ear of the Great Spirit Chief above, and that all people may be one people.

In-mut-too-yah-lat-lat has spoken for his people.

Washington City, D.C. Young Joseph

Additional Reading

- L.V. McWhorter, *Yellow Wolf: His Own Story* (1940).

- General Oliver O. Howard, "The Great War Chief Joseph of the Nez Perces, and His Lieutenants, White Bird and Looking Glass," *Famous Indian Chiefs I Have Known* (1908).

- General Oliver O. Howard, *My Life and Experiences Among Our Hostile Indians* (1907).

- Major General John Gibbon, "The Pursuit of Joseph," *American Catholic Quarterly Review* (April 1879).

- Major General John Gibbon, "The Battle of the Big Hole," *Harper's Weekly* (Dec. 21, 1895).

- General Nelson A. Miles, "The Nez Perce Campaign," *Personal Recollections & Observations of General Nelson A. Miles* (1896).

- General Nelson A. Miles, "The Capture of Chief Joseph," *Serving the Republic* (1911).

- Frank Carpenter, *The Wonders of Geyser Land* (1878).

ABOUT THE AUTHOR

Julia Sullivan started working on *Bone Necklace* more than twenty years ago, after visiting the Big Hole Battlefield in Wisdom, Montana. She first became interested in the Nez Perce story because of the great injustice the tribe had suffered. What kept her interested was their conduct during the war. While under attack, the Nez Perce won the respect of a society in which prominent members were unapologetic racists. At the end of the war, Canada offered them political asylum.

Julia is a lawyer in the United States and a solicitor in England and Wales. Throughout her career, she has worked to expose and root out injustice. Julia lives with her husband in Annapolis, Maryland, and Hamilton, Montana.

CPSIA information can be obtained
at www.ICGtesting.com
Printed in the USA
LVHW102155140622
721310LV00015B/153/J